Settle the Score

Nicki Edwards

DEDICATION

To all the first responders who put their lives on the line every time

they don their uniform and wonder if anyone notices.

We notice. We thank you. We care. You are never alone.

Acknowledgements

2020. The Year of The Nurse. The year of COVID-19. The year I turned fifty (without a party). The year when not much makes sense.

It's been a hard year to focus on writing, and there have been numerous times I've wanted to permanently close the lid of my laptop. If it wasn't for my readers who send me lovely encouraging notes, I might have given up.

But as my husband says, "it's not over until the fat lady sings." (An opera reference in case you're wondering.)

So, 2020 isn't over. COVID-19 isn't over. And my writing journey isn't over.

With the love of my local writer friends, Lisa Ireland, Delwyn Jenkins, Ellie O'Neill and Alli Sinclair; and with the unwavering support of Annie Seaton who has generously given her time and expertise yet again, I've managed to write more than I dreamed this year.

I also want to thank Belinda Williams who writes the best blurbs in the business, to Andrea Grigg who is the best writer friend a girl could dream of and Anna Welch who has excellent proofreading skills.

If you've read the acknowledgements in any of my previous books, you know my biggest supporters (and those I love the most in the world) are my family.

So, again, thank you Jeremy, Chloe, Zach (and Naomi) and Toby. It's been a big year of change for all of you and I'm so proud of how you've navigated huge interruptions to your plans. You are all incredibly resilient and positive and I love how you've embraced new seasons and directions during what will undoubtedly be the most difficult time of your lives. Soon, we will go back to "precedented" times (whatever they are) and I can't wait to see where you end up. I'm just looking forward to restrictions being over so we can gather together for a big group hug (without masks).

And finally, to Tim. My number one cheerleader in everything I do. I honestly do not know how you put up with me, but I'm glad you do. You clean up after me, you finish my sentences, you read my mind, you never roll your eyes—that I know of—and you love me unconditionally. Thank you for doing life with me, for continuing to dream of our future, for going along with my crazy hare-brained ideas (like getting a horse), and for never putting pressure on me to be anyone other than "me" —as messy as that sometimes is. I adore you.

Should you keep score when it comes to love?

As an adopted only child, Annabel Norton has always wanted children of her own. Having recently retired from playing semi-professional football for the AFLW, now would be the perfect time—except she's still reeling from the failure of her last relationship.

Special Operations Group police officer, Ben Naylor, loves the idea of a family, but with two marriages under his belt, he figures commitment isn't for a man like him. Especially as he needs time to process all he's lived through in his job. That's why it makes no sense that he falls head over heels for Annabel the first time he sees her. He does the right thing and keeps his distance … and then she moves in next door.

As their feelings become impossible to deny, Annabel starts to think that they might be made for each other. That is until she learns about an unexpected secret in Ben's past. For a chance at happiness, can she open her heart and accept that a future with Ben could involve more than children of her own?

Chapter 1

Current Day

Annabel Norton's idea of a relaxing Sunday morning was not standing at the altar. She preferred to spend her weekends sitting in a café sipping a latte, lazily skimming the papers, and watching the world go by. Right now, she should be at the *Box Office*, one of her favourite cafés in Geelong, enjoying her second, or third, coffee of the day. Not in church.

Perspiration prickled Annabel's skin as it trickled down her back. Was it hot in here? She glanced at the people in the front row of pews and when she caught sight of Georgina's mother, Jane, fanning her flushed face with the photocopied order of service, she realised it wasn't just nerves making her hot. It *was* stuffy in the little church.

She tried to shift from one leg to the other, but her thighs felt like they were glued together, and she cursed her decision to wear a tight skirt. She was more a jeans and T-shirt kind of girl. Her shirt clung to her back and she desperately wanted to tug it out of the waistband and give it a shake. She also wanted to get out of her heels.

She asked herself for the hundredth time why she'd agreed to this. Surely Jed and Georgina knew someone else better suited to being Daisy's godmother. She let out a soft sigh. Playing footy in front of a crowd of thousands was nothing compared to this.

Annabel snuck a peek at the congregation and her stomach churned more than it did before the first bounce. When she saw a few familiar faces of her friends from the footy club sitting amidst a sea of smiling strangers, she relaxed a little. She might be one of the five people encircling the baptismal font, but no-one was looking at her.

Annabel turned her attention back to the others gathered at the altar and smiled at Daisy asleep in Georgina's arms. Poor little darling had no clue some old guy in a cream-coloured linen robe was about to splash water on her head. She looked at Jed who stood head and shoulders above everyone else. Getting married and becoming a dad had been good for her friend, especially after he and Georgina had lost their first baby, Robbie, at nineteen weeks.

As the priest spoke about baptism and the role of godparents, Annabel zoned out and stole more glances at the man opposite her—Daisy's godfather.

Ben Naylor was a mountain of a man with dark eyes and a warm smile. From the moment Jed had introduced Annabel to him ten minutes before the service she hadn't been able to stop looking at him. He was gorgeous.

A mixture of concentration and reverence was etched on his face, and judging from the way he carried himself, Annabel bet a million bucks he was either a Catholic or he'd done this baptism-godparent-thing before. Or he was a darn fine actor.

Hmm. Maybe he *was* an actor. He was cute enough. Would have easily given one of the Hemsworth boys a run for their money. She stared at him. He seemed to be one of those men who either didn't realise how attractive he was or didn't care. The kind of man who commanded respect without being a jerk about it. Married? She'd stake her life on it. Guys like that rarely stayed single for long.

She'd seen him at Jed and Georgina's wedding last year, but unfortunately, they hadn't met. Another of Jed's friends, Charlie, had spent the night chatting her up and she hadn't been able to get away from him to introduce herself to Ben.

Jed had referred to him as "Nails". Was that just a shortened form of his surname, or did he have a reputation for being "hard as nails"? She stared at him again. Hard to tell. Right now, he looked like a big softie.

'And Jesus said: *"Let the children come to me for the kingdom of heaven belongs to such as these".* '

Annabel tuned back into the priest's words. She only had one job to do and if she wasn't careful, she might miss her cue because she was ogling the godfather. *That* had to be against the rules in church.

'Jed and Georgina, what do you want for your child?' the priest asked.

'Baptism,' they replied in unison.

Annabel bit her bottom lip to stop the smile from forming. Jed, who was still considered one of the best ruckmen to ever play in the AFL before his retirement after a career-ending injury, looked like a nervous rookie about to take his first kick for goal.

The priest traced the sign of the cross on Daisy's forehead. 'I baptise you in the name of the Father and of the Son and of the Holy Spirit.'

Daisy stared at him, eyes wide, and Annabel waited for her to cry. Instead, Daisy beamed and melted the hearts of everyone in the church, Annabel's included.

Ben stepped forward and received a lit candle from the priest, holding it like it was a Brownlow Medal before stepping back in line. Annabel followed his lead and accepted a white leather bible from the priest, hoping no-one noticed how much her hands shook.

The priest prayed for Daisy, then Annabel and Ben, cementing their titles of godparents or something along those lines, and then concluded the service.

Annabel exhaled softly. It was all over, and she hadn't done anything wrong or said anything stupid. Win.

After signing the baptismal register, she made her way outside into the mid-morning sunshine and stood on the edge of the group outside the church, watching Jed and Georgina mix and mingle with everyone. It looked like half the population of Glengarrick had shown up for the event. Grey-haired women in floral aprons bustled around setting up trestle tables and loading them with food until they groaned under the weight of plates. Men were unfolding chairs and putting them in a large semi-circle on the grass. Kids ran everywhere and Annabel lost count of how many prams she'd seen.

An unexpected wave of jealousy hit. She often felt uncomfortable being single and childless at events like this that screamed coupledom and parenthood. Usually she could tramp down her emotions, but today she struggled. Seeing so many people with babies was a stark reminder she'd fallen behind in a race she hadn't even had a chance to start. Even at the footy club it felt like everyone else had paired up and were popping out babies and she hadn't even heard the starter call of "on your marks". She sighed softly. Some of her friends in Geelong had even lapped her, now onto their second babies.

She looked over at Georgina rocking Daisy in her pram, cooing at her and smiling down at her. Like many of Annabel's circle of female friends back in Geelong, Georgina bemoaned the excess "baby baggage" she carried around her middle. Earlier today she'd told Annabel how lucky she was to still have her figure. But Annabel's size and body shape had less to do with the fact she was childless and more to do with the fact she'd been blessed with good genetics. And she was still fit from playing football in the Australian Women's Football League for the last three years.

Annabel's friends constantly told her how lucky she was, but as far as she was concerned, they were the lucky ones. They had what she wanted.

Jed came and stood alongside Georgina, draping his arm protectively over her shoulders. When he gazed down at his wife and daughter with a look that was something beyond love, a knot of emptiness and loneliness tightened in Annabel's stomach. There was a time when Scott had looked at her that way.

The knot tightened and she swallowed hard. Scott was the past. She pasted on a bright smile and looked at the positives. It had taken her three months to finally realise it, but now that he wasn't part of her future, she could be herself again. She could commit fully to the conversations ebbing and flowing around her rather than standing off to the side and watching him check his watch. Her ex had never pretended to like her friends.

Unlike Jed, who had been so excited to introduce her to his friends in Glengarrick.

Eighteen months earlier Jed had inherited his family farm and turned it into a rural campus for a private school in Melbourne. At her suggestion, Jed was currently doing his Master of Teaching qualification so he could teach outdoor education to the city students who spent a term living on the farm in Glengarrick. It was the perfect role for him, and she was so happy for her friend. He was also happy being home in the small town of Glengarrick, and she could see why.

Glengarrick, one of many small alpine towns nestled between the Murray River and the south-east coast of Victoria, was a picturesque town that, on first impressions, appeared to have been forgotten by time. When she drove in yesterday, the main street was bustling. Jed had said in the past ten years he'd been away, the town had doubled its population as Melburnians escaped the city for a tree change and that was evident by how busy it was. House prices had escalated, and new shops and businesses had opened.

What would it be like to live in a place where everyone knew everyone else and people were happy to strike up conversations with strangers? Annabel had lost count of how many people had stopped to greet her outside the church. It wasn't like that in Geelong.

She could see why Jed had been happy to give up a career as an assistant coach with Essendon to move back here. Plus, there was Georgina. She glanced across at them again. They were the perfect couple, and Annabel was glad they'd found each other.

Pushing aside the green-eyed monster, Annabel pasted on a smile as she watched Georgina working the crowd, greeting everyone with a hug and kiss. It was clear everyone loved her.

Ben worked the crowd too. Not that Annabel intended to watch him, but it was hard not to. Apart from his height and size, her eyes were drawn to him as though he had some magnetic superpower.

Like her, Ben appeared to be on his own, but maybe he had a wife or girlfriend somewhere. She hadn't noticed if he wore a wedding band, although not having one didn't mean much these days. She'd caught him looking her way a few times, and each time their eyes had locked, she'd had to quickly avert her gaze and ignore the warmth in his smile and the way it made her legs wobble.

From what she knew about Ben after quietly quizzing Jed, he'd also grown up in Glengarrick and left after school. The two men had been good mates at school but had gone their separate ways when Jed moved to Geelong to play football. It was only in the last eighteen months when they'd both returned to Glengarrick that they'd rekindled their friendship.

She glanced over at Ben where he stood with a group of men under a large peppercorn tree. One of the group held a phone and all heads were bent towards the screen. She smiled. They were probably watching the cricket.

Ben wasn't as tall as Jed—few people were—but he had broad shoulders that tapered into a narrow waist. He'd removed his blue jacket and rolled up the sleeves of his buttoned-up shirt revealing tanned, muscled forearms. His pale blue shirt was tucked into a pair of slim fit khaki-coloured chinos and his dark tan belt matched his leather boots. There was something about the way Ben dressed that suggested he didn't work in an office all day. And those clothes weren't from a discount department store either.

He turned and caught her looking at him. His gaze held hers for a few seconds and her face flamed. She quickly broke eye contact and spun on her heel, sighing with relief as Jed headed her way.

'I don't think she's had one cuddle with her godmother all day,' Jed said, handing Daisy over.

'She's been popular,' Annabel agreed as she rocked Daisy gently in her arms. She was a pretty baby.

'Look at you, you're a natural.'

Annabel looked down at Daisy's tiny face, watching in amazement at the way her little eyes fought sleep. 'She is adorable. And wasn't she an angel? She didn't even cry when the priest watered her head.'

'She is a darling,' Jed agreed. There was a beat of silence. 'Are you disappointed you didn't end up having children with Scott?'

She shook her head. Hindsight was a good thing. Scott's first marriage had ended in divorce when his daughters were in primary school and although Annabel was grateful that he'd never expected her to play an active stepmother role, she'd still wanted a family of her own. However, whenever she'd asked when they could start a family, Scott had always brushed her off, saying the timing wasn't right. Now, even though she'd give anything to have what Jed and

Georgina had, she was relieved Scott had never agreed to her prodding. It would have been disastrous.

'You're nearly thirty-five though, Bel. That doesn't bother you?'

Annabel didn't look up. 'And just like that you've crossed the line, Delaney. That should earn you a fifty-metre penalty.' She gave him a gentle shove.

Jed laughed and shoved her back. 'What are friends for?'

'Yeah, well thanks for pointing out that I'm getting older,' Annabel said, trying to ignore the heavy weight as it settled on her shoulders. Jed didn't mean any harm. He was a guy, and they often didn't think the same way as women when it came to having kids. 'Maybe I don't want kids.' She carefully handed a now asleep Daisy back to him.

'Yeah, right. How long have we been friends? You've been clucky as long as I've known you. I reckon that's why you like coaching so much—you get to hang around kids all day.'

She chuckled. 'I coach teenagers. Different from babies. Anyway, who knows. Maybe one day it'll happen.'

He gave Annabel a big smile. 'Thanks for everything today. You were great.'

'I know I wasn't your first choice, but I appreciate that you asked me.'

Georgina's best friend Zara was working overseas in the UK, and it had been too hard for her to come back to Australia.

'I'm looking forward to meeting Zara one day. Georgina said she's an amazing woman.'

'Zazu's pretty special,' Jed agreed, 'but George puts her on a pedestal sometimes. She's no different from anyone else.'

'Just smarter,' Annabel said. 'A top lawyer.'

'And yet I reckon she'd throw it all in if she found someone special. Zara's always wanted to find love, but so far, no luck.'

'Georgina said she's gay.'

Jed screwed up his face. 'She was. Didn't work out. Last time she was in town I thought she and Charlie were going to hook up. And at school she and Ben were always close.'

'Oh?' For some reason, the thought of Ben and Zara together annoyed her.

'Close. The way you and I are.'

She relaxed. She and Jed had never had anything more than a platonic friendship. 'Right.'

Jed smiled. 'Your friendship means the world to me, Bel, and I'm so glad you and Georgie have hit it off.'

'It's been great getting to know her and I'm just so glad she makes you happy. I was worried for you after you had to retire, so it's good to see you smiling and focused again.'

'All things work out in the end, don't they?'

'I hope so.'

Time to change the subject before Jed brought it back around to her single status.

'I also hope I'm a good enough role model for Daisy,' Annabel said, stroking the baby's downy hair. 'What happens if she turns into a wild child when she's a teenager? Will you blame me for being a bad godmother?'

Jed laughed. 'I promise I won't blame you. According to Georgie—who's read all the books on this stuff—children are a product of four things.' He held up four fingers and counted off. 'Their parents, their siblings—if they have any—their environment, and their friends.'

Annabel smiled and wiped her brow. 'Phew. No mention of godmothers. So, I'm off the hook if she turns into a ratbag?'

'Hundred percent. Your role is simply to take an interest in her upbringing and keep me sane when she hits her teens.'

'I'll bring wine and lock away your guns.'

They both laughed.

'Is she allowed to play football when she's old enough?'

'I'm all for it but ask me again when she's at the bottom of the pack or she gets knocked out like I was, and I might change my mind.'

'What if something bad happens to you or Georgina?'

'I've told you this already. My mum or Jane will step in.'

Annabel let out an exaggerated sigh. 'Thank God for that.'

As much as she loved children and wanted to have one of her own, there was no way she wanted to take on the responsibility of raising someone else's child. She had been relieved Scott hadn't expected her to be an active stepparent to his girls.

'I promise nothing's going to happen.'

'I'll hold you to that,' she said with a smile. 'I need to get going.' Standing on tiptoes, Annabel kissed Jed on the cheek. 'It's been a big day and I have a long drive back to Geelong tonight.'

'It has been a big day,' Jed agreed. A frown crossed his brow. 'I don't know why I didn't suggest you and Ben drive up together.'

It was her turn to frown. 'What do you mean?'

'Ben lives in Geelong too.'

Chapter 2

Ben couldn't stop staring at Annabel Norton. Her dress left little to his imagination, fitting her like a second skin, yet somehow it was still a suitable outfit for church. He spent far too long during the service looking at her legs instead of concentrating on what he was supposed to be doing. It was a wonder he hadn't done something stupid and made a fool of himself.

When their gaze had briefly met at one point during the service, a beam of sunlight coming through the stained-glass windows had illuminated her eyes and he'd been captivated. He wasn't sure if he believed in love at first sight, but if he did, he'd probably be in love with Annabel Norton.

Where his ex-wife, Chantelle, had watched her weight to the point of being too skinny, Annabel was slim but with an amazing athletic figure. But although she appeared to be fit, she also had curves and a softness about her. She was, to his mind, perfect.

And her auburn hair. When the light hit it, it reminded him of sunlight filtering through autumn leaves. Long loose curls fell halfway down her back, and he itched to run his fingers through it. Did it feel as soft as it looked?

As Annabel had stood at the altar nervously scanning the crowd, he couldn't fathom why every eye in the church wasn't on her. She wasn't trying to draw attention to herself, but he hadn't stopped gawking at her from the moment Jed had introduced them outside the church, just before the service had started.

And an hour later, he still couldn't look away. Annabel was magnetic, with that special something that made it impossible for him to pull his eyes away from. He'd spent the entire service watching her and was delighted when he'd caught her looking at him a few times. It had intrigued him when she'd blushed to the roots of her hair when she realised she'd been sprung.

It was interesting though; something about her gave him the impression she didn't want to be there. He was an expert at reading people and when they'd first been introduced, there was something aloof and slightly unapproachable in her manner. When she smiled, it never quite reached her eyes. He figured she was just nervous. Or perhaps shy. He wondered if it was more than that, then kicked himself for overthinking as usual. Other than Jed and Georgie, and maybe some of Jed's former teammates, Annabel probably didn't know anyone in Glengarrick, and she was feeling out of place. She'd only spoken a few words, but he'd been surprised by how sweet her voice was. In his professional experience, most people presumed quietly spoken women were timid or meek, but he'd learned that sometimes the quiet ones limited their speech so that when they spoke, people listened. When they had something to say, it was generally powerful. Was Annabel one of those types of women?

They hadn't had a chance to meet at Jed and Georgie's wedding because Charlie Sullivan, one of his mates from school, had stuck to Annabel's side like glue. At least Charlie wasn't here today to try his luck again.

When Annabel blew a kiss to Jed and hugged Georgie, Ben realised she was about to leave. He didn't want her to go without talking to her, so he made a decision, and headed towards her. He needed to do something before he regretted it.

'Annabel?'

She spun around and for a split second he struggled to remember what he'd wanted to say to her. Her assessment of him was so swift and unexpected he would have missed it if it wasn't his job to watch people's reactions closely. He bit back a smile. If he wasn't mistaken, her eyes had flashed with a hint of admiration. He relaxed a little. Up close, in heels, she was almost the same height as he was, and he was nearly six foot two.

He looked directly into her eyes. 'I'm not sure what the proper etiquette is when it comes to baby baptisms but isn't this the time when the godparents dance?'

If his question caught her off-guard, he didn't see it. She barely blinked.

'I think the waltz is reserved for weddings,' she replied with a flicker of a smile that revealed a dimple in her left cheek.

He pretended to pout. 'Really? No godfather-of-the-child dance?'

She shook her head.

He lifted his arms then let them drop to his sides. 'Darn. I only agreed to do this gig if I got to dance with the cute godmother at the end of the day.'

When she chuckled and both dimples made an appearance, a flash of warmth spread through him. Either she appreciated the compliment, or she was humouring him and counting down the seconds before she could escape. Either way, he wasn't giving up yet.

'Sorry, Ben, I don't dance.'

'What a shame. I was looking forward to dancing with you.'

Confusion creased her brow. 'Why?'

'It's what godparents do,' he said. 'It's in the rule book.'

Her eyes flashed again, doing something to him he couldn't put his finger on. Then she laughed. It was a sweet laugh and he wanted to hear it again.

'There is no rule book.'

'Georgina didn't give you a rule book?' he asked with mock seriousness.

She shook her head and the curls bounced. 'Nope.'

Ben lifted a hand and pretended to wipe sweat from his brow. 'Just as well you didn't do or say something wrong. Could've been a disaster.'

She tilted her head to one side. 'It's a bit hard to say or do anything wrong when all we had to do was stand there and smile and get prayed over.'

He scratched his jaw. 'Yeah, I need to talk to Jed about that. I'm not happy.'

Her eyebrows rose. 'About what? Being prayed over?'

'No, the fact we didn't get a chance to speak, say a few words, do something significant. I was hoping at least I'd get to tip the water on Daisy's head.'

Her eyes crinkled with withheld laughter. 'I'm pretty sure that's the priest's job.'

'Vicar,' he corrected, loving the easy banter with her, and loving the way her emotions flickered across her face. She was easier to read than a book.

'What?'

'Vicar. It was an Anglican service, not Catholic.'

'Does it matter?'

'I'd say yes, it probably matters to the vicar. And his wife.'

'O-k-ay. Right. Well, I'm glad I didn't have to say or do anything.'

'Not into public speaking?'

'Not into drawing attention to myself, no.'

'Then perhaps I shouldn't tell you that you failed miserably.'

Her eyes widened further, and she stared up at him, unblinking, as if wondering whether she'd heard him correctly.

He jumped in. What did he have to lose? If he didn't tell this woman how attractive he found her and she walked away from him without knowing, he'd kick himself for days.

'You were mesmerising, Annabel. Sheesh.' He let out a long, low whistle. 'Trust me, every man in this church, single or otherwise, in the sight of God as their witness, was not paying any attention to Daisy Delaney. And they definitely weren't focusing on the vicar either.'

Her face matched her hair and for a moment he thought he'd pushed it too far.

'They were *not* looking at me.'

'I beg to differ. I watched them.'

She playfully punched him in the arm. 'You should have been concentrating.'

'I'm a man who can multitask.'

She folded her arms across her chest. 'Do you have a comeback for everything?'

'Usually.'

This time her response was an exaggerated eye roll. 'Are you flirting with me?'

'I'm trying. Is it working? I'm a bit rusty.'

She laughed again. 'Too early to tell. I barely know you. This might be how you are with all the girls you meet.'

'Well, Miss Norton, technically you *do* know me. You know my name, and after today, we're practically related.'

'Yeah? How do you figure that?'

'Godparents. It's like a binding legal contract thingie.'

'Really?' She chuckled again. 'A thingie? I did not know that. Was that in the rulebook too?'

'Maybe not,' he admitted, 'but at my brother and sister's kids' baptisms it was protocol that the godparents danced together.'

'Ha!' She poked his bicep with her forefinger. 'I knew you weren't a rookie. How many baptisms have you been to?'

He held up four fingers. 'Four. My big sister Natalie and her husband Rob have two girls, Hannah and Rebecca. My older brother James and his wife Sasha have three daughters. Lily, and twins, Ava and Bella. You could say I'm a serial godparent.'

'Your siblings must trust you.'

He straightened and puffed out his chest. 'I happen to be very trustworthy, thank you very much.'

'I guess that's why Jed chose you. You're a trustworthy kind of guy.' Her tone held a hint of mockery, but he found it endearing.

He chuckled. 'Nah. I think Jed chose me because I'm the only bloke in Glengarrick other than Charlie without any kids. Everyone else has their hands full.'

'No kids by choice or circumstance?'

'Choice,' he replied automatically. After a beat, he added, 'my ex-wife didn't want kids.'

'Right. But what about you? Did *you* want kids?'

He was surprised at her personal question but didn't baulk. Sometimes he wanted a family, especially on days like today when he saw how happy his mates were.

'I'm not sure. Maybe. But it wouldn't be fair to have kids— not in my line of work.'

That was why Chantelle had left him. Or the reason she gave, at least. She told him she didn't want to go to bed worrying he'd be killed, and she'd be left a single mother. She'd also accused him of never communicating his feelings with her. He thought he was doing the right thing, shielding her from the stressors of his job, but that had obviously backfired. It wasn't that he hadn't wanted to be transparent with her, but sometimes it was better to shove down the pressure and get on with life. He got why so many cops ended up marrying cops. Very few people understood what they went through.

'What do you do?' Annabel asked, interrupting his circling thoughts.

'I'm a policeman,' he said, without elaboration. Too often he found once he'd told people what he did for a job they got all funny. He needed to change the subject and move back onto solid ground that didn't involve talking about himself. And he needed to lighten the mood. 'Anyway, like I said,' he continued with a smile, 'we're practically related and it's in the rules the godparents must dance. If not now, maybe another time. What do you think?'

'It's still a "no", sorry. I don't dance. Footy injury.'

She held up her foot and gave it a wiggle, flashing toenail polish and enough leg to cause his blood to overheat again. Until then he hadn't realised how high her heels were. No wonder she was so tall. He dragged his eyes back to her face.

'Footy?' he asked.

She nodded. 'I played for the *Cats*.'

No wonder she looked so fit. 'As in the AFL women's comp?'

She nodded. 'AFLW.'

His estimation of her skyrocketed higher. 'Wow,' he said. And he meant it. 'That's seriously impressive. Is that how you know Jed?'

'Yeah. I rucked for the women's team when he was rucking for the men. The club used us for a lot of promo stuff, and we became great friends when I was playing.'

'Was?'

'Retired now.'

'Injury?' He pointed to her foot.

'No.' She blushed. 'I fibbed about the injury. Age caught up with me. Time to let the younger girls have a go. I'll be thirty-five next year.'

'Do you still live in Geelong?'

She nodded but didn't elaborate, and he didn't want to appear too forward by basically forcing her address from her.

'Jed told me you live in Geelong too.'

He smiled. 'I grew up here, but yeah, I currently live in Geelong. I have a place in one of the new apartments on Western Beach.'

'Nice.'

They chatted for a few minutes about his apartment, how much Geelong had changed in the last five years, their favourite cafes and how much they loved the waterfront. They figured their paths had probably crossed at some point in time as they both seemed to enjoy going to the same places.

'Well, if you won't dance with me, it's my loss.' He sighed theatrically. 'I've been looking forward to it all morning.'

The blush crept up her neck again and he allowed himself the hope that maybe he hadn't lost his touch after all.

'Sorry, Ben. It's still a no.'

He sighed again. 'I guess I'm not going to win, am I?'

One eyebrow lifted. 'I wasn't aware it was a competition.'

Ask her out, a little voice shouted from his shoulder.

'Not a competition. But if you won't dance with me today, would you at least give me your phone number so I can take you out and buy you a drink some time?'

Before she could reply, they were interrupted by Jed barrelling past with a crying Daisy in one arm and a nappy bag slung across one shoulder—a father on a mission.

'Oi, Nails, stop chatting Annabel up. Seriously, you have the worst radar when it comes to picking up women. You know the rules. You're only meant to go after the available ones.'

Disappointment mixed with confusion and a weight of heaviness fell on Ben. He looked down at Annabel. The first thing he'd done was check her left hand—there was no ring. Still, he shouldn't have flirted with her until he knew she was single.

'You're seeing someone?' he asked.

'No…no. I'm not,' she stammered. She appeared to have shrunk in front of him.

She dipped her head, whether from embarrassment or something else, Ben couldn't tell.

'But you're not single,' he clarified.

'I *am* single. But Scott and I recently broke up and I'd just finished telling Jed I'm not ready to start seeing anyone yet. He's being sweet and trying to protect me, that's all.'

That made sense. And filled Ben with a shard of hope. 'How long were you and this Scott guy together?'

'Four years.'

He studied her closely. There was a funny catch in her voice and her eyes no longer shone the way they had earlier. She'd put up a mask and despite his years of work as a detective, and despite how easily he'd read her earlier, now he couldn't figure out what was going on in her head.

Annabel slipped her handbag over her shoulder and held out her hand. 'Sorry about my no dance rule.' She smiled warmly but it no longer reached her eyes. 'It was lovely meeting you, Ben.'

He caught her fingers in his briefly before letting them go. 'It was nice meeting you too, Annabel. I guess I'll see you round.'

'I guess.'

'Probably at Daisy's twenty-first,' he said, not wanting the conversation to end on this awkward note.

'Probably,' she agreed, taking another step back.

He smiled. 'Unless I bump into you sooner in Geelong.'

She didn't respond.

He followed her with his eyes as she waved goodbye to Georgie and tried to ignore whatever it was pulling at his stomach and fluttering in his throat. But he couldn't. The feeling was vaguely familiar and as he stood there, watching her, he realised what it was.

Yearning.

Chapter 3

One year earlier

Ben pushed open the door of *The Piano Bar*, stopped in his tracks and looked around. The moody hues and intimate setting felt like a New York jazz club. He let out a soft whistle. Full marks to Zara for choosing such a great venue for her 80s themed thirtieth birthday party.

He scanned the packed room for the birthday girl. When he caught sight of her, he couldn't help but grin. Typical Zazu. The venue might be sophisticated, but nothing about Zara was after she'd had a few drinks. Looking at her, she'd crossed the line from tipsy to sozzled hours earlier.

Her blonde, teased hair was dishevelled, her signature red lippy gone, and the top buttons of her white shirt had come undone, exposing her cleavage. She wore skin-tight acid wash jeans which left nothing to the imagination and although he couldn't see her feet, she'd be wearing killer heels. She always did. That was Zara. She wasn't the life of the party—she *was* the party.

She was dancing with a guy Ben didn't know and judging by the look on the man's face, he had plans with her for later that night. Ben chuckled to himself. The guy was going to be disappointed if he found out Zara sometimes batted for the other team.

He spotted a few familiar faces. He'd known Zara his whole life and they had many mutual friends. Born two hours apart in the same small hospital in Stockton, the nearest town to Glengarrick, they'd grown up on neighbouring properties, attended the local primary school together, then gone to high school together in Stockton, along with the rest of the gang—Jed, Georgina, Charlie, Jack, Emma and Kate.

After year twelve, they'd all left town. He and Zara went to Melbourne University and lived at Ormond College, one of the student residences, for two years before moving out and flatting together in Carlton. Theirs was a long history of close friendship and happy memories.

As much as their parents would have liked them to get together, Ben and Zara knew it would never work. They were best mates. Whenever anyone who didn't know them asked if they were a couple, they'd laugh and say they were more like siblings, only better, because they never argued.

When Zara eventually looked his way, Ben gave her a wave.

'Nails!' Her high-pitched squeal carried above the sound of the singing. She whispered something to the guy she was dancing with and headed towards him.

Ben fought another smile as Zara weaved her way through the throng of people to get to him.

'Happy birthday!' she shrieked, nearly piercing his eardrum as she leaned in for a kiss.

'Happy birthday to you too, Zazu.' He touched her teased hair. 'Looking a bit wild tonight.'

'And why not. You only turn thirty once.'

'True.'

'I'm glad you came. I know this isn't your scene,' she said. She looked him up and down, taking in what he was wearing. He wore his standard chinos and a button-up shirt, with the sleeves rolled to his elbows. 'I should have known you wouldn't dress up,' she accused.

'Acid wash, padded shoulders and lycra aren't my thing,' he replied. He'd rolled his eyes when he read the invitation. There was no way he was dressing up in 80s clothes and drawing attention to himself.

'At least you showed up,' she yelled into his ear.

It was hard to hear her over the pumping disco beat. 'Wouldn't have missed it for the world,' he said, gazing around. 'Bit different from the birthday parties of our childhood.'

Over the years as kids they'd shared parties at the park, McDonald's, and an indoor trampoline centre. As they got older, the parties moved to various pubs and clubs. This was the best venue yet.

She dragged him into an adjoining room where it was marginally quieter, and they found a vacant table and turned their chairs so they sat side by side.

'Do you want a drink?' she asked.

'Nah, I'm driving.'

She frowned. 'Why didn't you get an Uber?'

'I'm working tomorrow so I don't want a late night.'

She glared at him.

'Sorry. I couldn't get my shift covered.'

'Yeah, sure.'

'If I hang around looking like this, I'll cramp your style.' He pointed to the guy she'd been dancing with. 'Does he know about you and Kath?'

'That's finished. Long story. I'm done with women.'

He raised an eyebrow but didn't say anything.

'So, what's with him?' He flicked his head in that direction again.

'A bit of fun.'

'Let him down gently, won't you?'

Zara giggled. 'You're such an old soul, Nails.'

'Gee, thanks. I take it you don't mean that as a compliment. I'm already feeling ancient.'

He'd felt weirdly melancholic all day and nothing he'd done could shift the feeling that life was passing him by. By now he'd expected he would have been settled down with a wife and children. If only he'd had a crystal ball before he got married to Chantelle, he would have called it off sooner.

'Don't tell me you're having some sort of mid-life crisis,' Zara said, crossing her arms over her chest.

'At thirty? I hope not.' It wasn't a midlife crisis, but lately he'd felt restless and unsettled and didn't know why. 'I guess I just thought by my age I would have achieved something more than I have.'

The moment he spoke, he regretted his outburst. He was usually so good at holding his emotions in check. One of the things he liked about Zara was that she never held back from speaking her mind, but right now, he didn't need her opinions. When she stuck out her chin and glared at him, he braced himself for the verbal onslaught.

'Are you flipping kidding me? You're in charge of one of the most specialised units in the Victoria Police. Do you think responding to high-risk incidents shows a lack of achievement? Bloody hell, Ben, you save lives every day.'

'As do you,' he retorted.

Zara was a successful lawyer, and her speciality was working with domestic violence victims. He had no idea how she did what she did.

'When it comes to success, trust me, Nails, you have it in spades. Stop worrying about whether you've done anything worthwhile. You have. End. Of. Story.'

'I guess.'

'You know what your problem is?' Zara asked.

'I figure you're about to tell me.'

'You need to get back in the game.'

Ben bit back a reply. Dating was a game he didn't want to play again. He'd been wounded the first time and seriously hurt the second. And he was still recovering nearly three years later. It would take a lot for him to trust another woman.

Zara waved an arm around the room. 'There are plenty of single women here for you to choose. Why don't you live a little? Call in sick tomorrow. Let your hair down. Have a good time. It doesn't have to be forever.'

'First off, I'm not into one-night stands. You know that. And secondly, the last thing I need is another woman in my life. I swear, when it comes to love, I suck.'

She touched his arm, and her eyes became serious. 'That's because you never listen to me. Anyway, I think you're lonely and what you need is a woman to keep you company.'

'Ah, so *that's* my problem is it? I'm lonely.' He sighed. 'I dunno, Zazu. Why is it my dreams are so far from my reality?'

Zara's false eyelashes flickered. 'Well, aren't you Mr. Philosophical tonight? Maybe I should call the party off, send everyone home, and you and I can go through a couple of good bottles of red and commiserate about how we're both thirty and still single.'

'Sorry. I shouldn't have said anything. It's just that life has gone so fast and when I look back I see lost chance and opportunity and I can't shake the feeling I've missed out or that I should be doing something more with my life. Then I feel bad because I have a great life. My parents are both alive and we have a great relationship. I get along well with my siblings and their families. I have a fulfilling career I love. I live in a great house and have a reasonable degree of financial security. Other than two failed marriages, my life has been great. *Is* great,' he quickly amended.

'Oh, sweetie.' Zara put an arm around his shoulders.

'And here I am being Benny-Boring.' He put a hand behind Zara's neck and pulled her close, planting a kiss on her forehead. 'Sorry, Zazu. This is not how you want to spend your birthday— listening to me carry on like a misery guts.'

'*Our* birthday,' she reminded him.

'Yeah. Our birthday.'

They shared a smile.

Zara got him and he'd lost count of how many times he'd called her instead of Chantelle to download after a particularly difficult shift.

'Well, whatever you do, Nails, if you *are* having a midlife crisis, don't buy a leather recliner.'

Ben frowned at her. 'What?'

'As soon as you buy a leather recliner, that's it. You'll get fat and bored.' She put a hand on his arm and squeezed. 'And *that's* when life will be over. You know what I always say. You have to make every moment matter. We're all going to die one day, and that leaves you two choices. Either check out now and buy a recliner or go out there and get back on the horse.'

Ben smiled. If it was only that simple.

'Also, word of advice? Put a smile on your face. That grumpy face is a turn off. Find yourself someone to love and start living again. You checked out when Chantelle left you and if you keep going the way you are, you *will* be an old man sitting in your recliner before you know it.'

And that was Zazu. As tactful as ever.

'Maybe I'll buy a flashy sports car instead,' he teased.

She rolled her eyes. 'Then I'll know for sure you've lost the plot. Honestly, I've known you my entire life and I've never lied to you. Right now, you need to hear the truth. If you keep going down this path of self-doubt, you're going to have a ton of regrets in twenty years' time. That's not what you want.'

It wasn't.

'Discomfort isn't a bad thing. Neither is stress. And feeling unsettled can be a good thing too because it forces you to get off your backside and do something about how you're feeling. What you need is to do something different to break you from this funk.'

'If you're looking for a career change, you'd make a good psychologist.'

'It's basically what I do now, anyway.'

'So, what should I do?' he asked. 'Learn an instrument? Take up golf? Study French? Go to cookery school?'

She laughed. 'Nope.'

When Zara leaned forward and her eyes darkened, Ben's heart thudded in his ears. He recognised that look. When Zara got that look, she was up to something and it usually got someone in trouble.

'I'm thinking something bigger than that. Something *radically* different. Something altruistic.'

He went still. 'Like what?'

'Donate sperm.'

He sat back in his chair and stared at her. It wasn't often he was lost for words.

'I was going to ask you another time, but I need to say something now before I chicken out. I want to have a baby, Ben, and I want to use your sperm.'

If he'd had a drink in his mouth, he would have sprayed it everywhere. 'WHAT?'

Zara pushed on. 'I've always wanted a baby and I'm not getting any younger.'

His head felt like he was in a fog. 'You want to sleep with me so you can have a baby?'

'Ew, God, no!' Zara laughed. 'I just want your sperm. In a cup. In a jar. Whatever. I'll do IVF. That'll be the easiest way.'

He shook his head. 'How much have you had to drink tonight?'

'I'm not drunk.'

'Only a drunk person would ask their friend for sperm.' He ran his hands through his hair. She had to be joking. Any minute now she'd laugh and punch him in the arm and cry "Gotcha!" He swallowed. 'Hang on. Let me get this absolutely straight. You want *my* sperm to make a baby?'

She nodded.

'Are you insane?'

She stared at him unblinking.

He exhaled in a rush. 'I can't do that.'

'Why not?'

'It's just too weird.' He pointed to the dance floor. 'Why me? Why not that guy you were dancing with? He couldn't take his eyes off you. Ask him.'

'I don't even know his name.'

'Geez, Zazu. I don't know. Can I at least think about it?'

'Of course.' She beamed. 'I'll call you tomorrow for your answer.'

He stood. 'I'm gonna go.'

'You'll definitely consider it?'

'Yeah. I'll consider it.'

Or not.

Zara flung her arms around his neck again and squeezed so tight that for a second he worried that he'd pass out.

'Best. Birthday. Ever!' she screamed.

'All right, don't get carried away.' He gave her his best stern look. 'I didn't say yes, I just said I'd consider it. You get that, yeah?'

'Absolutely.' She held up two crossed fingers in front of his face.

He narrowed his gaze. 'What if I say no?'

'How long have I known you? You've never been able to say no to me.'

She was right. That's what worried him.

***

On Thursday morning Ben sat in a café in Geelong waiting for Zara. He'd slept badly again because her ridiculous idea kept pinging around in his head. The barista brought over another coffee and Ben stirred it while scrolling mindlessly through Facebook on his phone. It was impossible to concentrate.

Moments later Zara swept in and went straight to the counter to place her order before coming over to him. After kissing his cheek, she sat, leaning forward, both elbows on the table, eyes sparkling. 'So? Have you decided?'

'How did you pull up after your party?' he asked.

She rolled her eyes at him for answering a question with a question. 'I may have had a terrible hangover for a day or so.'

The waiter brought over a green smoothie. Ben laughed. 'I take it you still have a headache?'

'I'm detoxing,' she replied before taking a sip through the metal straw. 'For the baby.'

He stayed quiet. It was something he'd learned years ago, and it was one of the reasons he was so good at his job. He could quite happily sit in silence for hours if that's what it took. He never felt the need to pepper silence with words.

Zara tightened her grip on the glass. 'I know what you're doing Ben. Out with it. Yes or no.'

'I have a few questions.'

In truth he had hundreds. Thousands.

'I'm sure you do. I'm sure your first question is why I picked you.'

'I presume you picked me because I'm the only guy you could ask.'

'That's one reason.' She smiled. 'And also, because you come from good stock.'

'What am I now? A prized bull?'

She poked out her tongue.

'Okay. Start by telling me everything. What brought you to this point? I mean, seriously, where did you get the idea of a sperm donor? If you want kids this bad, why don't you foster or adopt. Or

God forbid, take the more conventional route—wait until you meet someone and fall pregnant the normal way.'

'You're such a man. You've got no idea. On Saturday morning, I stared into the mirror trying to tell myself thirty isn't old, but I knew I was kidding myself. My uterus is ageing and if I don't do something soon, I'm going to miss my chance.'

'But what if you meet someone tomorrow?'

'That's the issue, Nails. Even if I *did* meet someone, and even if I went through the whole dating-getting-to-know-you-circus, it would take months, years. I'd have to go through the hassle of an engagement, a wedding, the honeymoon. By the time I fell pregnant it could be another two years or more. And everyone knows how hard it is to have kids after thirty-five.'

'Hard, but not impossible.'

Zara took another sip of her green stuff and grimaced as she swallowed.

'What about adoption?' he asked.

'Too expensive and it's not easy in Australia, especially if you're single.'

'Fostering?'

'Too risky.' She smiled. 'And before you suggest it, I'm not going to sleep with a stranger and hope I fall pregnant. I've thought about it from every angle and I want to do it on my own.'

'With my sperm.'

'With your sperm.'

'Are you sure you can't use someone else instead of me—like an anonymous donor?'

She exhaled loudly. 'Well I *can* I suppose. They have a donor register, but the thing is I don't want some stranger's DNA in my child's blood. I know you. I know your family.'

'Good stock,' he repeated.

She let out a little laugh before tucking a strand of her hair behind an ear. 'Do you think I'm being selfish?'

Good question. Did he? If he was honest, it was hard to wrap his head around the whole thing. He was a traditionalist and in his way of thinking, every child deserved to know its parents. If he did this for Zara, there was no way he wanted the child to know he was the father.

'I know what you're thinking,' she said, 'but the reality is a baby doesn't ask to be born or get a say in who its parents are.'

'Yet you're deliberately, knowingly, *willingly*, taking that opportunity away from your child.'

'That's harsh.'

'It's just my opinion, Zars. Besides, in my line of work I've seen the impact on kids who don't have a father figure. You're putting a lot of pressure on a child to be raised not knowing their father.'

'But plenty of children are raised without a parent.'

'I know. But is that what you really want? It's not going to be easy raising a child on your own.'

'The thing is, Ben, families don't look the way they used to. The traditional family—the nuclear family like you and I grew up with—they don't exist anymore. Family doesn't have to mean those you're biologically related to. Different types of threads make up the fabric of families.'

Silence fell. In the kitchen they heard the sound of crockery and cutlery being washed.

'If you want to be involved you can be.'

'I don't think I'd want that.'

Zara shrugged. 'It's up to you.'

The silence lengthened.

'Is it legal?' he asked eventually.

'Of course, it's legal. I wouldn't ask you to do anything that wasn't above board. I'll even draw up a contract if it makes you feel better.'

'What will our parents say if they find out?'

Her head snapped up. 'You want to tell them?'

He shook his head. There was no way he would ever tell them. Family bloodlines were as important to his parents as the bloodlines of the cows and sheep they bred back in Glengarrick. If they had any inkling there was another grandchild of theirs out there, it would devastate them.

'I think if we do this, we need to keep it a total secret. Just between us,' he said.

She nodded. 'Fine with me. Maybe when the baby is old enough, we can tell it.'

He ran his hands through his hair. This whole plan was full of potholes. Large potholes. 'What will you tell it? How it was conceived? Or that I'm the father?'

'Whatever you want, Nails. It's up to you.'

Ben sighed wearily. 'If I say yes, it's a once off thing, okay. If you don't fall pregnant straight away, I'm not going back to do it all again.'

'But...'

'No buts.' He stared at her. 'And Zazu, if it *does* works, I'm serious. You don't tell a soul. I won't be there for you at the birth. I won't have people getting any hint that I'm the father.'

She folded her arms across her chest and glared at him. 'You won't be the father.'

'Just the sperm donor, right?'

'That's right.'

'I don't want this to ruin our friendship.'

'How could it?' she asked.

A million different ways.

'We're best friends. Nothing alters that unless you choose to walk away from me.' Tears welled in her eyes as she took his hands in hers. 'Please say you'll do it.'

He sighed heavily. 'Just promise me things won't get creepy between us.'

'They won't.'

'Okay,' he said finally, begrudgingly. 'I'll do it.'

'When?'

'I don't know. How long does it take?'

'You'll have to see a counsellor at the IVF clinic first. I can make an appointment for you.'

'I can do that. Just give me the number.'

'I'll text it to you.'

He stood and ran his hands through his hair again. 'Jeez I hope we're doing the right thing, Zazu. I don't know how you can be so certain.'

She threw herself at him and hugged him tight. 'We are doing the right thing, I promise you. And I also promise everything will work out. It's going to be perfect.'

'What if I meet someone? What am I supposed to tell her?'

'It's a moot point. You haven't met anyone.' She put a hand on his arm. 'Anyway, if she loves you, she'll understand.'

Chapter 4

The morning after Daisy's baptism, Annabel was back at the hospital where she worked as a nurse. Many people thought playing sport for a living was a dream come true. It was, but it came with challenges. Because of the semi-professional nature of the game, to earn an adequate income, all the AFLW players had to work other jobs.

It had been a tough three years and while she'd never regretted her decision to juggle her two jobs—nursing and playing footy—it had come at a cost.

Professionally she hadn't been able to concentrate on her nursing career because footy had always come first. Personally, she'd had to forgo a social life. It was probably no wonder her relationship with Scott had broken down—she'd given him her second, and sometimes third best.

For the last five years she'd worked in the emergency department of a hospital in Melbourne, fitting her shifts in around training sessions and games. It hadn't been easy, but she'd never complained. The only one who'd complained was Scott.

She loved nursing, but in the last few months, she'd struggled. It wasn't just dealing with the breakup that was weighing heavily on her. The workload was getting tougher and it felt like every shift was busier than the one before. It was rare to have a day like today when they weren't slammed. She should have taken time off after splitting up with Scott but going to work and picking up extra shifts kept her mind off all she'd lost. Not just Scott, but football.

It didn't help that she was also couch surfing—moving between friend's spare rooms and living out of her suitcase. But until she got some money from Scott as part of the settlement he'd promised her, she'd didn't have another option. She needed to work to eat.

Today's shift had been blessedly uneventful, allowing her plenty of time to reflect on what a great weekend she'd had in Glengarrick. If only Jed hadn't interrupted her conversation with Ben Naylor. She would have given her number to him and agreed to have dinner or a drink with him. But the look on his face when she told him she'd only recently broken off a long-term relationship said it all. He wasn't going to be a rebound. Not that she blamed him.

Still, it didn't stop her thinking about him constantly. She didn't normally feel nervous around new people, but every time she'd tried to smile, her lips had felt all wobbly and her breath had caught in the back of her throat. Even her skin had tingled where he'd touched her. She couldn't remember the last time anyone had made her feel that way. And the way he'd looked at her had made her think he wanted to pull her into his arms and envelop her in a warm bear hug. If he had, she would have accepted his hug, and returned it, willingly.

'Can't believe what a quiet shift we've had,' Adam, one of the other nurses, said, interrupting her thoughts.

They were standing side by side restocking the trolleys for the afternoon staff. At two-thirty-five, with only twenty-five minutes left of the shift before handover, there were only two snotty-nosed kids and their worried mothers in the waiting room.

Annabel rolled her eyes. 'I'll be cranky if you've just jinxed us.'

'Nah, we're all good. Waiting room's almost empty.'

'As if *that* means anything.'

'We can't complain. It's been a good day. The hardest thing we did was look after that little girl.'

'Oh my gosh,' Annabel said with another chuckle. 'She had the face of an angel and the strength of a devil.'

'How's your arm?'

Annabel rubbed the spot where the four-year-old had bitten her, almost breaking the skin. 'It's a wonder *I* didn't need stitches.'

Paige had cut her head open at day care and it had needed suturing. Her dad had taken her to their local GP, but neither the dad nor the doctor could hold Paige still and the GP had wisely sent them into the emergency department. The little girl's screams could be heard in the car park and they'd broken the monotony of the afternoon. In the process of trying to calm her down and give her some nitrous oxide, she'd bitten Annabel's arm.

As Annabel closed the drawer on the trolley, the bat phone—nicknamed after the phone in the 1960s Batman TV series—clanged, alerting everyone that an ambulance was on its way with a critical patient. Her pulse accelerated.

She glared at Adam and he groaned. 'I do it every time.'

They headed to the desk and waited while the nurse in charge took down the details of the call.

Terri hung up and looked at them. 'Hope neither of you are in a rush to get home. I'll need all hands on-deck for this one.'

Annabel waited.

'Police were called to a house where a guy had been smoking with his oxygen tank on.'

'How bad?'

'Beyond bad. He blew up half his face.'

Annabel winced. 'How far out are the ambos?'

'Probably five minutes, max. The cop I spoke with said he's in a real bad way. Neighbours called triple O and reported no-one had been near the house for years because of his dogs. When they got there, they couldn't get near the door. They had to shoot the dogs to get inside. The place reeked of animal urine and faeces and the guy was covered in his own crap too.'

Adam swore.

Annabel's heart went out for the police and paramedics as she imagined how bad this guy would look and smell. Some days their job was crappy and thankless. An image of Ben came to mind and she pictured him in uniform at the scene trying to negotiate with a pack of dogs to calm them down so they could get to the patient.

'Bel!'

She tuned back in. Adam was saying something.

'Sorry. What?'

'Let's go.'

She jogged to keep up with Adam as he strode towards the resus bay.

Not many things mobilised the emergency department staff like a trauma and it never ceased to amaze Annabel the way extra hands always seemed to materialise when a real emergency presented itself. The afternoon staff who had arrived early came from the tearoom the moment the message was passed around that a burns victim was on the way in.

As Annabel waited in resus, her mind went to the emergency algorithm, DRSABCD. A burnt face meant a burnt tongue, throat, and larynx, and swelling. Swelling on the outside was bad enough but inside the throat, it would close off the airway at once. His airway was their main priority.

When the patient arrived a few minutes later, Adam and Annabel shared a look. He was the sickest patient Annabel had seen in months. His heart rate was through the roof, his blood pressure was circling the drain and his oxygen saturation levels were less than fifty percent. The paramedics had scooped and run and although they'd tried to intubate on the way, they'd been unsuccessful. The man reeked of scorched skin and hair as well as a mix of cigarettes, alcohol and urine. Annabel almost gagged as she helped transfer him from the trolley to the bed.

Two doctors and an anaesthetist swooped and quickly sedated him and paralysed him and had the breathing tube down his airway almost before Annabel had time to turn on the ventilator and dial up the appropriate settings.

'I overheard one of the ambos say he needed his oxygen on full blast to muster enough breath to inhale his cigarettes,' Terri said.

'That's dedication to smoking right there,' Adam replied.

As time passed, the patient's condition went downhill quickly. The paralytic drug wore off and he began to squirm. As he did, his blood pressure and heart rate skyrocketed. He reached for the tube in his mouth and it took all Annabel's strength to hold him down and maintain his airway.

'We need more sedation,' she growled. 'If he pulls this tube out, he's gone.'

'He's probably gone anyway,' Adam mumbled under his breath as he gave a bolus dose of propofol.

'Is that his BP?' one of the doctors called out.

Annabel looked up at the monitor. Seventy-five systolic. She frowned. Moments earlier, it had been two-seventy-five.

Adam wrapped a blood pressure cuff around the man's upper arm and inflated it. He listened, frowning, before glancing up at the doctor.

'It's correct,' he confirmed. 'Eighty systolic.'

Annabel put her fingers to the man's wrist. His pulse was barely palpable beneath her fingertips. 'He's gonna crash.'

'Does anyone know his resus status?' Terri called out.

'No idea. Cops haven't been able to find his family yet,' one of the paramedics replied.

'Dammit.'

'What's caused his BP to drop so quickly?' Terri asked, staring at the monitor.

'Don't know,' Annabel replied. She was having enough trouble keeping the man properly ventilated to watch his blood pressure.

'He's going to need inotropes. I'll grab aramine and norad just in case.'

Terri dashed off and as Annabel secured the endo-tracheal tube with tape around the back of the man's head, she went through a list of possibilities. Was he bleeding from somewhere? Was the ETT in too far? Had it been pulled out too far? She put her stethoscope in her ears and listened to his chest. Equal air entry.

She checked the tube. Still at twenty-four centimetres to the lip. She rechecked the ventilator settings. They were appropriate. Yet his blood pressure continued to fall. What was going on? What had they missed?

She looked at Adam and he shrugged. 'I've checked all the lines and leads and double checked the drugs. Everything looks right to me. He probably just needs more filling.'

Neither of the doctors seemed overly concerned. They were more worried about covering his burns which was important too.

Terri returned with an armload of IV fluids, ampoules of Noradrenaline, pre-mixed syringes of Metaraminol, a half dozen extra IV lines and a drug chart tucked under her arm.

More possibilities raced through Annabel's mind. Had he had a heart attack? Had his emphysema caused a rip in his lung leading to a build-up of air?

Adam administered the Metaraminol and it brought his blood pressure up, but it was only a temporary measure. For a moment, an eerie silence fell over the room, broken by the whoosh and whir of the ventilator.

Everyone froze when the bat phone rang again.

Annabel massaged her temples. She didn't know how much longer she could keep up with the pace of this job.

Terri dashed off to answer the phone and returned a minute later, her face white. 'We've got two more coming in. MVA coming first. Cardiac arrest, second.'

In their small emergency department, it was rare to have two emergencies back to back and it stretched everyone tight. Three emergencies? They didn't have room. And they weren't equipped for trauma cases like this.

'Where the hell are we supposed to put them?' Liz, one of the doctors, called out.

'Is he stable?' Terri asked, pointing to the burns patient.

'He's stable enough for now,' another doctor replied. 'I've called the retrieval team and they'll get him to the burns unit at The Alfred. That's where he should have gone in the first place.'

'Move him into another cubicle and get these ones ready.' Terri touched Annabel on the shoulder as she rushed past. 'You and Adam can take the next one. The MVA. Your overtime is approved.'

'I don't want more overtime,' Annabel mumbled, but Terri was gone.

Everyone sprang into action again and within moments the burns victim was moved out of resus and the bay was restocked and ready for the next patient.

Four minutes later two female paramedics rolled a woman in. A third female paramedic was straddled over the patient on the stretcher doing chest compressions. The patient—Annabel couldn't tell whether it was a man or a woman—was ashen.

'I thought we were getting the MVA,' Adam muttered, face grim.

'Doesn't matter. Let's get this one sorted first,' Annabel replied.

'What've we got,' Liz asked as she entered the room donning gloves.

One of the paramedics consulted notes on his laptop. 'Ninety-four-year-old female. Husband heard a crash in the kitchen. By the time he got up, he found her on the floor and started CPR. Called us, and when we got there, he was still doing compressions. We defibbed her twice at the scene and unbelievably got a rhythm. Lost it again on our way here and started CPR again.'

Annabel looked at the woman and shuddered. Her lips were colourless, her skin pale and mottled. Annabel looked at Adam. He shook his head. This would not end well.

'Do we know her resus status?' Liz asked gently.

'Full,' the paramedic replied.

Annabel exchanged another look with Adam.

The paramedic shrugged. 'Husband said he wants everything done.'

'Her wishes or his?' Liz asked.

'He's at least ten years younger than she is.'

Adam swore under his breath. 'Does he have any idea how this will end?'

Annabel knew. Once she'd performed CPR on an elderly man and cracked his ribs. It was the most horrific feeling knowing that the pressure of her chest compressions on his aged osteoporotic bones had caused them to splinter. One bone tore into his lungs and it had caused a pneumothorax. With nowhere for the escaped air to go, the pressure had deflated the man's lung. The doctor had inserted a large bore needle directly into the chest wall and Annabel's only comfort was hoping that because the man was unconscious, he couldn't feel the pain they were inflicting on him.

The man's wife had sobbed that they had to "do everything they could" and in between compressions, they shocked his heart twice, but it had been futile. He had briefly regained a faint pulse then it was gone and so was he. He died with a tube in his trachea, a needle in his chest and four IV cannulas in his veins.

Annabel cried so much later that night. If only people understood what they were asking her to do to the ones they loved when they said, "do everything". She didn't want to have to do this again.

'Where's the husband?' Liz asked. 'I'll go and talk to him.'

The paramedic pointed towards the ambulance bay. 'Do you want us to keep going with CPR?'

Liz nodded. 'For now. Let me get the husband in so he can say goodbye.'

A commotion at the ambulance dock caused Annabel to gather her scattered emotions. The paramedics were wheeling in the patient from the car accident. She sensed the mood change and when she glanced over and saw how bad the woman's injuries were, she immediately ripped off her gloves, and threw them in the direction of the bin.

'Go,' Terri said. 'I'll stay here.'

The paramedic continued compressions on the ninety-four-year-old.

In the other resuscitation bay, the woman's wail filled the entire emergency like a broken siren. 'My arm, my arm. It hurts so bad. My arm.'

The reason the woman's arm hurt so much was it was missing. Annabel felt bile rise in the back of her throat. They weren't set up for this kind of trauma. Time stood still for a millisecond then the clock started again, and people began shouting orders across the room.

'Airway's intact,' Liz said, 'but let's hurry up and tube her.' She glanced at Terri. 'How far away is that retrieval team. They need to take this woman first. The burn's guy will have to wait.'

For the next hour Annabel watched the grim faces of the medical team as they moved around her. It was moments like these that she had the greatest respect for the dedicated professionals she was privileged to work alongside. Every one of them did everything they could to try to save the life of a stranger.

Unfortunately, not everyone could be saved.

The woman's blood pressure dropped and despite pumping her with blood products and fluids, she was losing blood faster than they could get it into her. Annabel's hand was on the woman's pulse as it ebbed slowly away until it stopped.

In the adjoining resus bay, the ninety-four-year-old hadn't made it either and before the retrieval team had a chance to load the smoker onto another stretcher to transfer him to the burns unit at another hospital, he passed away too.

The tears came before Annabel could stop them.

Adam put an arm around her shoulder and drew her aside. 'You okay?'

She sniffed and shook her head.

'Dumb question. Of course you're not okay. Is there anything I can do?'

She shook her head again. There was nothing anyone could do. She needed to do this for herself. Pulling her shoulders back, she blew her nose and gave Adam a watery smile. 'I'll be right. I just need a few days off.'

'You need a few months off. You've been burning the candle. I've watched you. How many extra shifts have you been picking up?'

'One or two a week.' At the least. Anything to keep her mind off her how much she missed football. And Scott.

'That's not good.'

Annabel sighed. 'I know.'

'Terri will understand you need time off. Do you have any leave?'

'Weeks.'

'So, take it.'

'I think I will.'

She'd take every last minute of it.

Chapter 5

A week later Annabel was officially on six weeks' annual leave. The break was just what she needed, and she was already contemplating handing in her resignation and looking for another job.

She softly hummed along to *Silent Night*, the song playing through the store's sound system. Ironic, because the early Christmas dinner with her parents tonight was likely to be anything *but* a "silent night".

Dinner called for a new outfit and she watched the teenage shop assistant wrap the black jacket in tissue paper and slide it carefully into the white paper bag emblazoned with the store's logo.

She didn't usually shop in high-end stores like this, but reconciled the fact the cost of the rose-pink dress and the jacket were worth it because she could wear the outfit again to a friend's wedding in March. Admittedly, the shoes weren't necessary—she already had a pair of black heels—but they were seventy percent off and what woman didn't love a bargain. Besides, for the last three years she'd rarely worn heels. She had flat shoes for work and runners or footy boots for every day in between.

'Credit or savings?' the girl asked, holding out her hand.

Annabel handed over her card. 'Savings, please.'

The girl glanced up moments later, snagging her bottom lip with her teeth. 'I'm sorry, it's been declined.'

Annabel frowned. She squinted at the girl's nametag. Ruby. 'That can't be right. I used it in the last shop.' She raised her arm and swung the bulging brown *Country Lane* bag in the air. 'It worked perfectly then. Can you try again please?' She smiled at Ruby. 'I probably entered the wrong PIN.'

Ruby pushed the EFTPOS machine back across the counter and Annabel punched in her PIN again. The machine spat out a slip of paper a second later and displayed a message on the screen.

Declined.

'Do you have another card?'

A chill slid down Annabel's spine. Since she and Scott split, she'd been so careful to monitor her finances. 'There's probably something wrong with it.' She let out a small laugh. 'I've given it a workout today.'

The music coming through the speakers changed to the upbeat *Joy to the World*, but there was nothing joyful about Annabel's mood now. She accepted the card back and slipped it into her wallet. Why had it been declined? She hadn't spent that much money today, had she? She mentally tallied up the dress, the jacket, the shoes, the lippy, the earrings. She was about to hand Ruby her rarely used credit card when she was filled with shopping regret.

'You know what? Forget it.'

Ruby froze, hand in mid-air, and stared at Annabel like she'd committed a shopping sin. 'Are you sure? It's the last one in your size. They've been so popular they're practically walking out the door.'

Annabel raised an eyebrow. At almost two hundred dollars, she didn't think the jacket was that popular, particularly because it was still full retail price. 'I'm sure. I really don't need it.'

She left the store, annoyed with herself. It wasn't the first time she'd spent too much money on clothes she didn't need so she could look the part and fit in with her parents and their lifestyle. It had been the same when she was with Scott. She'd always felt like she was trying to impress him. Scott had grown up in one of Melbourne's leafiest suburbs and, as she'd correctly guessed when she'd first met him, he had attended one of the best independent schools in Victoria. Like her parents, Scott liked the finer things in life and that included having a girlfriend on his arm who looked the part. When she'd met him, he already had the big house in one of the best suburbs in Melbourne, an expensive Mercedes coupe, a TAG Heuer watch, an MCC membership and a special climate-controlled cellar filled with Grange wines.

Unlike Scott and her parents, Annabel was content with a lot less. She didn't need to fill her life and home with material possessions, she just needed people. Growing up she'd had everything money could buy yet she never felt like she was loved.

Adopted out of the foster care system when she was eight months old, her parents told her that they'd wanted her, but she'd often felt like she was simply another possession to them. She'd been raised by parents who had a "be seen and not heard" approach to child rearing. That attitude or methodology had followed Annabel into adulthood. Her parents were happy to see her from time to time as long as when she spoke, she didn't voice her opinions. Hence, the reason she fully expected dinner to be the usual tense standoff between her and her parents.

As she exited the shopping centre with Christmas carols echoing in her ears, a pounding headache behind her ears and the hot sun beating down on her head, sudden tears threatened. But no matter how hard Annabel tried, this time she couldn't push them back.

***

Later that night in the Uber on the way to dinner, Annabel took deep breaths and forced herself to relax. Thankfully, when she'd checked her bank account, there was money in it. For some reason, her pay had gone in a day late. At least that was one less thing to worry about. She could have afforded the jacket, but she was glad she'd resisted. It didn't matter how much money she spent on new clothes, it was never enough. All she had to do now was smile and make sure she didn't say the wrong thing. If she could get through the next couple of hours in one piece, she wouldn't have to see her parents again for another month.

As the car travelled down Moorabool Street towards the waterfront, the lights of the floating Christmas tree lit up the night sky. It had stopped raining, but the occasional flash of lightning suggested another storm front was headed towards Melbourne. They'd had the weirdest weather this summer.

When the driver pulled up outside the waterfront restaurant at the yacht club, Annabel let out a long sigh.

'You okay?' the woman asked.

Annabel put her hand on the door handle. 'I'm fine.'

'You look like you're about to face a firing squad.'

'You're not far off the mark,' Annabel replied with a grimace.

She hadn't broken the news to her parents that as well as being single, she was also homeless, had no car, and was thinking about quitting her job. No wonder the thought of a root canal had been preferable to this dinner catchup.

'Family?'

Annabel nodded. 'In one.'

'Good luck with that.'

'Thanks.'

'Merry Christmas.' With a wave the woman drove off and left Annabel standing on the side of the road. She dragged in a deep breath, slung her purse over her shoulder and strode towards the entrance to the club.

Once inside, she immediately caught sight of her parents seated near the window overlooking the water next to a gaudily decorated fake Christmas tree. She arranged a smile and waved. Her father waved in return. Beside him, her mother smiled civilly, but as usual, it didn't reach her eyes. Too many skin peels and fillers. Although not even Botox could hide the deep grooves in Wendy's face caused by hours of lying in the sun in Noosa and the pack-a-week cigarette habit she denied.

Annabel weaved between the tables, relieved she'd chosen to dress up. Although most of the other people in the yacht club's restaurant wore casual clothes, her parents were overdressed.

Tonight, Dad wore a rust-coloured shirt which accentuated the ruddiness in his cheeks—the cheeks of a man who drank too much wine and had uncontrolled high blood pressure and refused to do anything about it. Her mother's jewellery probably cost as much as the yacht her father moored at the marina and her clothes were probably the latest fashion from her most recent shopping trip in Italy that Annabel would no doubt hear about ad nauseum during dinner.

As they got closer, her father stood. 'Right on time. Good drive? How was the traffic? Get a park okay? Where's Scott?'

Without waiting for a response to any of his questions, Dad kissed her clumsily on the cheek. She screwed up her nose at the reek of alcohol on his breath.

'Hi, Dad.' Annabel turned to her mother. 'Mum.'

Wendy embraced Annabel delicately, air kissing her cheek in a practised way. Her perfume barely covered the smell of nicotine.

'Hello, dear.'

She eased back and looked at Annabel, taking in everything from head to toe in one glance. Annabel resisted the urge to reach up and touch her hair.

'You look nice, although you could have chosen higher heels.'

Annabel bit down on her lip as she slipped off her old coat and put it over the back of the chair.

'New dress?'

Annabel nodded as she pulled out her chair and sat.

'*Country Lane*?'

How did she know that? 'Yes, it is.'

'I heard they had a *sale*.' Wendy let the word roll from her tongue like it was a travesty not to pay full price for something. 'You look tired.' She squinted at Annabel. 'Your skin is so pale it's making your freckles stand out more than usual.'

Annabel put her hands in her lap and clenched her fists. She kept her smile in place. The last time they'd had this conversation her mother had offered Annabel the name of a skin clinic and a "marvel of a man" who could help fade her freckles. When Annabel had politely refused, her mother suggested the name of a hairdresser who could tone down the colour of her mane. Annabel didn't have an issue with her chestnut hair colour. As a kid, she'd endured the usual taunts of redheads, but as she'd aged, her hair had deepened in colour and she loved it. It was thick and long and healthy and had enough wave to make it bounce when she walked.

Her mother leaned over and pinched Annabel's waist with two red-nailed fingers. 'You're not eating properly. You look scrawny again. I thought now you'd given up playing that ridiculous sport you might stop looking like you live on protein shakes.'

Annabel ignored the dig. If she put on weight, her mother would comment on that too.

She also ignored the comment about football. Neither of her parents had understood her decision to play women's football. They'd come and watched her play once, then found excuses for why they couldn't come again. Even when she was drafted to play for the Cats in the AFLW they hadn't been overly enthusiastic. They'd shown the minimal amount of interest, which had waned quickly before the season even got under way. In three years, she could count on one hand how many games they'd watched from the stands.

'How's work? Have you been doing nightshifts again?' Dad asked.

Annabel knew from experience as soon as she started talking about her job, her mother would politely cough and remind Annabel talking about medical emergencies in the middle of dinner wasn't appropriate table conversation. Her father wouldn't listen to anything Annabel said anyway. He'd always told her she was smart enough to be a doctor and she'd thrown away a perfectly good education—that he'd "paid good money for"—by becoming a nurse.

It didn't matter what the subject, her father always had an opinion and his was always the right one.

As usual, he didn't wait for her answer. 'You know nightshift causes cancer. If you were a doctor you could have chosen a speciality that didn't keep you up at night.'

The waiter arrived, saving Annabel from having to reply. He poured water, explained the specials on the board, took their drinks orders and left.

'Are we waiting for Scott?' Mum asked.

A cold sensation slid down Annabel's spine. She took a sip of her water before replying. 'No. He won't be joining us tonight.'

Thankfully they didn't ask for details, and for the next few minutes her parents pored over the menu. Annabel wasn't sure why they bothered. They'd have the same thing they ordered every time. Her father would have the steak, well done, and her mother would have the fish of the day and a salad—which she would barely touch.

The linguine was new to the menu, and Annabel announced she would try that.

'It has a lot of carbs,' her mother tutted.

Annabel forced a smile and bit back the retort that seconds ago she'd been accused of being too skinny. 'I'm sure I'll burn it off tomorrow.'

'Hmm. Well, the older you get the harder it will be to lose those kilograms, especially now you're not playing football. You're thirty-six next year.'

'No. I'm thirty-five next year.'

'Oh. That's right. I always forget what year you were born.'

Her mother's tone was dismissive, and Annabel had to close her eyes for a moment and push back the familiar hurt. Her parents didn't even celebrate the day she'd come to live with them either.

'When do you head off to the north coast?' she asked, changing the subject, and tamping down the hurt. Her parents had planned to spend Christmas this year in New York but because of the pandemic, international travel was still out of the question, so they'd decided to go to Pearl Beach in New South Wales instead.

'We're not going away now. I've decided to remodel the Lonnie kitchen instead.'

Annabel raised her eyebrows. 'Really? What's wrong with the kitchen?' From her recollection, there was nothing wrong with the kitchen in her parent's holiday house in Point Lonsdale. Not that Annabel had been there for at least a year.

'It's outdated. The French Provincial theme is so yesterday.'

Annabel worked on her smile. 'Yes, I suppose it is.'

A long silence followed.

Annabel placed her napkin on the table and pushed her chair back. 'Can you excuse me? I need to go to the bathroom.'

She needed air. Lots of air.

She left the restaurant and pushed open the glass doors to the road, shivering as the cool breeze wrapped around her bare legs. Dragging in a deep breath, she let it out slowly.

I can do this. Just another hour or so and it would be all over.

On the way back inside, as she was walking past the bar to the bistro, she froze. Even with his back to her, she'd recognise that tiny bald spot anywhere. Scott was leaning against the bar, talking to a woman, and their conversation didn't look like the type between two strangers.

Like a spectator in the cheap nosebleed seats at the Melbourne Cricket Ground, Annabel stared, wondering who his new woman was.

Scott looked relaxed, one elbow resting casually on the edge of the bar. When he touched the woman's cheek in a deeply intimate gesture, Annabel wanted to gag. Couldn't have waited a bit longer before he moved on? It hadn't even been four months.

When the woman turned sideways and kissed him tenderly on the lips, Annabel gasped. Her legs buckled under her and her heart slammed against her chest.

What the hell?

It was Nicole. Scott's ex-wife.

They kissed again, and Annabel shook her head, trying to dislodge the image of Scott tenderly stroking Nicole's cheek. Bile rose in the back of Annabel's throat. She took a deep breath and tried to walk away but her legs were rooted to the spot, her arms like dead weights hanging by her sides. Her legs trembled, and her chest tightened as though she was having an asthma attack, except she didn't have asthma.

She needed to move, to get away, to escape, but before she had a chance, Scott must have sensed he was being watched. He untangled himself from Nicole's clutches, turned, and saw her standing there. Their eyes met and their gazes locked. His face paled and it felt like time slowed.

Annabel had been shattered when he'd broken things off with her, but in the past three months she'd worked hard at moving on. Now, in one split second, her heart felt like it had been ripped from her chest afresh.

The son-of-a… Had he and Nicole been seeing each other while she was still with him? The thought made her want to vomit.

Spinning on her heel she sprinted out of the bar into the restaurant. Hot tears welled in her eyes before they streamed down her cheeks and blurred her vision. She angrily wiped them away. When she reached the table, she snatched up her bag. Without looking at her parents or offering them an explanation, she bolted from the club. Moments later she heard footsteps behind her, but she kept walking.

'Annabel! Stop! I didn't mean for you to see that. Let me explain.'

She lengthened her stride, as much as she could in her stupid heels and threw her reply over her shoulder. 'There's nothing *to* explain.'

Scott caught up with her, grabbing her by the upper arm and squeezing so tight she'd have a bruise tomorrow. He pulled her to a stop.

'You're making a fool of yourself, Annabel,' he said. 'It's not what it looks like.'

She jerked her arm from his and glared at him. 'Leave me alone!'

His eyes darkened menacingly. 'You're making a scene.'

'No. You are,' she snapped, raising her voice. 'With your *ex-wife*.'

He moved to touch her, and she jumped back, stumbling as her ankle gave way, but recovering quickly.

'Annabel?'

They both froze.

Annabel looked over and saw Ben Naylor on the other side of the road. Her heart hammered.

How embarrassing.

Ben crossed the street, covering the short distance in seconds. 'Everything okay?' His eyes searched hers.

'Fine.' Annabel forced a smile.

Ben's gaze flicked between her and Scott. 'Is this guy giving you a hard time?'

Annabel glanced at Scott, horrified at the mask of fury on his face. She glanced down at his clenched fists and shuddered. She'd never seen this side of him. If he hit Ben, he might be arrested for assaulting a police officer or something. Ben looked like he could handle himself in a fight without a problem, but Annabel didn't want to put him in that position.

She tried to step between the two men, facing each other like boxers in a ring, but Scott dodged around her.

'Back off, mate,' Scott growled.

Ben raised both hands. 'It's all good *mate*. Why don't you just walk away. You've said what you need to say. Let's not take this any further.'

Scott didn't take a hint. 'This is none of your business.'

'No, but if you keep harassing this woman, I'll make it my business.' Ben's tone was light but firm.

'Yeah?'

'Yeah.'

'He's a cop, Scott,' Annabel said.

The muscles in Scott's face went slack and he took a step back, unclenching his fists. Without a word he turned and walked away. Once he was gone, Annabel allowed herself to breathe again.

'You okay?' Ben asked.

'I'm fine. Thank you.' Humiliation burned through her. 'My ex and I had a little misunderstanding. Thanks for your concern.'

With fresh hot tears blinding her eyes, she walked away.

Away from Scott and away from her former life.

Nicole was welcome to him.

Chapter 6

Throughout his career as a "soggie"—a member of the Victoria Police Special Operations Group—Ben had dealt with all types of incidents involving armed offenders. He'd been threatened more times than he could count too, but until that moment, he'd never considered himself an angry or violent man.

He'd been out running along the waterfront when he'd spotted the altercation between the man and woman. The split second he realised it was Annabel, his blood reached boiling point and he'd responded without thinking. Thank God he hadn't had to pull out his freddy—his badge—and make things official.

By the time Scott had gotten in his car and driven off, tyres screeching, Annabel was fifty metres down the street walking in the opposite direction from Ben. How she walked in heels that high he didn't have a clue.

He jogged to catch her, stopping a short distance behind her so he didn't scare her again. 'Annabel?'

She slowed her pace in half and allowed him to walk beside her. He kept quiet. Her tears had left long black streaks down her cheeks and he ached to wipe them clean.

'Thank you,' she said finally.

'That's okay.'

They walked another fifty metres or so. Neither spoke.

'Where are you heading?' he asked.

'No idea.' She stopped and looked around before vacant eyes met his. 'Are you on duty?'

Police were never technically *off* duty, especially if a situation arose where intervention was required. Like tonight. He shook his head. 'I was just out for a run.'

She glanced at him again, this time taking in his running clothes.

When she began walking again, he easily kept pace with her.

'Scott wouldn't have hit you if he'd known you were a cop,' she said. 'He might be a jerk, but he normally respects the law.'

'Smart man. Wish more people did.'

They continued in silence as they walked along the waterfront. To their right, the water lapped against the concrete edge. In the distance, boats bobbed on their moorings, dark shadows on the water. Up ahead was the carousel, now closed. Beyond it, was the floating Christmas tree. Annabel headed that way like a moth drawn to light then stood, back ramrod-straight, staring out over the darkened water towards Melbourne.

'Is there someone you can call? Family? Friends?'

She rubbed her bare arms. Goose bumps dotted the surface of her skin. It hadn't been a warm day and the wind whipping off the water was cold. Typical summer's evening in Geelong. He was surprised she didn't have a jacket with her.

'No, there's no-one I can call.'

He waited for her to elaborate, but she didn't. The wind ruffled her hair, sending the floral scent of her perfume in his direction.

'Where's your car parked?' he asked.

'I don't have a car. I caught an Uber into town tonight for dinner.'

It had started to rain. Just a fine drizzle, but enough to be annoying.

'Can I drop you home?'

'Thank you, but I couldn't ask you to do that. I'm staying in Clifton Springs.'

'You didn't ask. I offered.'

She remained silent and he could almost hear the cogs turning.

'Look, while you think about it, why don't we go somewhere warm and grab a coffee?' He pointed to the Novotel.

She hesitated for so long he was surprised when she agreed.

As they stood at the pedestrian lights opposite the hotel waiting for the lights to turn, the wind sent another burst of her perfume towards him. When she shivered, he resisted the urge to pull her into a hug to keep her warm, instead opting for a light touch on her shoulder.

'Thank you, Ben.'

'I'm glad I was there.'

He knew he probably should leave her to sort her own life out, say goodnight and walk away. But there was a massive chasm between what he *should* do and what he wanted to do. He wanted to stay with her. For as long as possible without it being weird.

The lights changed, and Annabel took off too quickly, stumbling in her heels. It was an automatic response to hold out his hand to catch her and when her fingers grazed his, it sparked a jolt of electricity through him.

She didn't seem to notice.

'Stupid shoes. I don't know why I bother dressing up for my parents. That's where I was when I saw Scott,' she explained. 'Having my monthly dinner "meeting" with my parents at the yacht club.'

He sensed there was a lot more to that story too, but it wasn't the time nor place to ask.

At the entrance to the Novotel he managed to get to the door before her and hold it open. Once inside, their footsteps echoed on the tiles.

'Can we order two coffees please?' Ben asked a waiter who immediately appeared.

'Absolutely,' the waiter replied.

'We'll go and sit over there if that's okay.' Ben pointed to a dimly lit lounge area overlooking the waterfront.

'That's fine. I'll bring your drinks over. Won't be long.'

The waiter disappeared. Annabel was shivering harder and Ben strode over to the gas log fire. 'I don't think they'll mind if I turn it on.' He beckoned for her. 'Come and stand here and warm up.'

Annabel glanced past him. 'I think I'll use the bathroom first. Be back in a minute.'

Her shoes clicked on the tiles then quietness descended, scored only by someone playing the piano in the corner, the quiet voices of some nearby late diners, and the soft patter of rain against the windows.

By the time Annabel returned, she'd stopped trembling. She'd also washed all traces of mascara and makeup from her cheeks giving her an even more youthful appearance. She also looked sad.

Ben's heart snapped. If he ever saw that ex of hers again, he'd happily forget he was a cop and punch the living daylights out of the bloke for hurting her.

Their coffees arrived and neither of them spoke as they sipped them.

'Are you hungry?' he asked, after a while.

She shook her head. 'I'd be sick if I ate.' She took another sip of her coffee then glanced at her phone. 'Are you sure you don't mind driving me back to my friend's place? It's a half hour drive.'

She could ask him to fly her to the moon and back and it wouldn't be a big deal. 'I don't mind in the least.' He laid his hand gently on her arm and waited for her to look up at him. He searched her eyes. 'I want to drive you home, okay?'

She stalled for a moment as if debating whether it was safe to get in a car with him. Finally, she gave him a tiny smile. 'Thank you.'

'My pleasure.'

She tilted her head to one side. 'Do all police do this?''

'Do what?'

'Offer strangers a ride home?'

He chuckled. 'Not that I'm aware. Besides, you're hardly a stranger. Remember, we're practically related.'

She smiled and this time it reached her eyes. 'I suppose we are.'

Neither of them spoke for a while.

'How do you do it?' she asked.

'What?'

'Intervene in situations like that. What if Scott had hit you?'

'I'm a trained negotiator, Annabel. And I'm good at my job.'

'Fair enough.'

A thought hit him like a punch to the chest. He needed to be careful how he phrased his next question. He didn't want to scare her off.

'Has he ever hurt you?'

Annabel's head snapped up and her eyes flashed. 'No, of course not. Never! I wouldn't have stayed if he had. He's a jerk, but he's not abusive.'

Scott may not have physically hurt her, but it was clear he'd hurt her emotionally. Still, Ben believed her when she said he'd never laid a finger on her.

'Will you go back to him?' he asked.

She shook her head.

'Good.'

She checked her phone again. 'Sorry, Ben. It's getting late. Is it okay if we get going?'

'Sure.' He stood and patted his pocket for his car keys. They weren't there. 'Damn.'

She frowned. 'What?'

'I was out running. I don't have my car with me, but it's only ten minutes away. I don't live that far away. Are you okay to wait here? I promise I won't be long.'

She stood. 'Honestly, Ben, it's no big deal. I can get an Uber.'

'No, Annabel.' He softened his tone. 'I said I want to drive you, okay?'

Chapter 7

Twenty minutes later Ben re-appeared, dangling his car keys. His hair was damp from the rain and his skin was flushed. He'd changed out of his running clothes into chinos, a striped rugby jumper and leather boots.

'Sorry that took me longer than I planned,' he said. 'I wanted to shower first.'

'It's not a problem,' Annabel fibbed.

She'd left her jacket on the back of the chair at the yacht club and even though the gas log fire in the hotel was roaring, she felt like she did when they were playing football in the middle of a winter down at Kardinia Park. She was turning into an ice block.

'Crazy weather,' he said as they walked quickly to his car.

'Last week it was so cold they had snow in Tassie,' she replied, rubbing her hands together.

'Hard to believe it'll be Christmas next week.'

When they reached his car, he held the passenger door open for her and waited for her to settle into the seat and put on her belt before closing the door softly. Once inside, he reached behind her seat and pulled out a polar fleece blanket which he helped tuck around her. After starting the car, he pressed a button on the dash.

'Seat warmer,' he explained. 'If that's okay? You still look cold.'

'Thanks. I'm freezing.' She couldn't stop her teeth from chattering.

Ben pulled out of the hotel carpark and headed along the waterfront towards Eastern Gardens.

'What kind of policeman are you?' Annabel asked. With a half-hour drive to kill, she figured she might as well get to know him better. It was either that or sit in awkward silence for the car trip.

'I'm a negotiator on the Critical Incident Response Team.'

She glanced at him. He said it like it was no big deal, but she noted the way he lifted his chin with pride. She also noted that in profile he had a well-defined jaw.

Stop it, she warned herself.

'What does a negotiator do?' she asked, forcing her mind off Ben's appearance. And his fresh just-out-of-the-shower smell.

'Our primary objective is to negotiate a peaceful surrender to prevent the loss of life or significant injury without damage to persons or property.'

She chuckled.

He glanced at her. 'What?'

'I always think it's weird the way the police speak. It's so formal.'

'Yeah, I suppose it is.' He shrugged. 'I've been in the job so long speaking like that is second nature.'

'What do you *actually* do?' she asked. 'In laymen's terms.'

'I head up one of the teams who get called in whenever there's a crisis or a hostage negotiation or in the case of a situation which might turn volatile and potentially put lives at risk.'

'Oh wow.'

Not only impressive, it sounded dangerous, but she had a sense that Ben was good at his job. Maybe he did live up to his "hard as nails" nickname after all.

'Were you called in for things like the Lindt shooting in Sydney years ago? Or when that guy drove into the people in the Bourke Street Mall?'

For a long beat he didn't reply. She watched his fingers tighten briefly around the steering wheel before loosening.

'Yeah, things like that. It can be as serious as the Lindt shooting or Bourke Street, or it might be a case of domestic violence or someone with mental health issues threatening to take his or her own life. I guess at the end of the day they're all serious.'

'It would be a tough job.'

His Adam's apple bounced. 'Yep. Very tough.

'Have you always been a policeman?'

'Not always. I didn't join until I was in my mid-twenties. Up to then I worked on the family farm in Glengarrick, but I always wanted to be a cop. My uncle was a member and both my cousins joined too. My uncle was my inspiration. I wanted to be like him.'

'Are you?'

'I don't know. He died before I joined.'

'In the line of duty?' Annabel asked carefully.

Ben nodded. 'Yeah. Kind of. He took his own life.'

'I'm so sorry.'

He didn't elaborate, and Annabel felt awful for hitting what was obviously a raw nerve.

'Do you like your job?'

He nodded. 'Most days I love it. The best thing is every day is different. You get to see things the average person doesn't. Around every corner is the unexpected. One minute you're driving around and the next you're flying to a job to help someone. When you think you've seen it all, you quickly learn you haven't, and I like that. I also enjoy being part of the action. Never a dull moment.'

'Are you ever scared?' she asked.

He hesitated. 'I'm *always* scared. The day I stop being scared is the day I'll retire.'

'It must be dangerous.'

'I reckon general duties police are in more danger than us because they work in an uncontrolled environment. Our operations are planned, practiced and precise.'

She nodded. 'Makes sense.'

'What about you? Jed told me that as well as playing professional football, you're a nurse.'

'Semi-professional, and I've retired from playing now. But yes, I am a nurse.' It pleased her that he'd asked Jed about her. 'Emergency department.'

'Ah, an adrenaline junkie.'

She shook her head. 'Not really. I just enjoy the constantly changing environment like you do. I love how we never know who or what is about to come through the doors next.'

'I bet the whole COVID thing was a nightmare.'

She shuddered. 'I can't even begin to explain what it was like in the early days.'

'Which hospital do you work at? The public in Geelong?'

'No. I've been working at a hospital in Melbourne in the western suburbs.'

'Oh, right. Are you still there now?'

'Yes and no. I'm on leave while I figure a few things out.'

Like where she was going to live.

The drive from Clifton Springs to the western suburbs of Melbourne was tiring, especially after a nightshift. The only reason she was living on the Bellerine Peninsula was she had a friend who'd offered her a room for as long as she needed it after she and Scott split up.

'Once I work out where I want to live, I'll move and find another job.'

'Still in ED?'

She shrugged. 'Yes. No. Maybe. It's been a tough year and I think it might be time for a change of pace. Something a bit slower.'

'I totally get that.'

Something in his tone caught her attention but she didn't feel like she could ask him without being rude. They were getting along well and talking openly, but she didn't want to cross the line into too personal territory. Even if they were "practically related" as he kept joking.

'What's the craziest thing you've ever seen?' Ben asked.

'What?' Annabel glanced at him. It seemed like a strange switch of subjects.

'At work. What's the weirdest thing you've seen?' he repeated.

'Oh, right.' Annabel chuckled. She had a plethora of hilarious tales she could tell. 'Where would I start?'

For the next fifteen minutes she and Ben recounted stories, laughing as they tried to outdo one another with unbelievable tales of things they'd seen or heard in their lines of work.

Annabel was now glad her friend lived so far out of Geelong because the longer drive allowed them more time to chat and get to know each other. Ben was one of the easiest men she'd ever spent time with. He was intelligent and could easily hold up his end of the dialogue, but he didn't have Scott's annoying habit of trying to take over a conversation and make it all about himself. Ben listened intently when she spoke and asked well educated questions that showed he was genuinely interested in what she had to say.

'Why are you still single?' Annabel asked, after their laughter died down. She couldn't imagine why women weren't lining up for him.

Ben gripped the steering wheel and stared ahead at the darkened strip of road in front of them. Annabel mentally kicked herself. She had a shocking habit of forgetting other people's boundaries and she'd only just finished reminding herself earlier not to get too personal.

'Sorry, Ben,' she said, touching his arm lightly. 'I didn't mean to be nosy. You can tell me to butt out.'

'It's okay. I don't mind telling you. I've been married twice. Stuffed it both times. I'm clearly not good at relationships.'

She waited for him to continue.

He chuckled. 'God, that sounds worse than it is. My first marriage only lasted eighteen months. Sophie and I were young and stupid. We were barely out of our teens and had no idea what marriage entailed. We met at university and thought we were soulmates, but quickly discovered we couldn't live together. We parted on good terms. Soph's happily married now with three kids.'

'You stay in touch?'

'Only via Facebook.'

'And your second marriage?' She remembered him saying his ex-wife had left him because she didn't want kids. Was that Sophie or his second wife?

They passed under a streetlight and it briefly lit his face.

'Chantelle and I were married for four years. And we *didn't* part on good terms. She left me for a paramedic then fell pregnant. After telling me she didn't want kids.'

She heard the pain in his voice and wished she had the words to comfort him. Or wished she hadn't asked.

'I never saw it coming,' he said. 'That's the worst part of it. I thought we were happy.'

'Would you do it again?' Annabel asked, keeping her tone light even though with every question they were diving into deeper territory. 'Marriage, I mean?' she quickly clarified.

'I'd have to meet the perfect person first.'

Annabel chuckled. 'Is there such a thing as a perfect person?'

'I used to think so.'

'Yeah, me too.'

Silence fell.

As much as she wanted to be loved and to *be* in love again, she couldn't count on it happening again any time soon. Even though she'd grown up with parents who modelled a dysfunctional relationship, she'd always wanted marriage and a family. She loved the ideal of meeting someone, falling in love, getting married and having a baby or two or three. Simple as that. Unfortunately, she thought everything would fall into place without having to do anything to make it happen. But it hadn't worked out that way.

'Did you want to talk about what happened tonight with your ex?' Ben asked.

Her pulse quickened. 'Not really, but I feel like I owe you an explanation.'

He glanced sideways at her. 'You owe me nothing, Annabel.'

'Thank you.' She pulled a face. 'I caught *my* ex with *his* ex.'

'Oh.'

'Yeah. Awkward.' She dragged in a quick breath and blew it out through her nose. 'At least we didn't have kids. Much easier to dissolve a relationship when children aren't involved.'

'Would you have wanted kids with him anyway?'

Something twisted inside her heart like the tightening of a knot and she remembered how much she'd felt on the outer at Daisy's baptism. 'I thought I did,' she said softly, 'but Scott didn't. He already has two kids with Nicole. The ex.'

'You're a step-mum?' Ben asked.

'In name only. I've never had anything to do with his girls. They never stayed with us. I'm adopted and Scott knew I couldn't raise someone else's children. They lived with Nicole and he visited them every second weekend when I was at work.'

A shiver went through her. Perhaps Scott had been "visiting" Nicole every other weekend too.

'I'm sorry, Annabel. I know you're hurting, and I hope this doesn't come across as callous, but it sounds like you're better off without him. Just like I'm better off without Chantelle. There's no point being in a toxic relationship.'

She nodded. Yes, she was better off without Scott but the rejection and humiliation still hurt, especially after what had happened tonight at the restaurant.

Her phone vibrated and she glanced down at it and exhaled. Her mother, again. She had to tell them why she'd run out on them, but it could wait until later.

Music filled the gap between them, and neither of them spoke for the next few minutes other than when Ben asked for directions.

'You asked me before if I think there's such a thing as the perfect person,' Ben said finally.

She waited.

'My perfect person needs to be happy. Chantelle was never happy. She always wanted more. More from me. More from her friends. More stuff. Nothing was ever good enough. She was never content with what she had—always striving for something more. It never felt attainable, you know?'

'Yeah. I know.' He might as well be describing her parents. And Scott.

'No matter how hard I worked, I worked too hard. When I took time off, I should have been working. No matter what I did, it wasn't right, especially the shift work. She hated my job. Chantelle always wanted something she couldn't have.'

He slowed as he approached the roundabout then turned off the highway. They were only a few minutes away from her friend's house.

'I'm sure the perfect person for each of us is out there somewhere and if we're lucky, one day we'll find them,' Annabel said with as much confidence as she could muster.

'I hope so.'

'Me too.'

Moments later, Ben pulled up outside the house and turned off the engine. Her friend had left the curtains open and the lights on her Christmas tree flickered. Annabel and Ben opened their doors at the same time and met in front of the car. Annabel wrapped her arms around her. There was no streetlight, and it was so dark she could hardly see Ben's face, but he was close enough she could almost feel the warmth of his breath in the air between them.

'Do you believe in fate?' he asked.

'I guess. Why?'

He hesitated for a fraction. 'I'm not sure whether I did until tonight, but I think we were always supposed to meet again. I knew the moment I met you at Daisy's baptism that we'd see each other again. I think it was fate I was out running tonight. Like I said before, I'm sorry for what happened between you and Scott, but…Look, I don't want you to think I'm hitting on you Annabel, but I'm *not* sorry too, if you know what I mean.'

Annabel nodded, not trusting her voice. The way Ben looked at her made her stomach flip. Truth was, it didn't really matter that she'd seen Scott and Nicole together tonight. Her relationship with him had been over for a long time. Well before he'd called it quits three months ago.

She reached up and put a hand on Ben's shoulder. 'Thank you, Ben.'

Without stopping to think, she stood on tiptoes and went to kiss his cheek but somehow their lips managed to meet. She jumped back as if she'd been shocked.

'I'm so sorry,' she blurted, stumbling on the grass as she tried to step back further. 'I shouldn't have done that.' He must think *she* was hitting on *him*. 'Sorry,' she repeated.

He gently gripped her by the arms to stop her from falling and held her tight, his eyes boring straight into hers. 'You didn't do anything wrong. And don't be sorry. I'm not. If circumstances were any different and we'd met at a different time and place, I'd kiss you properly, but I get the feeling you still need to get over things with Scott first.'

Annabel's heart hammered. Slipping from his embrace, she blinked rapidly and tried to gather her scrambled thoughts. Thank goodness her friend wasn't home to look out the window or she'd have a lot of explaining to do.

'Thanks for everything tonight.' She clapped her hand to her forehead then waved her arm in a wide arc. 'I mean, for rescuing me. For the coffee. For driving me here. You know what I mean. Urgh. I don't know how to properly say thank you.'

Did he think she was thanking him for the kiss too?

'I think you already thanked me enough.' He leaned down and kissed her on the cheek, his breath as soft as butterfly wings.

She sagged against him for a second, but before she could change her mind and fall into his arms, she took two steps back. 'I should go,' she said, voice husky.

'Can I give you my number?' Ben asked. 'Just in case you ever need anything?'

'If I ever need rescuing again you mean?'

He shrugged. 'Something like that. In case you want to say hi. Or in case you want to grab a coffee or a bite to eat some time.'

She pulled out her phone, brought up her contacts list and with shaking hands, passed it to him. He entered his number then handed the phone back to her. She glanced at it and smiled. He'd added his name into her contacts as "The Godfather".

'I'll call you now, so you have my number too.' When their eyes met again, she smiled. 'Just in case you ever need rescuing.'

After calling his phone then hanging up, she slipped the phone into her purse. Breathing deeply, she blinked back sudden tears. Ben stepped closer and reached for her hands and when his fingers pressed hers, she felt strangely comforted and connected.

'If there's anything you ever need, promise me you'll call.'

He let go of her hands and she felt stranded again.

'Life doesn't always turn out the way it's supposed to, does it?' she asked.

'No, it doesn't,' he agreed.

'Thanks again, Ben. This has been the most bizarre night of my life. But it's late and I really need to go. If our paths ever cross again, let's see what happens.'

'You have a deal.' He smiled. 'Take care of yourself Annabel.'

'I will.' Because no-one else was going to take care of her.

Ben met her gaze, unblinking, and for a split second she worried that she'd spoken her thoughts aloud.

'I hope you find your perfect life partner one day, because you deserve to be happy.'

'As do you.'

'Merry Christmas, Annabel.'

'Merry Christmas to you too, Ben.'

She pushed open the gate and walked up the path to the front door, knowing he was watching her. Should she turn around? No. She raised her hand and gave a little wave before slipping into the house.

Once inside, she closed the door and sank against the wall, a flurry of emotions swirling inside her. There was a kindness in Ben's eyes which warmed her heart like nothing she'd ever experienced. She struggled to push the emotions down. Even though she and Scott were history, the last thing she needed right now was a rebound relationship.

Yet despite knowing it was crazy to think about him, Annabel drifted off to sleep that night dreaming of Ben Naylor and wondering how her life would look if he was in it at some point in the future.

Chapter 8

The late summer storm on the Australia Day long weekend brought torrential rain. Ben's wipers were set as fast as they would go, but visibility was reduced to next to nothing. The forecast storm seemed to come from nowhere.

Adrenaline pumped through Ben's veins as he drove, lights blazing, sirens screaming, up the highway from Geelong to a house in William's Creek, in one of Melbourne's western suburbs. Hot, stormy weather often set people off and they'd had three days in a row of temperatures in the forties and now this rain.

The tactical team was already assembled, and by the time he got there they'd cordoned off the entire street. He ducked under the police tape and jogged over to Sean, pleased his friend was working tonight.

Sean gave him a nod. 'How's it going?'

'Alright.'

They huddled under a tree that did nothing to stop the rain from soaking them through while Sean gave him a quick briefing.

Ben heard a woman screaming and crying from somewhere inside the house and he glanced in that direction. 'What've we got?'

'Twenty-six-year-old male. Armed with a knife. He barricaded himself and his ex-girlfriend in a bedroom earlier today,' Sean replied.

Ben's racing heart went up a notch. He hated domestic violence callouts. 'Who called it in?'

'Neighbours said they'd heard yelling all day, but no one made a call until about three.'

Ben checked his watch. Four-forty. 'What's the ex doing at the house?'

'No-one seems to know.'

'Does she have a restraining order out against him?'

Sean shook his head.

'Right. Do we have a name?'

'Hostage is Aliyah.'

'Offender?'

'Ahmed Deng.'

'Does he speak any English?'

'A little. They're both Sudanese.'

That made things interesting. And it also made it a political hot potato. Ben was surprised the media weren't already there. There was already enough fear around the Sudanese refugees. He hadn't had any issues with the community personally, but all it took was one bad egg and unfortunately, they were tarred with the same brush. It wasn't fair.

Someone handed Ben a heavy ballistic vest and he accepted it with a curt "thanks" before slipping it on.

'That's not all,' Sean said.

Sweat trickled down Ben's spine.

'There's a uniformed constable in there too. Unarmed.'

Ben cursed. He could picture what had happened. The constable had probably thought he was doing the right thing. He'd been sent out to the job—no doubt after the call from the concerned neighbour—had approached the house, put his gun down and gone in unarmed, attempting to diffuse the situation. It never worked. If anything, it usually inflamed things.

'Is he a hostage too?' he asked.

'Unclear.'

Ben triple checked he had all the equipment he needed, and the team were in position. 'Ready?' he asked Sean.

'Yep.'

'Let's go.'

They entered the house carefully. The smell of cooking oil, urine and cigarettes, combined with fear filled Ben's nostrils. "Once you've smelled fear, you never forget it," he always told the newbie negotiators. "It's as distinctive as the smell of a dead person."

The walls of the property were bare of any artwork, the carpets stained with who knew what and broken venetian blinds hung crookedly on the windows. The furniture looked like someone had purchased it from the local Salvos or picked it up off the side of the road. Ben took in his surroundings but ignored them. His thoughts had already raced ahead to what he would find and how he was going to deal with it.

After years on the job, there was always a small knot of anxiety in his guts about what it would look like if things went horribly wrong. And the potential for things to go wrong in a hostage situation was always high, particularly with domestic violence and when the perpetrator potentially didn't speak English.

The woman had stopped screaming but Ben heard her whimpering from a room somewhere at the back of the house. Everything within him wanted to rush, but he forced himself to move slowly and carefully. Sean followed him through the dingy lounge room into a hallway. They stepped over a door which someone had ripped from its hinges and broken in half. In the doorway in place of the door, a metal and wire bed base had been upended and pushed into the frame, forming a barricade. Shoved against the frame, holding it in place was a large pine tallboy, it's drawers and contents strewn across the room.

Through the wire Ben saw Ahmed—a tall skinny man with wild eyes, standing over a woman, presumably Aliyah, the ex-girlfriend. She'd been crudely tied to the mattress with a length of rope and Ahmed was shouting at her in what Ben assumed was

Sudanese, while holding an enormous kitchen carving knife to her throat. She wore a pair of tiny denim shorts and a tight yellow T-shirt which was stained with lines of her own blood. As Ahmed pushed the knife against her throat, it left a fresh crimson line in its wake. She started screaming again and Ben's anxiety went up another notch.

Ahmed turned and saw them. 'Who the hell are you?' he roared in heavily accented English.

Ben didn't answer, taking everything in.

'Get him out,' Ahmed screamed, waving the knife in the direction of the white-faced constable.

The young cop standing in the corner of the room didn't move but he shook like a dry leaf in a storm.

The woman shouted at him in broken English. 'Don't leave me. You cannot leave me here. Please. Help me.'

The cop looked pleadingly at Ben, clearly torn between duty, and freaking out. But even if he'd wanted to get out of the room, the bed base blocked his exit.

'We need to dial this down,' Ben murmured to Sean. He faced Ahmed and kept his tone light but firm. 'Ahmed, I want you to let the police officer out of the room.'

The constable gave a tiny shake of his head and nodded towards the woman. Evidently, he didn't want to leave her there. Ben reigned in his frustration. Cops made the worst hostages. It was just as well this one was unarmed. His presence wasn't helping—it was doing the opposite—escalating the tension.

Ahmed started screaming at the policeman again. It wasn't in English, but the message was clear.

Get out.

The constable edged backwards to the barricade, one slow step at a time towards Ben and Sean. Seeing him try to leave, Aliyah started crying hysterically. On the other hand, Ahmed, sensing he had gained a level of power in the situation, seemed to settle a little. The knife didn't leave Aliyah's throat, but the pressure against her neck eased off a fraction.

Ben took a good look at her, trying to assess how badly she was injured and whether her injuries were life threatening. There was a lot of blood and he couldn't tell where it was coming from. Apart from the stains on her T-shirt, there were long knife wounds to her thighs. If any of her wounds were life threatening, he'd give the call and the tactical guys would storm in and finish the business. But the risks in doing that were huge. Ahmed still had the knife to her throat and although they might take him out, if they weren't quick enough, he could slit her throat, and she'd be dead in a heartbeat. Another bead of sweat trickled down his back.

'Do you smell that?' Sean asked.

Ben sniffed the air. Gas. 'Get someone to turn it off at the mains.'

After deeming the slash wounds to Aliyah's skin were superficial, Ben talked calmly to Ahmed while the constable gingerly moved the barricade aside enough to ease out of the room. His back already ached from the weight of the twenty-kilogram vest he wore but Ben didn't move from his position, leaning casually against the doorway.

As rain pelted relentlessly on the roof, Ben talked for over an hour, trying to convince Ahmed of the logic in letting Aliyah go, of putting the knife down and of everyone walking out alive. While he spoke, Aliyah, thankfully stayed quiet. At one point, she closed her eyes and for a moment panic pushed against Ben's chest. Was she unconscious? When her eyes fluttered open, he exhaled in a rush. She was still okay. Terrified, but alive.

Occasionally Ahmed spoke to Aliyah in Sudanese and she replied, but the initial heat of their conflict seemed to have gone. At least he was talking. The first thing Ben always did was get the conversation started. If he could get them talking, it took their attention away from hurting themselves or someone else.

The hardest part of his job was the talking—the inane conversation. No, he corrected himself, the hardest part was not getting sick of the sound of his own voice.

He'd been a police negotiator for a dozen years and had worked on sieges where kids had been kidnapped by parents and on standoffs with mentally ill people who had locked themselves away with high-powered firearms. He'd talked countless unstable people down from ledges—metaphorical and physical—but in all the years on the job the most important thing he'd learned was that successful siege negotiations took time. They also took empathy and courage. Over the years he'd learned how to read the moment when the hostage-taker was engaged or when he or she was about to be pushed over the edge.

Every situation was different, and it didn't matter how good he was at his job. Nothing ever made it easier.

After Ben had admitted he often experienced flashbacks and panic attacks, Sean had suggested counselling, but he'd tried that, and it hadn't worked. But he'd promised Sean, and himself, that if things got too much and he couldn't handle it any longer, he'd retire from the force and move back home to Glengarrick.

Lately that felt like a smart choice. Life on the farm might be boring, but boring was precisely what he needed in his life right now.

Out of nowhere, he remembered his conversation with Zara on the night of their birthday. He'd been in a funk then and things hadn't gotten much better since. At least he hadn't gone out and bought a recliner.

It wasn't surprising thoughts of Zara had filled his head lately. Two nights ago, unexpectedly, she'd called to let him know she'd just found out she was pregnant. He shouldn't have been shocked, but he was. After doing his embarrassingly easy bit, he'd tried to put the whole thing out of his mind. He was glad for Zara's sake it had worked first time because he'd told her he wasn't doing it again and he meant it.

He still worried he'd made the biggest mistake of his life, but it was too late now. Zara would be holding their baby—*her* baby, he reminded himself—in September.

More thoughts filled his head—this time thoughts of Annabel Norton. And these ones made him smile. Since the awkward kiss outside her friend's house, he hadn't been able to get her out of his mind. When this was hostage situation was over, he would ring her and ask her out for dinner. He should have called her sooner.

His smile dropped. If he was going to pursue something with Annabel, he'd have to tell her about Zara and the baby, wouldn't he?

He changed position, stretching the kinks in his back. As much as thinking about Annabel was a welcome distraction from the hostage situation, he had a job to do and he needed to focus. And thinking about Zara and a baby was not going to help either.

While he'd talked about everything and nothing for two hours, trying to build rapport with Ahmed, looking for anything that would click with him and get him to tell them what was wrong, Sean had stood behind Ben, taking notes and relaying information back to Ben from the other members of the team outside. The local cops knew Ahmed well. He'd been apprehended twice already for break and enters and was awaiting a court date.

Finally, as the rain eased outside and the sun set, Ahmed yawned. Suddenly it was all over. He handed Ben the knife, pulled down the barricade and walked out of the house with his hands raised. The tactical guys rushed in, along with the paramedics to deal with Aliyah.

It was a perfect anti-climax—the way any good negotiation should end—but out of nowhere a dark cloud descended, crushing Ben's chest. His heart started pounding and he heard his blood passing through his ears.

Thump, thump, thump.

'That's it then,' Sean said, removing his vest and walking outside.

Ben followed him, but once he was in the front yard, his legs wouldn't move. He sucked in a lungful of air. The police vehicles lining the street were blurry and he wiped at his eyes with trembling hands. His heart felt like it was about to explode. He tried to take a deep breath, but his lungs were closing over, and each breath was too shallow.

Sean stopped and turned. 'You okay? Nails?'

Ben shook his head to clear it, but a voice kept telling him that he was dying. His mouth was dry, and his throat was tight. His vision narrowed as if he was looking through a kaleidoscope and he sank to the ground.

He had no idea how much time passed—it could have been thirty seconds or an hour—but by the time his vision cleared and his heart rate settled, he felt like life had been drained right out of him. He looked up into the concerned faces of his colleagues and he knew.

It was time.

****

A week later, on Thursday afternoon, Ben eyeballed his boss as he slid his badge and gun across Bob's desk.

'I'm done,' he said quietly. It had taken days of deliberation and a lengthy conversation with Sean over a few beers the night before, but his mind was made up. He should have done it sooner. Maybe if he had, the outcome of their most recent case would have been different.

Bob met his gaze with equal weight and pushed the badge and weapon back at Ben. 'Sorry, Ben. Your resignation is not accepted.'

'What?' Ben had imagined a dozen different conversations at this point, all variations on a theme of "I wish you all the best, mate", but he hadn't envisaged this scene. 'You can't stop me from—'

Bob held up his hand. 'Save it, Nails. And listen to me.'

As if Ben had a choice. Bob was a tough boss, but he was fair and well regarded by everyone on the team, Ben included.

'You're not seeing straight right now. You need to give it time. Yes, I know we all hated the outcome after last weekend, but I'm not losing my best negotiator to a pity party he's throwing himself.'

Ben started to rise.

'I'm not finished.'

Ben sat, but inside he seethed. Didn't Bob get it? A man had died last Saturday night, and two children were going to be traumatised for the rest of their lives because of Ben's failure to do his job. And the woman? She was still in a critical condition in ICU. Best negotiator? Hell, no. Right now, he was a liability to his team all because he'd pushed himself to keep working after his last panic attack, when instead, he should have resigned then.

'Have you talked to the psychologist?' Bob asked. He didn't give Ben a chance to respond. 'No. You haven't. Did you contribute to any of the debriefings? No. You barely said a word. Did you seek me out for a chat? No.' Bob shook his head. 'I thought we had a better relationship than that.'

Ben massaged the back of his neck. Bob was right but it didn't make it any easier to deal with.

'You're not the only person to lose a negotiation.'

'Yeah, but those kids—'

'Will have counselling and support. And they've still got their mother. I heard today she's out of ICU and on the ward. She'll make a full recovery. Those kids have you to thank for that.'

A full recovery. What a joke. The woman had been almost killed by her husband before they'd shot him dead in front of her kids. They'd be scarred for the rest of their lives.

'Sorry, Bob. I'm finished.'

Bob shook his head. 'It was a bad one. We all know it. And when women and kids are involved, it's extra tough. But you're not finished. You're burned out. And for that we have a leave of absence. Take as long as you need.'

As long as he needed? How long would it take before he was ready—*if* he was ready—to return to special ops? When he joined the academy fifteen years ago, he'd planned to be a cop for life but maybe it was time to consider a change in career. Choose another line of work. Find something with less responsibility, something that wouldn't be on his mind twenty-four hours a day, seven days a week. Something less demanding. Like farming. Hell, if he resigned, he'd be able to have a social life again. Perhaps even meet someone like Annabel Norton and fall in love again.

He couldn't afford to let Bob talk him out of his decision. Again, he started to get up, but Bob stopped him.

'One more thing,' Bob said.

'Yeah?'

'I want to hear from you every week.'

Ben raised his eyebrows. He already had a mother who insisted on the same thing, but Bob was his friend as well as his boss. 'I'll call you.'

'And you'll call the psychologist.'

Ben nodded.

'What are you going to do?'

'I'm going to head back to my folk's farm in Glengarrick. Start doing jigsaw puzzles and find another career.'

Bob chuckled. 'Yeah. Good luck with that. I'm telling you; you'll be bored in under a week.'

Chapter 9

By the end of January Annabel had used up all her annual leave and was back at work. She'd had a good break and the time away had cleared her head and helped her regroup.

Ever since bumping into Scott and Nicole before Christmas, she realised she needed to put permanent distance between them or risk seeing them again. Geelong wasn't small, but it was small enough.

Moving seemed like the perfect solution. As well as getting her out of Scott's orbit, it would put some much-needed space between her and her parents. After telling them she and Scott had split up, they hadn't held back their disappointment. Not in Scott. In her.

When Jed called and said he'd heard the new GP clinic in Glengarrick was looking for a part-time practice nurse, it seemed too good to be true. Even though she had never worked in a GP clinic, she put in an application and, surprisingly, had an interview next week. If it all went to plan and she got the job, she'd move to Glengarrick and instead of an hour or longer to commute to work, the drive would only take her minutes.

Ever since applying for the job, the idea of renting a little house in the country, growing her own veggies, and keeping chickens, grew bigger and better in Annabel's mind. The fact that Ben Naylor came from Glengarrick might have had something to do with her decision too. They occasionally texted each other and in the last message she received from him he said he was thinking of spending some more time on the family farm. He hadn't elaborated, and she hadn't asked, but the notion that they might bump into each other when he came home to visit was a nice thought to hold onto.

On Saturday morning Annabel was having coffee with her friend, Tracey. She'd just broken the news that she was planning to move out of her friend's spare bedroom.

The furrow in Tracey's brow deepened. 'But you're welcome to stay with me as long as you need,' she said. 'You're not a difficult flatmate, if that's what you're worried about.'

It wasn't just that. As much as she liked Tracey, her friend was getting married next month and living with a pair of newlyweds was not on Annabel's agenda.

'And Sam wanted me to make sure you know the invitation is from him, too, not just me,' Tracey continued earnestly. 'We don't want you to think we're kicking you out.'

'You're not. And I get that. But you two need your own space and I'd be cramping your style.' Tracey had made no secret that as soon as the ring was on her finger she and Sam planned to try for a baby. Annabel shuddered. She did not need to hear what went on in the bedroom next to hers.

'We love having you stay here with us.'

Because she paid half the rent, Annabel thought, but kept it to herself. When she and Scott split up, Tracey had opened her heart and her home without hesitation, and she had been a good friend.

'Thanks, Trace, but it's time I moved on.'

'What are you going to do? Where are you going to go?'

'I'm thinking of a tree change. Maybe a move to the country.'

Tracey stared at her like she was mad. 'What? Where?'

'The High Country. Glengarrick. It's a little place in the Victorian Alps.'

Annabel didn't add that before she went there for Daisy's baptism, she'd had to Google it. It was barely a blip on the map.

'Why on earth would you want to do that? You won't know anyone there.'

'Which makes it perfect for starting again. And I do know people there. My friend, Jed, lives there with his wife, Georgie, and when I was there recently for their daughter's baptism, I met some of their friends. It seems like a lovely place to live.'

'Escape, you mean.'

'Call it whatever you want. I need a break. A change of scenery, both personally and professionally will be good for me.'

'Maybe you'll meet someone in Glengarrick,' Tracey, ever the romantic, said.

Annabel laughed. 'Are you kidding? It's a town of less than a thousand people. They're probably all related. Anyway, that's not why I'm going. I'm not focusing on men; I'm going to concentrate on a new career direction and a new life.'

'If the perfect person showed up, would you ignore him?'

An image of Ben flashed through Annabel's mind, but she flicked it away. 'I don't know, Trace. Perhaps I'm not as optimistic as you. All I want to do is take each day at a time.'

'Promise me though, Bel, if love comes your way—'

Annabel put her hand up. 'I promise I'll think about it. That's all.'

***

On a Friday morning in the first week of February, Annabel slowed her car as she hit the fifty-kilometre speed limit. This was it. Glengarrick was one of many small towns nestled between the Murray River and the southeast coast of Victoria. A little pocket of Victoria that the tourist brochures said promised a simpler life. Which was why Annabel had already decided it was the perfect place to move to. Right now, she needed simple. Lots of it.

The moment she'd turned onto the road heading out of Geelong with the music cranked up in her car, she'd begun to relax. Although she'd had a few second thoughts—mostly because her parents had tried to put them in her head—she had a feeling that moving to Glengarrick would be the balm she needed to heal her heart. She could put down roots and make the kind of friends who could become the family she desperately craved. She gave herself a little shake. Before she got too ahead of herself, she needed to get this job, then she had to find somewhere to live.

As she'd driven into town this time, she noticed things she hadn't seen when she'd driven here for Daisy's baptism earlier in the year. She was surprised how many houses were being built in a subdivision that had once been a farmer's paddock. And as she drove down the main street, she noted that both the primary school and high school appeared to have new buildings and most of the shops in the main street looked like they'd been recently revamped. It felt smaller than she remembered from her last visit, but every bit as pretty.

When Jed told her about the job, he said the practice, and Glengarrick, would be the perfect fit for her now she'd retired from football and was looking for a change of pace and scenery. Not only was the town in the middle of the pristine wilderness of Victoria's High Country, it was full of the most genuine people on earth.

She exhaled slowly and lifted her eyes to the mountains in the distance. Jed said his favourite thing about Glengarrick was the views. He reckoned they had the power to right wrongs, rewind time, and glue all the broken pieces back together. Was that true or had he just said that as a selling point? She was about to find out.

She found a spot to park over the road from the GP clinic and stepped out of the car. The forecast was for temperatures in the mid-thirties again today, and it already felt hotter than that. Slipping on her sunglasses, she crossed the street to the town's only real estate agency which, from what she could tell, also doubled as the newsagent and post office. Her interview wasn't for another hour so she figured she might as well check out the rental property market.

She pushed open the door and almost crashed into a man who was about to leave the office.

'Sorry,' she said, holding the door open for him to allow him to pass.

If there was a checklist for the typical alpha male with a commanding presence, this guy ticked all the boxes. He exuded self-confidence and a fleeting hint of self-assuredness that suggested he knew how good-looking he was.

'I'll call you if I hear of anything, Nick.'

Annabel dragged her attention from the man at the door—Nick apparently—to a much older, well-dressed man standing in the frame of a doorway that led to an internal office. He might as well have been wearing a sign around his neck that said, "real estate agent".

'Thanks,' Nick said to the older man. He turned back to Annabel and smiled. 'Hi. I'm Nick.' He held out his hand and she waited for his eyes to stop looking her up and down before she shook it.

'Annabel,' she replied, extracting her hand quickly.

His smile widened. He was a walking talking advertisement for teeth whitening. 'You're my eleven o'clock, right?'

Annabel frowned. 'Pardon?'

'My eleven o'clock appointment. You're here for the job interview.'

'Yeah, yes, I am,' Annabel stammered.

'I'm Nick Young. The doctor. I'll be interviewing you.'

'Oh. Okay. I'll see you soon, I guess.'

His lack of formality made her feel slightly awkward. Was he being too familiar, or did she just have her radar turned up?

Something about him reminded her of the type of guy who'd followed her football career with a little too much interest—she'd come across a few of those over the years. They would send messages to her through social media telling her how they loved watching her play. She ignored them all. They were the type of men Scott would have gone ballistic about, had he known.

The real estate agent coughed, and it broke the weird moment.

Nick slipped past her, softly closing the door behind him and Annabel turned her attention back to the man in front of her.

He smoothed his tie before offering his hand. 'Good afternoon. John Hansen. How can I help?'

She shook his hand. 'Annabel Norton. As Dr. Young said, I'm applying for a job here.' She smiled. 'I might be getting ahead of myself, but do you have any available rental properties?'

John held out his arm and gestured for her to go ahead of him into his office. 'Tell me what you're after,' he said after he'd waited for her to sit on the other side of the desk.

'I'm not fussy,' Annabel said, 'although I like to cook so it would be great if it has a decent kitchen.'

'I'm not going to lie, Annabel. There aren't any available properties that would suit a single person. That's what I was just saying to Dr. Young.'

Annabel's heart sank. 'Oh.'

John leaned forward. 'Would you like a cup of tea?'

'Ah. No thanks.'

'Coffee?'

'No, thank you.'

'Anything?'

'Sure. Yes. A glass of water would be fine. Thankyou.'

John picked up the phone, put it to his ear and pressed a button. 'Linda, could you please bring me two glasses of water?' He put the receiver back in the cradle and smiled at Annabel. 'Tell me about yourself. What brings you to Glengarrick?'

Annabel licked her lips and considered how much to tell this stranger. She didn't generally like to talk about herself, but even with his crisply ironed shirt and perfect manicure, there was something grandfatherly about John too. She sensed he wanted to help her, and she also had the feeling she could trust him.

Before she could reply, a woman entered with two tall glasses of water. With a smile she placed one in front of John and the other in front of Annabel before closing the door gently behind her.

'You've had a challenging time lately, haven't you?' John asked.

Annabel blinked.

'Relationship issues?'

She found herself nodding. 'Boyfriend. It ended months ago but I still need some time and space to think about what the future's going to look like for me without him in it.'

'You need time to heal,' John said in a matter of fact manner.

'Something like that.'

Annabel reached for her water with a shaking hand and brought the glass to her lips. After swallowing she set the glass back on the desk. She needed to get back to the reason she was here and away from discussing her personal life.

'So, you're telling me there are no rental properties?' She could always find somewhere to live in Stockton or another town, but she had her heart set on living in Glengarrick.

'We have a handful, but they'd all be too big for you and too expensive. Unless…' He sat back in his chair and steepled his fingers. 'I know someone who has a furnished cottage they rent out to the right person. The cottage is attached to the main house but it's self-contained and very private.'

If she got the job, she didn't want to live in someone's granny flat, but it sounded like she might have no choice. It wasn't like she'd seen another real estate agency in town.

Before she had a chance to tell John she might consider it, he picked up the phone again.

'Linda, can you call Jock or Heather and tell them I might have someone suitable for *Wandana?*' He disconnected the call and when he looked at Annabel, his brown eyes twinkled. 'This might be exactly what you're looking for. If Jock or Heather are around, we can go out and have a look now if that suits. It won't take long.'

Annabel checked her phone. Ten-twenty. She still had time before the interview, but it could be jumping the gun. 'I haven't got the job yet.'

'Ah, yes. The interview.' John glanced at his watch. 'Perhaps best to have the interview first then we can go out to the farm. If Heather is there, we'll get stuck chatting.'

Linda reappeared. 'I couldn't get through to Jock or Heather, but I spoke to their son and he said you can pop in any time. He's there now.' She handed John a set of keys. 'He said he's happy for you to head over whenever it suits. His parents will be home this afternoon if you want to catch them too.'

'Perfect.' John smiled at Annabel as he stood. 'Come back after your interview and I'll drive you out to *Wandana* for a look.'

'But what if I don't get the job.'

John chuckled. 'You'll get the job, won't she, Linda?'

'There's no doubt. You're just who Dr. Young is looking for.'

Chapter 10

Annabel sat in a chair in the empty waiting room of the GP clinic feeling more nervous than a teenager getting ready for a first date. A door opened and a woman around Annabel's age appeared, smiling warmly.

'Annabel. Hi, I'm Melissa, the practice manager.'

Annabel stood. 'Sorry, I'm a bit early.'

'Not a problem. Linda called and said you were already in town. No point having you sit around waiting.'

'I could have stayed longer at the café and had another coffee.'

Linda had obviously called the *Silver Spoon* café too, because when Annabel went in to get a coffee and see if Georgie was working, Renee, the woman behind the counter, wouldn't let her pay and wished her all the best for the interview. The benefits—or were they negatives? —to small town life.

Melissa smiled. 'Don't stress at all. Come on in.' She beckoned for Annabel to enter the office. 'Your resume looks great.' She closed the door behind them.

Annabel took the offered seat. 'Thank you.'

Melissa shuffled the papers in front of her. 'I see you don't have any practice nurse experience, but Nick's called your referees, and they all say you're a quick learner.'

'Really?' Since when were references checked before an interview?

Melissa must have seen the look on her face. 'Nick said he just met you at the real estate office and knew you'd be a perfect fit for us.'

Annabel raised her eyebrows. 'We barely had a ten second conversation.'

Melissa smiled. 'Nick's a good judge of character.'

'Am I the only person who applied?' Annabel asked.

Melissa didn't reply immediately but the flush on her cheeks was enough of an answer. 'Yeah, but we wouldn't employ anyone. Your experience is exceptional. We couldn't believe it when we got your resume. We couldn't wait to meet you.' The blush deepened. 'I've watched you play footy too. You were phenomenal.'

'Nick mentioned *he* was going to interview me,' Annabel said. It wasn't that she wanted to ignore Melissa's question, but it didn't seem right to get drawn into a conversation about her former football career when she was interviewing for a job.

'He was, but he got called out.' Melissa shrugged. 'Happens all the time. A kid fell off a swing at the school and they think she's broken her arm. He's gone out to check. We don't have a local ambulance station.'

'Oh, right.'

Melissa tapped Annabel's resume with a finger. 'Nick thinks you'll be great, but I have to be honest, I'm worried you might be bored working here after coming from the emergency department. And Glengarrick's not forward when it comes to women and sport. Although we *do* have a women's team here now. Maybe you could join them and give them a few pointers.'

Annabel smiled. 'All good. I'm ready for a change of pace and that doesn't include playing football. I've hung up my boots.'

She spent the next couple of minutes convincing Melissa why she had no hesitation about walking away from ED and her football career.

'You know it's just a maternity leave position, don't you? We don't know what our current practice nurse's plans are after she's had her baby. Rachael might decide to come back to work at the end of twelve months or take longer. But it's at least for a year.'

'That's fine. I'm not sure what my own long-term plans are.'

'How soon could you start?'

'Immediately.' She stopped. 'Presuming I can find a place to live. Options are limited according to the real estate agent. I'd rather not have to drive too far out of town, but I suppose if I had to, I could live in Stockton and drive here.'

'Oh, yeah. Nick's having trouble finding a rental too.'

'He's not a local?'

'No. He comes in from Stockton every day. It's only half an hour.'

'How long has he worked here?'

'Six months. Since we opened the new clinic. Before that, there was an old GP who worked out of his car and did a lot of home visits. He retired, thankfully.'

'Well, I'm looking at a place this afternoon, so if that works out, I could start in the next few days. I'd just have to get myself settled.'

A few days was all she'd need. It wasn't like she had much stuff, and she didn't have too many people she'd want to catch up with before moving. Most of her friends turned out to be Scott's friends.

She was still waiting for Scott and his lawyer to work out the financial arrangements of their breakup. Scott had already told her he wanted to keep all their furniture and artwork—which didn't surprise her—but that she could expect significant financial remuneration as part of their settlement. Once she received the money, she could decide what to do with it.

'Rachael will be thrilled you can start so soon. Her baby's due in three weeks and she's already finished work. If you can start straight away, she can come back in and give you some training.'

It was all happening quickly, but it felt right. Still, she hesitated. 'Can I let you know later today?' She'd give Jed a call and run it all past him. He'd been her sounding board on a lot of things over the years.

'Sounds perfect.' Melissa stood.

It was Annabel's shortest interview ever.

'It will be good to have you join us. I know Nick is looking forward to working with you. He said every practice needs a good nurse.'

'Right. Well, thanks. I'll call you this afternoon and let you know.'

Annabel had her hand on the door handle and was about to exit the clinic when a woman entered, doubled over in pain. She took two steps and collapsed on the floor in the middle of the waiting room.

'Michelle!' Melissa rushed over to her. 'What's wrong?'

Annabel paused, wondering if she should step in to assist. She had no idea whether Melissa had any medical background. For all she knew, Melissa might be a nurse too. But the moment Melissa looked up at her, panic in her eyes, Annabel knew she had to help.

She turned to Melissa. 'Can you call Nick and get him back here?'

Melissa nodded. 'I can try.' She dashed behind the reception desk and picked up the phone.

Annabel squatted down beside the woman. 'Hey, Michelle, I'm Annabel. I'm a nurse. What's going on?'

Michelle put her hands on her stomach and looked over at Annabel. 'I don't know. I've been having stomach cramps since yesterday morning. It's just getting worse.'

'Do you think you can get up and walk?' Annabel glanced around the small waiting room. Three closed doors led off a small hallway. 'Melissa, which one is Nick's room?' Annabel asked.

Melissa pointed. 'Last door at the end of the hallway is the treatment room. Take Michelle there.'

'Did you get hold of Nick?'

Melissa nodded. 'He's taken the kid into the hospital in Stockton and he's at least half an hour away. He said to call him if you need him. I'll call Rachael and see if she can come in and give you a hand.'

'That'd be great,' Annabel said. She was in an unfamiliar setting and had no idea what was wrong with Michelle; the combination was a recipe for trouble.

She helped Michelle stand and supported her as they shuffled down the hallway to the treatment room. Annabel opened the door, and one glance calmed her tingling nerves. The room was light filled and well-equipped. Everything was labelled so if she had to find something in a hurry, it shouldn't be too difficult. Hopefully it wouldn't come to needing emergency equipment, but if she did, there was a large red trolley in the corner with oxygen and suction and a defibrillator.

'Can you get up onto the examination table so I can have a listen to your tummy?' she asked.

Michelle nodded. Annabel was about to close the door to the treatment room to give Michelle some privacy when a man burst in. He was flushed and sweating and breathing heavily. He stopped when he saw Annabel and the groove between his eyebrows deepened. 'Who are you? Where's Rachael?'

'I'm Annabel. I'm a nurse. Rachael's on her way.'

'Right. Good-oh. Bloody hell, it's hot out there. What do you think it is? Appendicitis?'

'I've had my appendix out when I was a kid,' Michelle said. 'I told you that, Dave.' She turned to Annabel. 'This is my husband, Dave.'

'Nice to meet you.'

'Maybe it's kidney stones, Shell. When I had kidney stones, I felt like I was in labour.'

'Like you'd know how that felt.' Michelle grimaced.

Dave shrugged. 'Well, you know what they say. It's just like giving birth.'

'I wouldn't know,' Michelle replied, breathing heavily, each word an effort.

'Can you tell me a bit about yourself?' Annabel asked. 'Have you ever had anything like this before? Any operations? Any past medical history you can tell me about? Are you taking any medications?' One of her favourite parts of her job was putting the clues together to work out what was wrong with a person. But she'd never done it without the support of her team at the hospital around her. And not without access to pathology and radiology.

'Nothing relevant.' Dave answered for Michelle. 'I can't even tell you the last time she went to the doctor. She's never sick other than having that gastro bug last year.'

'I know I'm a bit overweight, but otherwise I'm fairly healthy,' Michelle said. Her brow was less furrowed as though the pain was easing. 'Maybe it's something I ate.'

Dave smoothed her hair back from her forehead with his hand. 'Stop going on about your size. We've both put on some weight lately.' He planted a kiss on the top of her head. 'Blame that cruise we took for our wedding anniversary last year.'

Michelle smiled at him. The pain was evidently easing. 'I'm *never* going on a cruise again. All that food.' She groaned and rolled her eyes.

Annabel found a blood pressure monitor and slipped the cuff around Michelle's upper arm. While it pumped up, she palpated her pulse. Slightly fast.

'So, you've otherwise been well? Any changes in your bowel habits?' Annabel asked.

'None. Everything's fine. Just the usual things when you get older.' She smiled at Annabel. 'Not that you would know about that yet.' She rolled her eyes. 'Peri menopause *sucks*.'

'How old are you?'

'Forty-seven.'

'Any pregnancies?'

Michelle shook her head. 'Dave and I didn't meet until two years ago.'

'Any burning or stinging when you go to the toilet?'

Another head shake. 'I just need to go to the toilet more than usual. And earlier today there was blood in the toilet.'

'What do you think it is?' Dave asked.

Annabel went through the possibilities. Might be pancreatitis. More likely gall bladder. Could be kidney stones. Or a bowel obstruction? But that didn't explain the bleeding Michelle had reported, did it? Ovarian cysts? Kidney infection? Perhaps Michelle could give her a urine specimen.

She was about to ask for one when Michelle started groaning again, clutching her abdomen.

Dave took her hand and spoke soothingly to her before glancing up at Annabel, eyes flashing with fear. 'When's the doctor coming? Shell needs to see a doctor now.' He stroked his wife's hair. 'Shouldn't we call an ambulance?'

Annabel had no idea. What was the protocol out here? How long would it take an ambulance to get here from Stockton? If

Melissa was there, Annabel could ask her, but she hadn't reappeared.

'Nick will be here soon and Rachael's on her way.' Annabel found a stethoscope. 'Do you mind if I quickly examine you?' she asked Michelle. She needed to listen to her chest and abdomen and see if she could figure out what was going on.

'What do *you* think's wrong with me?' Michelle asked after Annabel stood back and wrapped the stethoscope around her neck.

It was impossible to tell without a scan, but Michelle fit the Five-F criteria: fair, female, in her forties, possibly still fertile even though she claimed she was peri-menopausal. And, as much as it was politically incorrect to say, fat. Annabel would never call anyone fat, but Michelle was at least forty kilograms overweight, carrying most of it around her middle. And what troubled Annabel most was the size of Michelle's distended abdomen. Although she had bowel sounds, her stomach was too firm for Annabel's liking which might mean some sort of bowel obstruction which was a medical emergency that required surgical intervention.

'It might be your gall bladder. But I wouldn't want to make any guesses,' Annabel hurried on. 'How bad is the pain?'

'It's okay now,' Michelle said. 'It comes in waves.'

'When you get it, how bad is it. On a scale of one to ten. Ten being so bad you want to curl up in the corner?'

'When it's bad, an eleven.'

'And now?'

'Nothing.'

'Hmm. What does it feel like? Sharp and stabbing?'

Michelle shook her head. 'No. More like a squeezing pain and it goes right through to my back.'

'Okay. What else has been going on? Any nausea? Vomiting? Diarrhoea recently?'

'Nothing.'

'You were sick the other day,' Dave said. He hadn't left Michelle's side, holding her hand or stroking her arm or pulling her hair back from her face.

'That was just something I ate.'

Dave looked over at Annabel. 'She's been off for months. Ever since we got back from that cruise.'

'Probably caught Coronavirus.' Michelle chuckled. 'I keep telling you, it's just the joys of getting old. I used to be able to lose weight easily, but now I can't.' She screwed up her face and groaned. 'The pain is coming back.'

'Can you give her something?' Dave asked.

'I'm sorry, I can't.'

'Where the bloody hell is the doctor?'

Good question. And where the heck were Melissa and Rachael?

Dave stood. He towered over Annabel and for a moment she felt a flush of alarm. She didn't know these people and there was no sign of a panic button. Even if she pressed it, who would come?

'She needs a *doctor,* not just a nurse.'

'Let me go and find Melissa.' Annabel ducked out of the room and headed for waiting room. Empty. No sign of anyone. She opened the front door of the clinic and glanced up and down the street. It was empty too.

Dave's shout got her attention and she spun around and ran back to the treatment room where she found Michelle collapsed on the floor on her knees, blood-stained fluid pooling between her legs.

Annabel swore loudly. 'I need help in here!' she shouted. Melissa had to be somewhere in the building.

By the time Annabel and Dave had helped Michelle back onto the bed, she was groaning in pain.

Annabel heard footsteps and moments later a heavily pregnant woman entered, puffing. Rachael.

'Hey Michelle. Dave. What's going on?' Rachael asked.

'Where's the doctor?' Dave asked her.

'Nick's on his way back from Stockton. I've just spoken with him.' She finally looked at Annabel, eyebrows raised. A small smile played across her lips. 'Hi. Sorry to have to meet you like this. Melissa told me you're going to take my maternity leave position.'

Annabel nodded. Although after all this, they might reconsider hiring her, especially if things didn't end well.

'What happened?' Rachael asked.

'She walked in about twenty minutes ago in severe pain,' Annabel explained softy. 'Abdomen is firm and distended.'

'How long has she been like this?' Rachael asked.

'Since yesterday morning.'

'Bowel sounds?'

Annabel nodded.

'I can feel something down there.' Michelle pointed between her legs. 'It's coming out.'

Dave's fingers were white from her grip.

Rachael's eyes widened. She glanced from Michelle to Annabel. 'Vaginal prolapse?' she whispered to Annabel.

Annabel had considered almost everything except *that*.

'Can I examine you?' Rachael asked.

Michelle nodded and Annabel and Dave helped her slip off her trackpants and knickers.

Rachael swore under her breath and her friendly demeanour disappeared. 'You forgot to mention she's pregnant,' she said under her breath.

'She is?' Annabel gaped at Rachael then looked up at Michelle. '*Are* you pregnant?'

Michelle tried to laugh. 'No. Definitely not.'

'She's not pregnant,' Dave said, shaking his head. 'Definitely not.'

'I'm too old to be pregnant.'

'Looks like a cord to me,' Rachael whispered to Annabel.

Annabel squatted beside Rachael. She'd never seen an umbilical cord except on YouTube videos but that's exactly what looked like was hanging between Michelle's legs.

She dropped the F-bomb.

The umbilical cord was the baby's lifeline and if it had prolapsed, Michelle's unborn child was in grave danger of having its vital oxygen supply cut off.

'Are you sure it's not a vaginal prolapse?' Annabel whispered to Rachael.

'Hundred percent that's a cord.'

'What are we going to do?'

'We hold it in while we wait for the ambos.'

'I've called them,' Melissa said, from the doorway. Her face was pale.

'Where's Nick?' Rachael asked.

'I'm here. What's going on?' Nick barrelled into the room. 'Sorry, this hot weather has brought everyone out. The roads are atrocious. Took me longer than I thought.'

'She's got a prolapsed cord,' Rachael said quietly, 'although she claims she didn't know she was pregnant.'

Dave, stunned, hadn't moved or said a word. He looked from Nick to Rachael to Annabel. 'How is this possible?'

'I can't be pregnant,' Michelle said, through gritted teeth. 'I haven't had a period in nearly a year. *And* I'm forty-effing-*six*!'

'Have you rung triple O?' Nick asked calmly.

'Melissa did.'

'How far along do you think she is?'

'I'm guessing full term,' Annabel said.

'Right.' Nick rolled up the sleeves of his shirt and calmly went to the sink to wash his hands. 'Melissa, get me AV on the phone. Annabel, help her get on her knees on the bed. Knees to chest. To keep weight off the cord, her pelvis and legs need to be elevated. Rach, get things ready in case we have to deliver this baby.'

Annabel gently helped Michelle roll over into the position Nick wanted. Her pelvis was in the air, her head on a pillow. She looked awkward and uncomfortable.

'What's going on?' Dave asked. 'What are you doing?'

'We have to keep the baby's head off the cord,' Nick explained. 'If your wife lies like this, there's a chance it won't compress the cord any further.' He pulled on a pair of latex gloves. A thin sheen of sweat covered his brow but he still managed to give Dave a reassuring smile and he moved like he didn't have a care in the world. Annabel found a level of respect for him. If he was this calm in a crisis, he would be good to work with.

'I can't be pregnant,' Michelle repeated after the next contraction eased. Tears streamed down her cheeks. 'I can't be.' She groaned again, as another contraction started.

'You're doing great,' Rachael reassured her. 'This bub is in a hurry to meet you.'

Annabel heard the optimism in Rachael's voice but one look at her face and there was no question she was as petrified as Annabel was.

'I have the operator on the phone,' Melissa said from the threshold of the room. She held a cordless phone in the air. Rachael took the phone from her, put it on speaker and held it near Nick.

'This is Nick Young in Glengarrick. One of my patients is in labour and I can see the cord. How far away is the ambulance?'

'We have two units on their way. They should be there within five minutes.'

'Bloody well hope she's got that long,' Dave muttered.

Annabel glanced at Michelle. She was ghostly grey. *Hurry up*, she begged the ambulance. If she were a praying person, she'd be on her knees right now.

With Michelle and Nick still in position, there was nothing anyone could do except wait in near silence. Dave held Michelle's hands and whispered in her ear. Another contraction gripped Michelle and she cried out in agony, the sound mingling with the whooshing sound of adrenaline in Annabel's ears and the distant sound of ambulance sirens, headed their way.

Minutes later the room exploded with people.

Annabel exhaled in relief as the paramedics took charge and within minutes they'd taken over from Nick and loaded Michelle onto a stretcher with a paramedic sitting on top of her with his hand inside Michelle's body, attached to the unborn baby like a human lifeline.

Outside, it had started bucketing with rain and they stood watching the ambulance leave, sirens shrieking, as it headed towards Stockton where a team were waiting to take Michelle straight to theatre. A retrieval team were on their way from Melbourne just in case they had to transfer mum and bub to the Royal Women's or Royal Children's hospital by helicopter.

Annabel trailed back inside after Nick and Rachael and followed them into a small staffroom. Melissa was pouring cups of tea and putting food out. The last thing Annabel wanted was food, but she could use a strong cup of tea.

'How is it possible to not know you're pregnant?' Melissa asked Rachael.

Rachael rubbed her belly. 'I have no idea. This one kicks continually and keeps me awake at night. How would Michelle have explained away not feeling that? Let alone the morning sickness, the sore boobs, and no periods. It's so weird.'

'Do you think she was in denial?' Annabel asked, 'or do you think she genuinely had no idea?'

'Hard to know,' Nick said, 'but although it's rare, it's not as rare as you think. They're called cryptic pregnancies. I've never seen one before.'

'Will the baby be okay?' Melissa asked.

Nick shrugged. 'If they got Michelle to theatre in time. We just have to hope that cord wasn't compressed too long.'

'You did great, Annabel,' Rachael said. 'What a baptism by fire. I bet you thought country town nursing would be boring.'

'I'm not sure what I expected, but this wasn't it,' Annabel said with a laugh.

'I hope you haven't changed your mind about wanting to work here,' Melissa said.

Annabel shook her head. More than anything she wanted to be part of the team here. 'As long as Nick says he's happy to have me on board, then yeah, I still want the job.'

'When can you start?' Rachael said, running her hand over her belly again.

'I think she already did,' Nick replied with a laugh.

He held out his hand, looked deep into her eyes and shook Annabel's hand. A tiny shiver of unease raced up her spine, but she pushed it away.

Nick's phone rang, breaking the moment. He released her hand and answered. Listening to his side of the conversation, it was obvious he was talking to someone at the hospital. When he gave a thumbs up, Annabel and the others let out a collective sigh. Michelle and her new baby daughter were safe. Dave, on the other hand, had fainted and missed the whole thing.

Chapter 11

Just before two o'clock Annabel left the clinic and headed back to the real estate agency. She hoped it was still okay to go out and see the place John had mentioned. When she pushed open the door, he called out from his office.

'Come in, Annabel. Linda's still at lunch.'

When Annabel entered his office, John looked up and smiled. 'Busy morning.' It wasn't a question.

'You heard?'

'Country town grapevine. You get used to it.' He stood. 'Plus, I saw the ambulances. You still want to head out to *Wandana*?'

'Only if that suits you and the owners.'

'I've just gotten off the phone with Jock and Heather. They can't wait to meet you.'

'Sounds good. I can have a quick look then head home to Geelong.'

'You in a massive hurry to get back?'

'Not really.'

'Good. Because Heather's invited you to join them for an early dinner.'

Annabel opened her mouth to say something, but John held up a hand. 'Trust me, once you've met Heather, you'll realise there's no point arguing with her. She heard what you did today, and she wants to thank you. Heather's way of thanking people is feeding them.'

Ten minutes later, Annabel parked her car behind John's, switched off the engine and gazed around her in awe. *Wandana* was breathtaking. It was nestled at the foot of a mountain and commanded views over the entire valley. The striking two-story bluestone mansion overlooking a manmade lake was like something from a magazine.

She stepped out of the car and took a deep breath. The sun was high in the sky and still generating a lot of heat but surrounded by green grass as far as she could see, it felt cooler out here. In the distance she heard the tick-tick of a sprinkler and the growl of a lawn mower. A light breeze tickled the liquidambars lining the drive and yellow leaves fell like confetti over them.

'What do you think?' John asked. 'Spectacular, isn't it?'

'I've never seen anything like it.' As they walked towards the house, gravel crunched underfoot.

'The gardens were designed by William Guilfoyle, of Melbourne Botanical Gardens fame,' John boasted as if the property were his own.

Annabel gazed out of the rolling green lawns. To the left of a perfectly pruned dark green hedge, she spied a tennis court and to the side of the house a swimming pool sparkled and glistened in the sunlight.

A dog barked and Annabel turned to see a Border Collie sprinting towards her. A man followed behind. She squinted and put a hand up to shade her eyes from the sun. Her heart raced.

'Ben?'

'Annabel!'

She strode towards him and they met in a warm embrace as the dog danced circles around them.

'What are *you* doing here?' she asked Ben after he let her go.

He grinned. 'I could ask you the same thing.'

'Ben is Jock and Heather's son,' John explained, extending his hand. 'Nice to see you again.'

'And you,' Ben said, pumping John's hand and slapping him on the back at the same time.

'How do you two know each other?' John asked.

'Oh, we're practically related,' Ben said, with a chuckle.

Annabel giggled at the look on John's face.

'We're co-godparents to Jed and Georgina Delany's daughter, Daisy,' Annabel explained. 'We keep bumping into each other in the most random places. I knew Ben was from Glengarrick, but I had no idea he was back home, or that this was his parent's property.'

'Well, what do you know,' John said as he reached down to pick up the ball the dog had dropped at his feet. He tossed the ball, and the dog took off after it. 'Since you two already know each other, why don't you do the honours, Ben, and show Annabel around while I head indoors and say hello to your folks.'

'I'd love to,' Ben said. 'Mum's in the kitchen. You know the way.'

'No doubt cooking up a storm.'

'You know Mum. You staying for dinner too?' Ben asked John.

'Not tonight.'

The dog circled around John, ball in mouth, tongue lolling. Ben laughed as he ruffled her ears. 'That dog would chase a ball twenty-four-seven if we let her.'

John left them and crossed the lawn towards the house.

'It's good to see you,' Ben said.

'And you.'

'How have you been?' he asked.

'Great. Good. You?'

'Yeah. Good. Okay.'

There was something about his tone that made Annabel look over at him, but his face was inscrutable.

'What are you doing in Glengarrick?' he asked. 'Here to visit Jed?'

'Actually, I'm having a tree change or whatever you want to call it. I've just accepted a job at the new GP clinic.'

Ben stopped walking and faced her. 'Really?'

'Yep. The nurse who works there is taking maternity leave.'

'Rachael Black?'

Annabel nodded.

They started walking again. 'Didn't even know she was pregnant. I'm so out of the loop. Haven't been home for a while. I used to spend a bit of time with Rachael and her husband Dan. I heard there's a new doctor in town too. I haven't met him, but I'm told he's good.'

'After what I saw today, I'd agree. Very good.'

'What happened today?'

Annabel quickly filled him in.

'Wow. Full on.'

'Not what I expected when I came down here for a job interview.' She smiled. 'So, tell me about this place. What's the deal? John didn't give away much. He just said your parents have a cottage they rent out. Is it like a granny flat?'

Ben chuckled. 'They do rent out the cottage from time to time to the right person, but it's slightly nicer than a granny flat. Come on, I'll show you around.'

He led the way again and just before they reached the main house, he veered left through an opening in the hedge and headed towards a smaller red brick building.

'This is the place they rent out. It was the original maids' quarters and it's connected to the main house, but as you can see it's quite separate. You'd have your own entry.'

'It's so pretty.'

'It's simple inside, but yeah, it's cute. Mum and Dad established a trust fund years earlier and the income they receive on the property is based on a sliding scale depending on a person's circumstances.'

Annabel stopped walking. 'What do you mean?'

Ben shrugged. 'They don't always charge people to stay here.'

Annabel lifted her chin. 'I'm not looking for a handout.'

Ben touched her arm briefly. 'Relax. No-one's saying you are. Sometimes Dad collects full rent on the cottage because money isn't the overriding issue. It's kind of hard to explain. Dad asks John to find the right person for the cottage, regardless of whether they can afford to stay here or not. John knew this place would be perfect for you to get yourself back on your feet. And I'm not just talking financially.' Ben smiled. 'I happen to agree with John. This place will be just what you need.'

A tingle raced up and down Annabel's spine. The moment John met her it was if he'd seen deep into her soul and known she was still hurting.

'What if I say no?'

They arrived at a pale blue timber door. On either side of the door were two potted box hedges shaped into perfect balls. A "welcome" doormat greeted her. Ben pulled a set of keys from his pocket, slipped one into the lock and instructed the dog to sit and stay.

'When you see inside, you won't be able to say no.'

He was right.

After they'd looked around the cottage, which didn't take too long because it was, as Ben had explained, very small, Annabel was ready to sign whatever paperwork was required. Still, she was concerned that Ben's parents thought she was some sort of charity case.

'I wouldn't want anyone to think—'

Ben lifted his hand. 'No one other than John or Dad know who is renting the cottage or how much they're paying. Your privacy is totally guaranteed.'

She still wasn't completely sold on the idea, but the cottage *was* cute, and the location was idyllic. If she lived here, every tree-change dream would come true. She stood at the front door and glanced across the paddocks that sprawled out as far as she could see. She could see herself living here. It would be the perfect place to start over.

Ben closed the door, locked it, and pocketed the keys. The dog picked up the ball and followed them. 'Renting out this place is

Dad's way of paying it forward.' He put out his arm and indicated she walk ahead of him.

Annabel felt his hand brush the small of her back briefly and a shiver ran through her.

The path wound through a rose garden before turning through another gap in the perfectly groomed hedge leading to another garden.

'When Dad's parents died, he was left with *Wandana* and a truckload of money—more than he could spend in a lifetime—and he wants to make sure other people get to enjoy the property and the gardens.'

'That's an incredibly generous thing to do.'

A niggle of doubt went through her. Were Ben and his parents just like Scott and her parents? Focussed solely on financial gains?

'It sounds altruistic but wait 'til you meet Dad. And Mum. You'll love them.'

If they were anything like their son, she knew she'd like them immediately, but she was strangely nervous about meeting them. What if they were like Scott's parents? Every person she'd ever met with money acted like they were better than everyone else and she had no reason to believe the Naylors would be any different.

'Am I really invited to dinner?'

'Absolutely. Mum loves guests.' Ben grinned. 'But I have to warn you, the whole family will be here tonight.'

'*Your* whole family? Why?'

He didn't reply immediately and once again Annabel felt like he was holding something back.

'I had a slight change in plans a couple of weeks ago and decided on my own tree change. I moved back last week, and Mum's arranged for the family to get together for a meal. I haven't caught up with everyone since Christmas. We used to all catch up for a family dinner once a month.'

Annabel wasn't quite following. 'You've moved home? Here?'

Ben pointed and she followed his gaze.

'See those stables?'

Ahead of them on the other side of the orchard was a bluestone stable block.

'That's where I live. There's a unit above the stables. Looks like we're going to be neighbours.' He grinned. 'Close neighbours.'

Chapter 12

The moment Ben's parents found out he and Annabel already knew each another, they took Annabel into the fold as if she was a long-lost daughter. When his mum gave Annabel a hug, Ben noticed neither of them let go for a long time and it made him wonder what type of relationship Annabel had with her own parents. She told him she was adopted, but for some reason he'd pictured a loving family picture. Maybe that wasn't the case.

Annabel tried to excuse herself from their family dinner, but Mum wouldn't hear of it. Ben wasn't surprised. His parents were well known for their warmth and hospitality. And he wasn't going to complain. He didn't mind having Annabel here. Not one little bit.

Since the day of his breakdown, he'd been so consumed by his own issues, that he hadn't given too many thoughts to Annabel, but now she was here he remembered he'd been planning to call her and ask her out for dinner. Thank goodness yet again, fate—or God, or the Universe—had intervened and brought them together again. This time he wasn't going to let her out of his sight.

Dinner was the usual crazy affair. The formal dining room was ablaze with lights and the table groaned under too much food. Mum always catered for extras and it was a rare family dinner night that there wasn't someone extra around the table. Tonight it was Annabel's turn to experience the Naylor family at its best.

His family had a strong bond, but that didn't mean they didn't enjoy a few heated debates. A few times he caught Annabel watching the verbal banter between him and his siblings with a worried expression and he had to keep reassuring her the teasing was all in jest.

His sister, Natalie, was the quietest in the family and she and Sasha, their sister-in-law, made sure Annabel was included in the conversations flying around the table. He smiled when he overheard Natalie and Sasha making plans with Annabel to have a movie and pizza night some time.

The only slightly awkward moment came when Natalie's husband Rob asked how long he was on leave for. He hadn't been totally truthful with his parents about his reasons for coming home. He'd let everyone assume he was taking long service leave rather than the truth, which was he was on stress leave.

It wasn't that he was ashamed to admit he was suffering PTSD; he just didn't want to open up the floor for everyone to offer an opinion on what he should do to get over it. He had enough support through Bob, Sean, the Police Wellbeing Unit and the Code 9 Foundation which had been established to support first responders with PTSD, anxiety, depression and other mental health conditions that resulted from their service to the community.

After dinner with his parents his first night back home, Ben had slept until noon the next day which for him was unbelievable. Maybe cutting out caffeine was key, but he didn't think so. He'd given credit to inhaling the fresh country air and being in a place of good memories and happy times.

He'd had an amazing childhood growing up at *Wandana* and always loved being out on the farm. It helped too, that he had a great relationship with his parents and siblings and their families.

Years earlier, Ben and his brother James had turned the attic space above the stable block into a two-bedroom self-contained unit and that was where Ben stayed when he came to visit. There was more than enough room in the main house, but it was nice to have his own place away from his parents.

When he'd arrived home with his car loaded to the roof with clothes and personal belongings Mum had raised her eyebrows at how much stuff he'd brought with him but hadn't said a word. Her hug was longer than normal though. Dad's gaze had narrowed but neither of them had pushed him for more information. He'd tell them the real reason he was back home when the timing was right. After just two counselling sessions via phone with the psychologist, he already felt better, although he had a sense that he still had a long way to go.

For now, he had everything he needed—his solitude, some groceries, a thousand-piece jigsaw given to him by his colleagues as a joke, and a change of environment. The combination seemed to be working well so far.

But with Annabel moving to town, things just got a whole lot more interesting. And a whole lot better.

He was about to answer Rob's question as honestly as he could, while remaining as vague as possible, when his oldest niece was regaling her younger cousins with a story at the other end of the table and accidently knocked a bottle of wine flying. Thankfully, everyone's attention was diverted to mopping up the stain and they forgot about Rob's question and Ben's reply.

He glanced over at Annabel and caught her looking at him. The look on her face said she wasn't fooled.

After a magnificent dinner, which included a dozen more stories told over nearly as many bottles of top-quality red wine, his parents offered to take Annabel on a tour of the property while the others cleaned up the kitchen. He joined them, laughingly correcting his mum with every recollection she had of his childhood.

'I can't believe how close you all are,' Annabel said as she put her arm through his and they followed his parents outside. 'It's hard not to be jealous.'

'Do you have siblings?'

She shook her head. 'Adopted only child. A psychologist would have a field day with me.' She smiled but it didn't reach her eyes and he made a note to raise that subject another time. Seemed like both of them were hiding some deep hurts and he made a pact that if their friendship was going to progress, he wouldn't hold things back from her.

'I'm very blessed,' he said. 'We get along well. Always have.'

'It's how families are supposed to be.'

'Trust me, I know how rare it is.'

'Remember when you were playing hide and seek, and fell asleep in the hedge,' Mum said when they caught up to her and his dad.

Ben laughed. 'I didn't stir until I heard the sirens.'

'Sirens?' Annabel asked.

'We laugh about it now but at the time it wasn't funny. We had to call the police and arrange a search party. We'd been looking for him for hours. I was worried he'd fallen into the dam and drowned,' Dad said.

'That must have been terrifying for you,' Annabel said.

'It was, but Ben was in his element. I think that's when he decided he wanted to be a policeman.'

Annabel glanced at Ben. 'Was it?'

'Yeah, I reckon it probably was. I remember Uncle Dave finding me.'

'How old were you?' Annabel asked.

Ben looked to his mum for clarification. 'I dunno. Five or six?'

'That's about right.'

They continued their tour, and he couldn't stop smiling at the way Annabel's mouth kept dropping open.

'The whole place looks like it should belong in the Royal family,' she gushed.

Ben laughed. 'Mum's considered local royalty round here.'

His mum blushed. 'Don't be silly, darling.'

'It's true.'

'Anyway, Annabel, as you can see, the original four rooms and central passageway are still evident, but additions were made over the years including a portico over the front door, the bay-windowed drawing room, four more bedrooms and an indoor kitchen and bathroom.' His mum stopped and put a hand on Annabel's arm. 'I hope I'm not boring you.'

Annabel shook her head. 'Not at all, I'm fascinated by history and I love watching those home renovations shows. Go on.'

'Maybe we should get Chip and Jo to Australia to do one of their *Fixer Upper* shows. Costs a bleedin' fortune to maintain it,' Dad grumbled good-naturedly.

'Don't listen to him,' Ben said. 'Dad knows he's part of history and he loves it. Not long ago he and Mum were asked if they wanted to feature in a coffee table book about grand homes in the Western district. Dad couldn't say yes quickly enough. Even went out and bought a new pair of jeans and had a haircut before the photographer arrived.'

'Alright, alright, mate, don't tell stories. You make me sound like I'm lord of the manor or something.'

'It's an incredible home,' Annabel said once they'd returned to the cosy sitting room off the kitchen and everyone had cups of tea in hand. 'Does it ever feel too big?'

'Yes and no. When everyone comes back to visit like this weekend it feels like a home again, but when we're getting ready for open days and events it feels like we're visitors in our own place.'

Seeing her confused look, Ben explained. 'Mum runs open gardens and rents out some of the main rooms in the house for weddings and special events.'

'Has this property always been in your family, Jock?' Annabel asked.

Dad nodded proudly. 'Five generations of male Naylors have lived at, and run, *Wandana* as a working farm.'

'All with the first name James too,' Mum added.

Annabel looked from Ben to his dad. 'But your name is Jock.'

'I've been called Jock since I was a whippersnapper and it's stuck. I was christened James.'

'If you want to stay on his good side, don't ever call him James,' Ben warned.

Everyone chuckled.

'Will James take over the farm from you when you retire?'

'Bloody oath. I'm not handing it to anyone other than a blood relative. Yes, James will take over the farm from me. He already works with me, as does Sasha, and when I'm ready to hang up my boots, which isn't for a long time, the farm will go to him. Unless of course Ben has changed his mind about being a cop.'

Dad narrowed his gaze and stared at him, making Ben squirm.

'And that's a question you keep dodging,' Dad said, looking directly at him.

'I've told you, Dad, I'm on leave.'

'So, you haven't changed your mind?'

Ben bristled. 'I haven't made up my mind.'

One of the things he struggled with when considering retiring from the force was feeling like he'd be labelled a quitter. By nature, he wasn't one to give up.

'Jock,' Mum warned. 'Not now.' She stood. 'Darling, how about we let these two young ones catch up. Come and give me a hand in the kitchen with the dishes.'

His dad grumbled good naturedly and followed his mum to the kitchen.

Although Ben was grateful for time alone with Annabel, for a second he couldn't think of a single thing to say. He reached for his cup of tea then realised it was empty and set it back down on the coffee table.

'Ben—'

'Annabel—'

'You first,' she said.

Ben knew it was possible to fall in love at first sight. That's what had happened to his parents. He saw it in every look and touch between them. They were in love. Still, that didn't mean he ever expected it would happen to him.

Had he been so focused on *not* looking for love that it had crept up on him? Was Annabel the one? If so, it scared the hell out of him. He wasn't sure if he was ready for another relationship but everything within him wanted to know Annabel better.

After Chantelle, he'd decided a good long break was what he needed. Maybe that long break was ending. He'd always hoped that one day he'd find a woman to be his partner in life the way his parents were partners. And maybe if they were lucky, they'd have a couple of kids.

But when he'd moved home, he hadn't thought those things were part of his foreseeable future. Maybe they were. Or perhaps he was jumping the gun. But from the moment he met Annabel he knew she was special. Problem was, he didn't want her to feel pressured into a relationship with him just because they were living next door to each other on the farm.

He was known for his patience—it was why he was so good at his job—but where Annabel was concerned, it felt like his patience had flown out the window. He didn't want to go slow. Didn't want to wait and see if things developed. He wanted her to know how he felt. Now. Annabel had walked into his life and it was like a curtain had parted and the sun was shining in again.

'This is so awkward. I feel like I'm a teenager asking the most popular girl in school on a date,' he said.

Annabel raised her eyebrows at him as she tilted her head to the side. 'Really?'

He cleared his throat. 'It's just been a really long time since I've done this.' He coughed again. 'Sorry I feel like a foal trying to stand for the first time. What I'm trying to say is I'd like to see you. As in I'd like to spend more time getting to know you.' He closed his eyes and put his head in his hands. This was all coming out wrong. He sounded like a fool.

After seconds that felt like minutes, she touched his thigh. He looked up and met her gaze.

'I'd like that too.'

He exhaled. 'At least we're on the same page.'

'Very much so.'

'Remind me to thank John later for thinking of *Wandana* for me. It's perfect. Until I saw you today, I was wondering how I was going to arrange to bump into you again.'

'You could have called.'

'Yeah, I could have. Should have. Was going to. But some work stuff got in the way.'

'Are you okay? I noticed you avoided all the questions. Do you want to talk about it?'

'Yeah, I do, but not tonight. It's late.'

Annabel pulled out her phone and checked it. 'Oh, wow. I'd better get going.'

Ben looked at his watch. It was nearly nine o'clock. 'Why don't you stay tonight and head off tomorrow? It *is* late and it's a long drive back to Geelong.'

'Thanks, Ben, but it's fine, I don't mind driving.'

'Stay,' he insisted. 'Please. In the cottage,' he added, in case she'd misunderstood him. 'I'm not asking you to stay out of obligation or politeness. I really want you to stay. We can hang out tomorrow. Unless you have other plans.'

'I don't have any plans, but I haven't brought anything with me, not even a change of clothes.'

Ben laughed. 'Trust me, between Mum and my sister, they'll rustle up whatever you need.'

Thankfully, Annabel didn't take much more convincing.

'I'd love to stay.'

'Awesome. I'll let Mum know.'

'She won't mind?'

'She'll be thrilled. Trust me. Any chance to have people stay. Mum loves it. Do you want to stay in the cottage or the main house?'

'The cottage please. Only if that's convenient. I heard your dad say something about it needing a fresh coat of paint.'

'It'll be fine. Give me a minute to get some clean sheets and things for you.'

Annabel put a hand on his arm. 'Please don't go to too much trouble.'

'Trust me. It's not an issue.'

On impulse, he gave her a peck on the cheek before going off to find his mother and tell her Annabel was staying the night.

Chapter 13

After making up the bed in the cottage with fresh sheets, Annabel and Ben returned to the main house for a cup of tea. Rob and Natalie and their girls had gone home—they lived on the property next door—but James and Sasha and their daughters were still there. Jock and Heather had retired to bed. The lounge room fire was roaring, and everyone was relaxed, sitting around with their feet up on the oversized leather couches enjoying hot drinks and snacking on chocolate and lollies. The girls had pulled out a card table and were working, heads bowed, on Ben's jigsaw.

'Are you joining us tomorrow?' Sasha asked after Annabel and Ben sank onto a couch opposite Sasha and James.

Annabel looked to Ben. He hadn't mentioned any plans. She'd presumed first thing in the morning she'd head back to Geelong and pack.

'We're crutching the sheep,' James said, 'and the more the merrier.'

'You mean more hands make light work,' one of the twins—Ava or Bella? —called out from the other side of the room. She rolled her eyes. 'Dad's always looking for extra people to help. I'm sure he plans the crutching when we're home from school.'

'What's crutching?' Annabel asked.

As Ben explained, Annabel screwed up her face. 'So, if I say yes, you want me to help by picking up all the poo covered bits of wool?' she clarified. 'Doesn't sound like a fair deal.'

'It's not,' Sasha replied, 'and we wouldn't expect you to say yes. It's one of those things that just has to be done.'

'It's so gross,' one of the twins said.

'Now's the time to back out,' Ben said with a smile. 'No-one is forcing you. It's hard work and you'll either love or hate sheep by the time we're done. And your back will ache for days.'

Sasha chuckled. 'I might grumble about it, but I couldn't imagine doing anything else. My fondest memories are of Mum and Dad pulling us kids out of boarding school for two weeks at a time to help with shearing. When I was old enough, I'd get up early and drench the sheep before they went into the shed for shearing. I'd spend the day being one of the roustabouts then help Dad move the sheep back to the paddocks that night and bring the next lot in. I used to go back to school with more blisters than the rowers.'

'Say you'll hang around, please, Annabel,' the other twin said. 'It'll be fun.'

'Ava, don't lie,' Ben said with a laugh. He turned to Annabel. 'Don't believe my niece. There's nothing fun about crutching.'

'I'd love to stay,' she'd said. 'It sounds great. Count me in.'

She wasn't afraid of a bit of hard work, but it was the chance to spend more time with Ben that was the main drawcard. Plus, his family were special, and she wanted to get to know them better too. Now that she was moving to Glengarrick, it would be nice to make some friends. One of the hardest things about giving up football was that she no longer had the close daily contact with her teammates, many of whom had become tighter than family to her over the past few years.

'Wear something warm,' Sasha warned. 'It's freezing down at the sheds in the morning. At least until the sun gets over the trees, then you'll be stripping off.'

'Yeah. Wear layers,' Ava advised.

'And don't forget sunscreen,' Bella added.

Were they making fun of her? 'How many seasons are you expecting tomorrow?' she asked.

Everyone laughed.

'I hope you're fit,' James said.

'Yeah, I'm pretty fit,' Annabel replied with a grin. Clearly Ben hadn't mentioned to his family that she'd played football.

Ben chuckled. Their socked feet were up on the coffee table and he nudged her foot with his. 'Liar. You're fitter than the lot of us. Tell them.'

Sasha and James gave her a questioning look and she felt her cheeks flame.

'Annabel used to play for the Cats.'

At the jigsaw table, three heads snapped up. 'The women's team?' Bella asked, reverently.

Annabel nodded. 'AFLW.'

'Wow, that's sooo cool.'

'Do you know Daisy Pearce?'

'I do.'

'What about Tayla Harris? She's amazing.'

Annabel smiled. Tayla's impressive kicking technique had helped redefine the image of women playing football. Her trademark split kick had been captured in photographic freeze frame mid-match and become instantly iconic.

'How long did you play for?' Ava asked.

'Three seasons,' Ben said, answering for her, 'and from what I've heard, she was very good. Wish I'd seen her play.'

Annabel's chest expanded at the genuine compliment. She glanced at him, and his smile melted her heart.

They spent the next few minutes talking about football and how quickly the women's competition had taken off in Australia, but her mind was on the pride in Ben's voice. She wished he'd seen her play—unlike her parents or Scott, he might have actually cheered her from the stands as well as the sidelines.

'Why did you stop playing?' James asked.

'A lot of reasons,' Annabel replied. 'Age being the biggest one. I was in the inaugural group of girls to be selected for Geelong and I was one of the oldest picked. I always knew I'd only get a couple of years out of it. I wanted to end on a high, and I did.'

'She won the best and fairest for her club and they reckon she was the best ruck to play.'

Annabel blushed again but to hide her flaming cheeks she leaned into Ben and shouldered him. 'Who have you been getting your info from? Jed?'

'Maybe.'

'He's always been my biggest and loudest supporter so you can't believe everything he says. He's totally biased.'

'Your parents must be so crazy proud of you,' Sasha said.

Annabel's good mood soured a little. Even after spending this small amount of time with Ben's family, it had heightened her awareness of how lacking her relationship with her own family was. Not that she could do anything to change it—she'd tried many times over the years and given up. It wasn't worth getting worked up about it and she couldn't change them.

'I'm sure they were proud of me in their own way, but my parents are old school. Dad doesn't think women should play a men's game. He probably would have been happy if I'd just kept playing netball.' Not that he'd ever cared about her promising netball career either. She shrugged. 'I guess women's footy remains a blind spot for a lot of people. Your dad would probably be the same as mine. It's that generation, I suppose. They don't want to see women doing a man's job.'

Sasha and Natalie gaped at her. Ben shook his head. The girls murmured that that wasn't the case at all with Jock.

'No way,' James agreed. 'Not Dad. If you'd told us tonight at dinner that you played footy, I guarantee Dad would have pulled up YouTube videos or something to watch you play. He would have wanted to know all about it.'

'Absolutely,' Ben said. 'Mum, too.'

'Do you miss it?' Sasha asked.

She hesitated before replying. It was always hard to explain that on one hand she missed it dreadfully, but on the other hand, it was a chapter of her life that had ended, and she was okay with it.

'I do miss it, yeah. Those three years were hard though. They taught me, they tested me, they challenged me, and they also upset and frustrated me at times too. But I wouldn't change any of the experience for quids. The last three years were great.'

Professionally she'd kicked big goals, even if personally her love life was a train wreck. But she didn't need to bring Scott into this conversation.

When the girls started arguing about something, Sasha stood. 'Time to get you two home and into bed. Go and get your coats and put your boots on.'

They grumbled about wanting to finish the jigsaw, but one look from James and they left the room.

James glanced at Annabel's feet then up at Sasha. 'Speaking of boots. Annabel's going to need a pair for tomorrow.'

Sasha nodded. 'I was already thinking that. And clothes. Can you please drop off a pair of my old gumboots to Annabel at the cottage later tonight?' She turned to Annabel. 'Lily is about your size. I'll get James to bring you a bag of clothes too and you can go through that.' She chuckled. 'We can't have you crutching sheep in your interview clothes.'

'Thank you. That's very thoughtful of you.'

Ben left the room to take their dirty cups to the kitchen. Annabel offered to get up and help, but he told her to stay put.

'You don't have to get your hands dirty to make a good impression on my brother,' James said with a chuckle.

'That's right,' Sasha said, 'he's already besotted.'

Warmth washed over her, and it took all her strength not to grin. She was kind of besotted with Ben, too.

'I can hear you,' Ben said, entering the living room again. 'Come on, Annabel, let's get you back to the cottage before my brother and sister-in-law start match making. They're not known for their subtlety.'

She smiled at him, surprised by the ruddiness in his cheeks. Maybe Sasha was right—he *was* smitten.

If bumping into each other once that night after the disastrous dinner had been "fate", as Ben had suggested, what did it mean that they'd bumped into each other a second time? Serendipity?

If serendipity was the unsought and unexpected discovery of something by accident, this might be it. She hadn't been looking for love. She'd been looking for a new start. A new job, a new place to live, the chance to start over and make new friends who could become family. Yet, if she was honest with herself, it felt like the love she wasn't looking for was staring her in the face.

***

That night, before she slipped between the crisp hotel-quality sheets, Annabel sent Tracey a text to tell her she'd accepted the job and wouldn't be home that night. She omitted telling her friend about bumping into Ben again—that would require too many answers to questions she was still trying to get her head around herself. The biggest one being: was it too soon after Scott to consider jumping into another relationship?

Even though it was late, she called her father too, knowing he would still be up. As expected, he was shocked by her news, questioned why she would want to move to the middle of nowhere and told her he hoped her contract at the clinic wasn't set in stone. When he suggested he get her mother on the phone to "talk some sense into her", Annabel said she needed to go and told him she'd call her mother later.

Chapter 14

Early the next morning, as the sun began to turn the navy night into a lighter shade of blue, and pinks, oranges and reds coloured the sky, Annabel walked silently across the dew-covered paddock towards the shearing sheds where Ben had said to meet everyone.

In the dark distance, a horse whinnied, followed by another one. A cow bellowed then it was quiet except for the swoosh of her borrowed boots as she cut through the long grass. She rubbed her cold hands together. She wore multiple layers, at everyone's suggestion, and was glad she had. It was much colder than she'd anticipated. The last time she had felt this cold was when she went skiing.

The rattle of a truck penetrated the stillness. Seconds later, a dirty ute pulled up near the shed, brakes protesting. The headlights were cut, and the interior light came on. Annabel glimpsed Ben behind the wheel and James in the passenger seat.

Behind them, on the tray of the ute, a jumble of dog's heads appeared including the Border Collie she'd met the day before, and two chocolate brown Kelpies.

James leapt out of the passenger side and onto the tray in one fluid movement. Seconds later the dogs were released, and they tore off barking, grinning at the prospect of chasing some sheep.

Ben jumped from the cab too and slammed the door. In his peaked cap and khaki overalls tucked into gumboots he looked like he belonged on an episode of *Farmer Wants a Wife*. He grinned when he saw her and jogging over to her, he greeted her with a hug that lasted slightly longer than it needed to. No complaining from her. She hugged him back, thinking how easily she could get used to a man who hugged like that.

'How'd you sleep?' he asked, rubbing his hands to keep warm.

'Great thanks.' In truth, it was the best night's sleep she'd had in months. From the moment her head hit the pillow, she didn't stir until her alarm went off.

'Have you eaten?'

She nodded. Heather had left a basket with assorted goodies to make a quick breakfast in the kitchen of the cottage, but although she'd enjoyed a cup of tea along with the muesli and yoghurt, she'd give almost anything for a latte to wrap her hands around.

'The sheep won't miss you in that jacket.' He plucked at the hot pink fabric of the puffer jacket and his eyes crinkled with teasing laughter.

She rolled her eyes. 'It feels weird wearing someone else's clothes.'

From the bag of Lily's clothes James had dropped off at the cottage the night before, she'd chosen a pair of faded denim jeans with non-designer rips in the knees which she'd tucked into the gumboots Sasha had loaned her. Under the pink Kathmandu jacket, she had on a white long-sleeved T-shirt, a green and blue plaid flannel shirt and a black woollen jumper that had seen better days. Nothing matched and she didn't care.

'I can assure you; this jacket wouldn't have been my first wardrobe choice.' She touched her hair and chuckled. 'With hair this colour, I usually avoid pinks and reds.'

'Looks good to me.'

Ben grinned, and his open admiration—and his ease in telling her—set sparks off inside of her.

'Thought you might have changed your mind and slept in. Or at least stayed inside where it's warm,' he said.

'No way. I didn't want to miss the fun.' She shoved her hands deeper into the pockets of the coat and wished she had a beanie, gloves and a third pair of socks.

'Fun?' Jock asked, appearing on her left with Heather. 'What lie did my son tell you?'

Heather gave Annabel a quick hug. 'Hope you slept well, sweetheart. Now, have the boys told you what we're doing today?'

Annabel shook her head. 'Not specifics.'

'I'll leave you to explain, Mum.' Ben touched Annabel briefly on the shoulder before loping off with his dad.

As Ben and Jock headed over to the shed to find James Heather turned to Annabel and explained what would happen. 'Just don't get in the way, okay,' she finished. 'And if anyone yells at you to move, then move and don't be offended.'

Annabel swallowed nervously. What had she gotten herself in for? 'O-k-aay.' She had no intention of getting in the way. Or of being yelled at.

'Right then, let's go and see what those men are up to.' Heather took off like a woman a quarter of her age, and Annabel jogged to keep up with her long strides.

As they came through a break in the line of dark green pine trees surrounding the timber-fenced yard, the paddocks opened in front of Annabel, revealing endless open space. She exhaled softly. She didn't think she'd ever tire of these magnificent views.

There was no sign of any of the men, but Sasha stood with Natalie's twins at the fence line looking out across the paddock.

'Where's Nat?' Heather asked.

'She and Lily went into town to get coffees for everyone,' Sasha replied.

Annabel's mouth watered.

'Hope you like a latte,' Sasha said. 'I guessed you'd be a coffee drinker and that's what I asked Natalie to get you.'

'You guessed right. Thank you.'

Movement out of the corner of her eye caught her attention and she turned and spotted a moving mob of sheep, specks of creamy white against the green grass. A man on a red horse was slowly moving the mob towards them and behind him were the dogs, yapping at the sheep's heels. Two men on quad bikes brought up the rear.

She squinted. 'Is that Ben?'

Sasha chuckled. 'He didn't tell you he was practically born on the back of a horse?'

'No.' There was clearly lots Annabel had to learn about him. She leaned against the post and rail fence in between the twins to watch. She didn't know a single thing about horses, but Ben and the red one—chestnut, one of the twins called it—seemed to move as one. She wished she'd thought to bring her phone to take photos.

When Ben rode the horse close to the fence, Annabel's heart kicked against her chest when he looked straight at her and grinned. It was obvious he was trying to impress her, and it was working. Despite her hesitation last night about getting into another relationship so soon after Scott, there was something special about Ben.

Clicking his tongue, he cantered off back towards the sheep with the dogs racing alongside him, trying to keep up. One of the sheep darted left, quickly followed by the others. Ben dug his heels into the horse's side, and they took off. The one in front jumped, all four feet off the ground at the same time, and the others followed in a long single file line.

Annabel burst out laughing and pointed. 'What are they doing?'

'Being sheep,' one of the twins—Ava, maybe—said with an exaggerated eye roll. 'Dumb animals.'

'They're not as dumb as your poddy calves, Ava,' the other twin—Bella, obviously—argued.

'My poddy calves are smart. At least they know when to line up to get fed. Not like your stupid lambs.'

'Girls,' Sasha cut in, rubbing her forehead. 'It is far too early to argue.'

'Ignore my granddaughters when they're bickering,' Heather said. 'They've never agreed on anything from the moment they were old enough to talk. Some days I think they disagree with each other because that's what they've always done. If Bella says she hates sheep one day, be assured she will love them tomorrow if Ava announces *she* hates sheep.'

'What's a poddy?' she asked after the laughter died down. For all their bickering, the twins actually seemed to get along well, and it reminded Annabel again of how much she'd missed out on, not having a sibling.

At her question, Ava stared at her, aghast. 'You don't know what a poddy is? It's an orphan calf.' She might as well have added, "how could you not know that?" but Annabel refused to be offended by a kid. 'Why are they orphaned?' she asked.

'Sometimes the mothers die, or they mismother them, so we have to hand rear the babies. We do it for lambs too, not just calves,' Sasha explained.

For a second, Annabel pictured tiny baby calves drinking bottles of cow's milk bought from the supermarket. 'What do you feed them?'

'They have to get colostrum in the first few days, or they'll die. If we can't get that from their mothers or from another cow, we can get it commercially. It saves their life. After that they generally get fed a specifically formulated powdered calf milk which we give them with a bottle and teat.'

'And you must feed them properly,' Ava added with a serious expression. 'Their head has to be tilted back the right way or the milk curdles and doesn't get absorbed properly. That's right isn't it, Aunty Sasha?'

Sasha nodded.

'Do you get many poddies?' Annabel asked.

'A couple a year usually. Despite Bella's opinion, they *are* cute. They follow you around like a dog or hang around in the backyard.'

'What happens to them after they grow up?' Annabel asked. Farm life was totally unfamiliar to her.

'We wean them when they're about three to four months old.'

'Do they go back out into the paddock?'

'Yep. That's the hardest part. They get put out with the other weaners in the paddock. Some of them are grateful you hand reared them and devoted a huge portion of your life to save theirs, and they come up and greet you and let you give them a scratch and a cuddle. Others are plain obnoxious and totally ignore you.'

'Which is why lambs are so much better than poddies,' Bella interjected. 'At least they don't forget you. Cows are stupid.'

Ava pushed her sister off the fence. 'They're not stupid.'

'At least with the lambs you don't have to teach them how to bottle feed. Poddies are so dumb,' Bella retorted.

A car pulled up behind them and Annabel turned to see Natalie and Lily get out. Lily carried a tray with four takeaway coffees and Natalie carried another tray. She wore a beaming smile and layers of clothing.

Handing Annabel a coffee, she smiled. 'Good morning. Told you it'd be cold. This one's for you. Extra hot. Hope you don't take sugar.'

'Thanks. That's perfect.' Annabel inhaled the coffee as she clasped her frozen fingers around the warm drink.

The twins continued to argue about the merits of their favourite animal while sipping on their hot chocolates. Annabel listened, trying not to laugh. Heather was right—the girls disagreed on everything.

When their drinks were finished and the sheep were penned, Sasha took Annabel over to the sheds where the men were setting up a portable shute, connecting it to the larger holding yard which was currently empty of any sheep.

'Oh my gosh,' Sasha said when they were out of earshot. 'I love my nieces, but those twins drive me bonkers sometimes. I often think Natalie and Rob should have stopped after they had Lily. That girl is an angel compared to her younger sisters.'

Annabel laughed. 'They're lucky—all of you are lucky—to be part of a big happy family.'

'I know you said last night your parents didn't approve of your decision to play football, but you must be close to them if you're an only child. What will they think about you moving up here?'

'Actually, we're not close at all. And as for what they think? They weren't impressed, but that's nothing new.'

Sasha raised her eyebrows.

Annabel exhaled slowly. 'Not only am I adopted, I'm an only child. These days my parents wouldn't be approved for a rescue dog. Let's just say my mother isn't known for her maternal instincts. I often wonder why they actually wanted a child unless it was to look good on their resume.'

Sasha rested her hand on Annabel's arm. 'I'm sorry. That must be hard on you.'

'I've had years to get used to it. But when I see all of you together, I'll admit it does make me a bit jealous.'

'I promise I won't complain again. And don't get me wrong, we *are* a happy family, but sometimes I want to strangle my nieces. I'm sure they'll grow out of it. Or it'll be rubbed out of them at boarding school next year.'

'They sound like typical pre-teenage girls to me,' Annabel said. She'd coached teenagers in football and spent time with girls that age in the school's programs she'd participated in when she played for the Cats and she understood what they were like.

'You're right. Maybe because my girls are older, I've blocked out the memory of their teenage years.'

They stood side by side at the fence and watched the men work. While they were talking someone opened the gate and some of the sheep were herded into the yard.

'Sash, we need your help over here,' Rob called out, waving her over.

'Be right back,' Sasha shouted.

'Is there anything I can do?' Annabel asked. She didn't want to stand around doing nothing.

'Not yet. But when we're ready to get the sheep onto the crutching cradles, we'll probably get you to drench them,' Sasha said. 'I'll show you how. It's not difficult.'

'Okay.'

A few minutes later Sasha called her over. Annabel climbed through the fence and jogged over to where Sasha stood in the middle of the yard.

'When Ben shouts, you need to open the gates as quickly as you can, then let a dozen or so through, then quickly shut the gates again. Reckon you can handle that?' Sasha asked.

'No worries.' How hard could it be? All she had to do was open and close a gate when she was told. She nodded, but her legs shook as she headed back to the gate.

The sheep, which had been walking sedately seconds earlier, suddenly picked up speed and headed straight towards her. Knowing she couldn't afford to stuff this up, anxiety started low in her stomach, spreading its fingers. She pushed it away. If she could stand in the centre of the ground and face her opponent, she could face some sheep.

Ben whistled to get her attention and she looked up.

'Open the gates!' he shouted.

She thought the sheep would explode through the gates in a rush but as they approached and saw the small enclosure they were being herded into, they slowed. Behind them, the dogs and Ben on his horse kept them surging forward.

Ben whistled again, and the dogs barked and nipped at the sheep's heels. A few of them bucked and kicked but the dogs danced out of their way as if it were a game.

Slowly the sheep moved into the yard. After about a dozen sheep had passed her, Jock shouted, 'Shut the gates, Annabel!'

She slammed the gate closed.

'That's it. Atta girl.'

She beamed at the compliment. Five minutes with Ben's dad and she felt more comfortable with him than she did with her own father.

For the next hour Annabel opened and closed the gates until all the sheep had passed through into the yards. By the time they'd finished with the sheep, she'd stripped down to her T-shirt, glad she'd taken the advice to layer up.

When they were finished, Ben vaulted off his horse and headed her way, the horse following him.

'Good job. You're a natural.'

'Thanks. Speaking of natural. You look okay up on that horse.' She grinned at him. 'Kind of sexy in a *Man from Snowy River* way.' She pointed to the horse. 'What's his name?'

'Monty.' Ben made a clicking sound and the horse stepped forward.

'Whoa.' Annabel giggled nervously and took an involuntary step back. 'You can stay right there, big fella.'

Ben chuckled as he affectionately rubbed the horse's white blaze. The horse rubbed his head against Ben's shoulder.

'You ever ridden?' he asked.

'Nope. And before you get any ideas, I'm not sure I want to. He's too big.'

'Don't worry. I'd never put you on Monty, but there are plenty of other horses here that are perfectly safe if you ever want to give it a try.'

'Maybe. Not sure I want to make a fool of myself. You and your brother look like you were born in the saddle.'

'I don't remember not being able to ride,' he admitted.

Monty rubbed his head against Ben's shoulder again leaving a smudge of dirt and horsehair on his jumper.

'We match,' Annabel said, running her hand over Monty's smooth neck. 'His colour is almost identical to my hair.'

Ben smiled. 'I knew there was a reason I was attracted to you.'

Annabel laughed. 'Because I remind you of your horse? Not sure that's a compliment.'

'Trust me. It is. But I can assure you as I like my horse, I'm not attracted to him like I am to you.'

A wave of warmth whooshed through her. There was no misinterpreting the look in Ben's eyes.

'I'll be sore tomorrow.' He grinned. 'But whatever you do, don't tell anyone or they'll roast me.'

'Your secret is safe with me.'

James rode past on a quad bike, slowing as he neared them. 'Stop your gas bagging, Nails,' he called out. 'We've got more work to do.'

For a moment Annabel was worried James was serious, but when he grinned and revved the engine before taking off, she laughed.

Ben laughed too. 'You heard my brother. There's work to do. Feel free to head back to the main house with the girls for some lunch. We'll be here for a while. After lunch, let's go for a drive or something before you have to head back to Geelong.'

'I'd like that.'

He searched her face. 'You're not bored?'

'Gosh, no. I'm not bored. It's fun. Sheep are hilarious.'

'Good. I'm glad you're enjoying it. If I ever give up being a cop, this is where I'll be.'

'I was thinking about that when I watched you ride. You seem at home here.'

'I am.'

'I have a feeling I'm going to love living here.'

Ben grabbed her hand. 'I have a feeling I'm going to love you living here, too.'

They both looked down at his hand holding hers.

All the breath left Annabel's lungs as their eyes met. Then, not caring who was watching, she possibly did the dumbest thing she could do. Reaching over she cupped Ben's face in both hands and kissed him firmly on the lips, leaving him no doubt she was attracted to him too.

Chapter 15

When Annabel touched his face, Ben's first thought was that he was going to have a lot of explaining to do to his family.

But when Annabel *kissed* him, his second thought and every one after that vanished. Before he could get a handle on his reaction, her lips were on his again. They were soft and tentative at first as if she was scared she was overstepping the boundary, but when he kissed her back, she reached up behind his head, buried her hands in his hair and directed him closer, deepening the kiss.

He didn't hold back. From the moment she'd walked into his life he'd ached to kiss her. He pulled her tight and pressed his lips to hers, trying to hold back and not crush her mouth beneath his. The kiss—their first *proper* kiss—was beyond anything he'd imagined.

Her soft moan of response sent tingles through his body and he shifted closer. What was it about this woman? She smelled so good. And she tasted good too. A faint taste of coffee and a hint of mint toothpaste.

But it wasn't only that. It was how Annabel made him feel. Whenever he was around her, he felt happy. Like a weight had shifted. He brought his hand up to cradle her face, stroking her cheek as they kissed again, before traveling a lazy journey down her jawbone to her neck. When Annabel shuddered in response, he forced himself to pull back.

'Wow.' His voice was low and raw, his breathing ragged. 'You have no idea how much I want to keep kissing you. But not here.'

He loved his family, but if any of them had caught them locked in an embrace like this, he'd never hear the end of it. As much as he wanted to spend more time getting to know Annabel—which included kissing her again—he wanted to do so without his family bringing out the popcorn and taking front row seats for the show.

He took her hands in his. His heart hammered so much he felt like he was about to ask her to go skydiving with him. But this wasn't simply an invitation to have dinner with him, it was more. He felt it in his gut. Still, he also sensed the need to go slowly.

'Are you in a hurry to head back to Geelong tonight?' he asked.

She shook her head. 'Not especially. Why?'

'Can you stay another night?'

'I don't see why not.'

'Good. Let's have dinner. Just the two of us.'

Annabel tiled her head to one side and her grin formed slowly. She tucked a loose curl behind one ear. 'Are you asking me out on a date?' she asked coyly.

'I am.'

The smiled widened. 'I'd love to. I told Melissa I'd start work on Wednesday. I'll stay tonight and head to Geelong first thing Monday, pack up my stuff at Tracey's, stay there the night and be back here by lunchtime Tuesday. How does that sound?'

'Perfect. The local farmer's market is on tomorrow too. It's only held once a month. You'll love it.'

'What time tonight then?'

'Six. Six-thirty. I'll cook. Do you like risotto?'

'That sounds lovely.'

He pressed a tender kiss to her forehead rather than kissing her lips again because once he started, he wouldn't be able to stop. Pulling away, he squeezed her hands. 'I'd better go, or James will come looking for me.'

***

The next morning, Ben swung past the cottage just after eight to pick Annabel up. When she left his place the night before to return to the cottage, he'd told her to skip breakfast, promising her they'd grab something to eat at the farmer's market.

'Where have all the people come from?' Annabel asked. 'Glengarrick has a population of less than nine hundred people. There's more than that here right now.'

'You'll see why there's so many people. It's one of the best markets for miles.'

Rows of cars lined each side of the road leading up the hill to the primary school where the market was held.

They got out of the car and he took her hand as they walked up the centre of the road. A steady flow of people of all ages ebbed around them, many with dogs on leads or pushing babies in prams. Country music pulsed through the playground and Ben found himself walking in time to the beat. With Annabel's warm hand in his, he couldn't remember the last time he'd been this happy.

As they turned into the schoolyard, a voice over the sound system declared there were bargains to buy at the cake stall.

'We have to buy one of Mrs Kennedy's prize-winning chocolate mud cakes. They're to die for,' Ben said, lengthening his stride. 'But we'll need to be quick. They always used to sell out first.'

'Sounds good.'

The aroma from the Rotary Club tent, with its sausages and sizzling onions made his stomach growl. 'Hope you're hungry.'

'Famished. And there's nothing better than a snag for breakfast.'

As they headed that way, the smell of freshly brewed coffee wafted towards them. He spotted a coffee van and tugged Annabel in that direction. 'Sausages and cake can wait. I need coffee first.'

She giggled. 'You speak my language.'

'Nails!' A man's voice boomed.

Ben turned. 'Mate. Good to see you.'

Dan clapped his hand on Ben's shoulder before drawing him into a warm hug and back slap.

'Annabel, this is Dan Black.'

'Nice to meet you, Annabel,' Dan said shaking her hand. 'Heard all about you already.'

Annabel frowned.

Ben chuckled. 'You'll get used to living in a small town. Dan's married to Rachael, the nurse you're taking over from at the clinic.'

'She said you were great the other day,' Dan went on. 'Sounds like the clinic's in safe hands with you taking over her job.'

'I hope so.'

They chatted for a few minutes, then with another handshake for Annabel and a hug for him, Dan said goodbye and sauntered off.

A group of half a dozen giggling girls dressed in Scottish kilts dashed past, heading towards the stage where the band had finished playing. It felt totally natural to reach for her hand again, and they walked aimlessly through the stalls towards the stage, stopping periodically to taste or smell or check something out.

'Dan's a top bloke,' Ben said. 'Growing up we hung out a lot and when I was with Sophie, we used to catch up occasionally as couples.'

'I must admit I feel a bit like everyone's looking at me. Are they checking me out and saying: there goes Ben Naylor's next wife?'

Ben stopped to stare at her. When she looked up at him with wide brown eyes full of uncertainty, his heart galloped in his chest. She bit her bottom lip and he felt terrible to think she wasn't enjoying herself. 'Is that what you think?'

'I'm not usually insecure, but it feels like everyone's watching me and wondering who I am. Or comparing me to—'

He cut her off. 'To Sophie or Chantelle?'

She nodded.

'Trust me, no-one would be doing that. Chantelle hasn't been on the scene for years and most of these people never met her. And those who did, never warmed to her. One day ask Jed or Georgie what they thought of her.'

'But why does it feel like every second person is smiling at me? It's not my imagination.'

Ben chuckled as he draped an arm over her shoulders and pulled her close. 'Everyone is smiling because this is the country and they're friendly folk. Also, most of these people feel like they already know you because they know me. They're smiling because they genuinely want to meet you. Plus, they would have all heard about what you did at the clinic the other day. They think you're a hero. And don't forget word spreads very quickly round here. They'll all know you're an AFLW superstar. I'm surprised there aren't kids lining up for selfies.'

'Oh.'

He gave her shoulders another squeeze. 'Trust me, no one is judging you or looking at you weirdly or comparing you to my ex-wife.'

'Ex-wives.'

'Touché.'

They kept walking and headed towards the stage. On the small, elevated platform, the group of young Irish dancers danced, backs straight, arms bent, stomping their feet in time to the music and flicking their legs in a complicated movement. They watched for a while, before Ben tugged her hand and they walked on a bit further.

'Your dad said something at dinner the other night—about you thinking of quitting the force. Is that true?'

He needed to choose his words carefully. 'I won't quit. I'll retire. When the time comes,' he added.

He hadn't breathed a word to anyone other than his psychologist about his thoughts on early retirement. He'd always said if he wasn't handling the job, he'd retire in a heartbeat. He just never thought it would happen.

She stopped walking.

'*Has* the time come?' she asked gently.

He nodded slowly. 'Yeah. I think it has.'

It was best to be honest from the get-go. He liked Annabel a lot and if it was worth pursuing something with her, she deserved to know how broken he was before things went any further. She already knew about his ex-wives, so she might as well know about his anxiety and PTSD.

He should have brought it up last night over dinner, but they'd been too busy getting to know each other. He'd been enjoying himself so thoroughly—especially after dinner when they'd sat in front of the fire kissing—that he hadn't wanted to bring up such a serious topic and put a dampener on their incredible evening.

'I haven't told my family yet, but I've taken stress leave from the job.'

Annabel's eyebrows rose, but she stayed quiet, waiting for him to finish. Once again it hit him with how different she was from Chantelle. She would have pushed him to the edge then pulled hard to get the information out of him.

He cracked his knuckles. 'I had a panic attack after the last case, and the flashbacks got worse and I knew it was time to step away.' He told her what had happened the night of the last hostage situation.

'Sounds like it ended well for everyone but you. Were you forced to take leave?' she asked.

'Not forced. But it was highly recommended.'

'How often do you have the flashbacks?'

He paused to think. Funny thing was, since coming back to the farm he hadn't had any more flashbacks or nightmares—the kind that woke him in the middle of the night, lathered in sweat, the sheets twisted around his legs in damp knots. 'It's been awhile now.'

'What are they like?'

Great question but so hard to answer. Unlike Hollywood movies, his dreams weren't an instant replay of an event or situation. 'They're mostly a bad feeling in my gut. A feeling of dread combined with the knowledge that something bad is going to happen and there's nothing I can do to stop it.'

'Do they last long?'

'Sometimes a few seconds, sometimes minutes.'

'What triggers them?'

'I wish I knew. Sometimes it's little things like sights, smells, the weather. Other times it's easy to see what triggers them. Like watching a movie and seeing someone in a hostage situation. That always sets me off.' The things that always guaranteed a bad night's sleep were the suicides.

The last suicide negotiation happened at sunset on a clear, cold, winter's night and he'd spent six hours on the roof of a Melbourne apartment building, lying on his back, holding onto a young man's headphone cord, talking him off the window edge. The man had eventually agreed to come down, but as a result, sometimes clear winter sunsets combined with the smell of the city and traffic noises set Ben's brain off.

'Are you seeing someone? A GP? A counsellor?'

'Psychologist.'

'I'm glad. It's good you have help. How long has it been going on?'

'It's been months, but things were escalating, and I kept ignoring the warning signs. Mostly I was able to cope when I was on the job, but I was a mess at home. When I lost it at work one day, I knew I needed to do something.'

'If you do retire from the police force, what will you do?'

He shrugged. 'Maybe country policing. If a job came up here in Glengarrick or even in one of the nearby towns, I'd take it in a heartbeat.'

'If there aren't any positions, is farming an option? You sure looked at home on that horse rounding up the sheep.'

He smiled. 'Now you're moving here, yeah, I'd say it's definitely an option. I'm going to do whatever I can to make sure I'm wherever you are, even if that means begging Dad or James to let me work on the farm.'

Annabel's cheeks were pink from the fresh air, her eyes sparkled, and she looked so darned pretty he wanted to kiss her right there in front of everyone and let the entire town of Glengarrick know he'd fallen in love again.

She closed the gap between them and leaned into him. The contact made his already tight stomach twist further into a ball of need and he swallowed past the lump in his throat. He had to take things slowly. Didn't he?

'Ben, I know we've barely spent any time together, but I feel like we've really connected and I'm really looking forward to seeing where this goes,'

Unable to speak, but in total agreement, he nodded.

She took a step back and he resisted the urge to close the gap between them again. Forget slow. He wanted to take Annabel in his arms and kiss her right now and make certain she knew he wanted exactly what she wanted.

'Me too,' he said finally.

When he looked up, Annabel's smile was huge, and it made hope bloom in his heart.

Maybe, just maybe, third time round, he would be lucky in love.

Chapter 16

A group of farmers were gathered in the shade over near some machinery along the line of pine trees. Annabel followed Ben's gaze in their direction.

'Okay with you if I go and say G'day?' he asked.

'You don't need to ask my permission. Go.' Annabel smiled. 'I'm going to get a bag of donuts and see what else I can find.'

'You'll be okay on your own?'

'Like you said, everyone's friendly.' She gave Ben's hand a squeeze. 'I'll be fine. Jed sent me a text to say he and Georgie are on their way, so I'll keep my eye out for them. Go on. I'm happy to wander and explore.'

'Can you please get me one of those chocolate mud cakes I was telling you about?' He patted his rock-hard stomach. 'Although I probably shouldn't.'

'I think you worked off enough calories riding that horse yesterday to earn a piece of cake.'

'It's not one piece I'm worried about. The problem is you can never stop at one. It's incredible.'

She gave him a little shove. 'Go and talk to your friends. I'll catch up with you.'

But despite Annabel's assurances that she'd be okay, the moment Ben left her side, irrational anxiety nipped at her. She moved slowly through the throng of people, at first trying to avoid eye contact but it was impossible and in the end she gave up and smiled back, finding her fears dissipated. Ben was right, people were just being friendly.

She found the cake stall and surveyed the mouth-watering goods. It took her a while to decide and as she was deliberating between the lamingtons, the vanilla sponge cake, and the scones, and wondering which one was Mrs. Kennedy's famous chocolate mud cake, when two older women approached the cake stand and stood beside her.

'I heard Ben Naylor's thinking of quitting the police force and moving back home,' one of the women said.

'Is that right?' the second woman replied.

'And he's got a new woman too. Brought her home to stay with his parents for the weekend. Must be serious. Maybe it'll be third time lucky for him.'

Annabel's heart raced. Were they talking about her?

'What a shame he and Zara Pritchard didn't end up together. I always thought those two were perfect for each other.'

Annabel's good mood was suddenly ruined as she remembered Jed once said everyone thought Ben would end up with his friend Zara.

As the women moved off out of earshot, Annabel turned her attention back to the cake stand and tried to ignore what she'd heard.

'No-one talks about it, but Mrs. Kennedy uses a packet cake mix,' a voice beside Annabel said.

Annabel turned and saw Georgie. They greeted each other with a hug.

'Where's Jed and Daisy?' Annabel asked.

Georgie pointed. 'Jed has her in the pram. I swear he loves to show her off more than I do.'

'He's such a good daddy.'

'He is,' Georgie agreed.

'So, which one of these is Mrs. Kennedy's famous cake I've been told I need to try?'

Georgie leaned and lowered her voice. 'They're good, but she charges like a wounded bull just because she wins first prize every year at the local show. It's gone to her head. People pay her a bucketload of money to make cakes for special occasions and she uses a packet mix from Coles then claims she's made the cake from scratch.'

Annabel chuckled. 'Well, I've been told I can't leave until I've bought one of her cakes.' She wasn't ready to admit to Georgie that it was Ben who wanted the cake in case Georgie read too much into it. Then again, if news travelled that quickly in town, Georgie might already know she and Ben had seen each other.

'I'll have one of those mud cakes please,' Georgie said to the woman behind the table.'

After handing over her money she accepted the brown paper bag. Georgie linked her arm through Annabel's, and they started walking.

'Are you enjoying yourself? Isn't Glengarrick wonderful?'

'I love it.'

'When Jed told me that you were applying for the job at the clinic, I was so happy for you.' She glanced at Annabel. 'How did the interview go? I've had my fingers crossed.'

'I start next week.'

Georgie stopped walking and bounced on the spot. 'Amazing. So good. Do you know where you'll live?'

'I'm going to rent the cottage at *Wandana*. At the Naylors,' she added, although she knew Georgie would know exactly what cottage she was referring to.'

'Oh my gosh, that's awesome. So good. It's the perfect little place for you.' Georgie's smile widened and Annabel watched the cogs turn. 'I heard Ben's moving back home too. That'll be interesting having him as a neighbour. Have you seen him yet?'

A blush crept up Annabel's neck. 'Yeah. Last night.' She held up the brown paper bag. 'The cake is for him.'

'Is he here?'

Annabel nodded. 'He went off to chat to some guys he knew.'

'I can't wait to see him. We'll need to arrange a time for the four of us to have dinner.'

'Great idea,' Annabel said, 'but that'll set tongues wagging.'

'What do you mean?' Georgie stopped walking.

'If you listen to the local gossip, apparently I've already moved in with Ben and it won't be long before I'm wife number three and you'll be able to hear the pitter patter of tiny feet.' She was exaggerating of course.

Georgie chuckled and started walking again. 'Good old small-town gossip. Ignore it.'

'I'll try.'

'Honestly, most of the old women in town have nothing better to do than matchmake. Most of them wish they had daughters they could marry off with Ben.'

'I can see why.'

'It'll be so good to have friends our age back in Glengarrick. You'll have to meet Charlie. He's moved home too and is running the local pharmacy.'

'And I'm looking forward to meeting Zara too.'

A shadow passed briefly over Georgie's face. 'She doesn't get home much these days. Although once she has the baby, I dare say she'll move home.'

Annabel stared at Georgie. 'Baby?' Now she really needed to know more about this woman. And her relationship with Ben. 'Ben didn't mention she was pregnant.'

Georgie shrugged. 'He may not know. He and Zara used to be tight, but in the last couple of years as far as I'm aware they haven't had much to do with each other.'

'Did something happen?'

'I have no idea. I've never asked either of them.' She smiled. 'You know how it is—sometimes you just go in different directions.' She glanced up and groaned. 'Speaking of which,' she muttered. 'I wish we could go in a different direction now, but we're stuck.'

An elderly woman approached, leaning heavily on her walking stick with each step she took.

'Ignore what she says,' Georgie said under her breath. 'She's trouble.'

The woman fixed her dark eyes on them, reminding Annabel of a crow.

'Will I see you and Benjamin at church next Sunday?'

Annabel blinked.

Georgie stepped forward. 'Hello Dorothy. Nice to see you. Have you met Annabel Norton? Annabel's going to take over from Rachael at the clinic and she's moving into the cottage at the Naylors. Annabel, this is Dorothy Taylor. President, Secretary, Treasurer and Chief Elder of the Glengarrick Uniting Church.' Georgie lowered her voice further. 'And town busybody.'

'Don't get sassy with me, Georgina. I might be old but there's nothing wrong with my hearing.'

'Nice to meet you, Mrs. Taylor.' Annabel offered a polite smile.

Georgie hooked her arm into Annabel's again. 'We need to keep going. I think I can hear Daisy crying.'

They rushed off.

'Sorry,' Georgie said when the woman was out of earshot. 'You've just met our number one town odd-bod today.'

'There's more than one?'

'One day I'll tell you about Bruce Saunders but that would take hours. Talk about *mad*. Come on, let's go find the boys and arrange a time for dinner with the four of us. It's going to be so much fun having you in town. Just promise me you and Jed won't get stuck talking football all night.'

Annabel chuckled. 'I can't promise, but I will try.'

Chapter 17

On Friday night, a few weeks after Annabel had moved to
Glengarrick, she and Ben were having dinner at Jed and
Georgie's. Ben was looking forward to the night with his friends
and was hopeful that Annabel and Georgie would hit it off. It
would be nice to spend time hanging out with them.

'Can I give you a hand?' Ben asked Georgie. He had
followed her into the kitchen after they'd all made a fuss of Daisy
before she was put to bed.

Jed and Annabel had headed out onto the deck to put the meat
on the barbeque. Judging by the hand signals and body language,
they were talking football.

'I'd love a hand, thanks.' Georgie pointed to the bag of
tomatoes with a knife. 'Can you start on those, please.'

He took the knife from her and began chopping the tomatoes into quarters.

'It's good to see you looking so happy,' Georgie said. 'Annabel too. Things are going well between you two obviously?'

He drew in a deep breath and let it out slowly. '*So* well.' Since she'd arrived, there wasn't a day they hadn't spent together. Sometimes they went for a run, other days they just cooked an early dinner together then watched TV. Or not, as was often the case. Sometimes they started kissing and time slipped away, and they ended up missing most of the show they'd started watching.

'How serious is it?'

He felt his face warm. 'Very.'

'You're not worried about how fast things are moving?'

He smiled. Georgie had always been the serious one in the group of friends. 'It feels right.'

'Annabel is a sweetheart and I'm happy for you, but don't rush into anything, Nails. You know what happened last time.'

As if he needed reminding. He'd rushed into both his marriages with disastrous results.

'Hardly rushing, George. It's been years since I've dated anyone, let alone thought about getting serious.'

Yes, things were moving quickly, but they hadn't slept together yet, so in that sense, he'd kept the brakes on. The thing was, he'd fallen hard for Annabel from the moment he met her and as crazy as it was, he pictured himself spending the rest of his life with her. If going slowly meant he didn't stuff things up, he'd do that. But the more time he spent with her, the more he knew it was only a matter of time before he couldn't keep his hands off her any longer. And it was clear she felt the same way.

He gazed out the window. Annabel and Jed were deep in conversation and something told him they were having a similar discussion to the one he and Georgie were having inside. Annabel had told him that Jed was one of the few people she trusted for advice. At first, he'd felt a flicker of jealousy before he remembered that he and Zara used to have that type of friendship.

'Does she miss playing football?' Georgie asked.

'Sorry? What?' He'd been miles away, thinking about Zara.

'Do you think Annabel misses playing football?' she asked. 'Apparently she was one of the best.'

'She said she doesn't miss being constantly sore,' he replied. He and Annabel had talked a lot about her football career. 'Yes, she misses playing, but mostly she misses her friends. Sounds like she was closer to her teammates than she was to her own family. She doesn't have any siblings.'

'Jed says the same. He misses the guys, the mateship.'

'She's happy she doesn't have to balance work, sport and her private life though. It must have been hard juggling two careers. To be honest I don't know how she managed shift work at the hospital as well as training and games. She said life was hectic back then and I'd say that was probably an understatement.'

'Will she play this weekend?'

Once a year the Glengarrick Saints Football and Netball Club held a fundraising sports carnival. There was a tennis round robin, soccer and netball games and the day culminated in a fun football game. Anyone could play—men and women—and there had been years when both eight and eighty-year olds were on the ground at the same time. It was always fun whether you were a player or a spectator. Quarters were only ten minutes long and the rules were everyone had to play fairly and avoid being injured. Ben had fond memories of playing every year through high school. He wasn't much of a footballer, but he'd kicked a few goals in his day.

'I don't think she knows about it,' he replied.

Georgie laughed and pointed out the window. 'I guarantee that's what the two of them are talking about now. They're probably coming up with a game plan or something.'

'I hope she *does* play. I'd love to watch her in action. What about Jed? Will he play?'

After too many serious concussions, Jed had been forced to retire from his professional football career.

'He says he's playing. But he's promised me he'll wear a helmet and be careful.'

'Doesn't stop you from being worried.'

'No, but he's a grown man and I know he's sensible. Will you play?'

'Don't see why not.'

They watched Jed and Annabel a bit longer.

'How do you think she'll find the change of pace up here?' Georgie asked after a while. 'It'll be hard for her going from a busy emergency department to a quiet GP clinic in a country town. Jed knew what he was coming home to, but Annabel's a city girl. You don't think she'll struggle?'

'I don't think so. She had a ball out on the farm the other day when we were doing the sheep.'

'That's one day. The novelty might wear off.'

He shrugged. 'Or not.'

They continued preparing the salad in silence.

'Hey, what's going on with Zara?' Georgie asked after a while. 'Have you spoken to her lately?'

He froze. 'Ah…no, I haven't.'

Georgie faced him and frowned. 'You know she's pregnant, right?'

'Mm…yeah. I heard.'

'So, she hasn't told you who the father is?'

Cold slivered down his spine. 'No.' He swallowed past the lump in his throat. Was their secret not a secret? Zara was Georgie's best friend, and it wouldn't surprise him if she'd told her. 'She hasn't told you?'

'Not a word. When I asked again the other day, she snapped at me and told me it was none of my business.'

He raised his eyebrows but didn't say anything. Even though he and Zara had promised each other that his agreement to be her sperm donor wouldn't create a rift between them, it had. Their friendship was irrevocably changed because of their decision. It was killing him to keep her baby's DNA a secret but telling anyone was unthinkable.

After a few months when he'd heard nothing, he'd figured Zara must have changed her mind and decided not to go ahead with the IVF. When the clinic contacted him to let him know she was pregnant, which was their protocol, he'd been furious with Zara. She should have been the one to tell him, not a stranger on the end of the phone.

It took him a week to contact Zara and even then, he was still so mad he couldn't bring himself to call her. As impersonal as it was, he'd resorted to sending her a text.

His message had been short and to the point.

'Hi Zara. Heard the news. Congrats. Hope you're well. BTW, wanted you to hear this from me first before you hear it from someone else. I've met someone and it's serious. Her name is Annabel. Let me know when you have the baby. All the best. Cheers. Ben.'

In hindsight, his words were too blunt and impersonal, but he hated the way one crazy spur of the moment decision had put a huge wedge in their relationship. Exactly as he'd worried it would.

After a lifetime of friendship, there were days he felt like he was missing a limb. They'd gone through so much together and been there for each other for all the important occasions and it felt wrong that he wasn't there for her this time. But what was he supposed to do about it? He'd told her he didn't want anyone to know what he'd done, and she'd kept her end of the deal.

Ten weeks passed and when he had no word from Zara, not even an acknowledgement of his text, he wondered if she'd miscarried and didn't know how to tell him. For her sake he was glad that hadn't happened.

'How far along is she?' he asked.

'Nearly halfway apparently.' Georgie frowned. 'You haven't seen her?'

'No. She's been keeping to herself,' he lied.

Now he felt worse than guilty for sending her a text and not calling her. What kind of friend was he? The problem was, the longer it went without either of them speaking to each other, the harder it had become. As far as he was concerned, he'd tried, and the ball was in Zara's court.

He was more annoyed that Zara had lied. He still remembered her words in the office at the IVF clinic.

I'll let Ben know when I fall pregnant and as soon as the baby's born, he'll be the first person I tell.

He wasn't even sure who to blame for the rift: Zara for wanting his sperm or himself for agreeing to give it.

But blaming wouldn't help anyone. Zara was pregnant. And he had to somehow explain it to Annabel because there was no way he would keep a secret this big from her even if he'd wanted to.

***

Dinner was thoroughly enjoyable. Ben loved the way Annabel easily slotted into the existing friendship he had with Jed and Georgie. As Georgie predicted, Jed *had* told Annabel about the upcoming sports carnival and she was keen to play. They spent the night chatting about sport and finding other areas of common interest. When they went home, it was with full stomachs and hearts.

Thankfully, the only time Zara's name came up, he was able to steer the conversation away from her. The last thing he wanted was Annabel asking questions about Zara until he had the right answers.

Chapter 18

It had been three years since Ben had been home for the sports carnival. As he entered the football grounds, everyone greeted him warmly. A few asked if he was back home for good—they'd obviously heard some rumours—and he gave the same answer to everyone. He was taking long service leave from his role on the force and considering his options. A few people asked if his reason for hanging around had to do with a certain new nurse in town and he laughingly admitted that that might have something to do with it too. Even though he'd left town years earlier, he'd always felt a sense of belonging when he returned and never more so than today.

'Ben!'

He turned and saw Annabel jogging towards him. In her short shorts and tight-fitting football jersey, it was impossible not to gawk at her athletic body. She might have retired from playing, but she'd kept herself in incredible shape.

'I was wondering when you were going to get here,' she said, greeting him with a kiss and a hug.

He'd spent all morning on the farm getting jobs done with Dad and James so they could all get down to the oval for the game. Dad was nudging seventy, but nothing would stop him from getting out on the ground for a kick.

'Have you had fun?' he asked, knowing she'd been here all day with Georgie.

'It's been great. I even got roped in to play netball and I shot four goals.'

He chuckled. 'You're not competitive, are you?'

'Not when it comes to netball. But footy? That's another thing altogether.'

He reached out and tousled her hair which hung loose and curly down over her shoulders. 'If you run around the oval looking as hot as this, the other side won't be able to concentrate.'

She grinned. 'My teammates used to say my hair was my secret weapon. One of my superstitions is to leave it down until the last minute.'

'Hey, Nails.'

Ben turned and greeted Jed with a handshake and back slap.

'You ready?' Jed asked.

Ben patted his gym bag. 'Got my boots and mouthguard. What more do I need?'

The three of them headed towards the brick clubhouse.

'Do we have enough to make two teams?' Ben asked. Some years they'd had to rope in netballers to make up the numbers.

'As long as your dad and Rob and James are playing, we've almost got a full side although we won't be able to have anyone on interchange. The other team have an extra couple of players. We thought it was only fair.'

'Dad should already be here, and James is coming in with Sash. No idea about Rob.'

'I can't believe your dad still plays,' Annabel said.

'That's because he forgets his age. Until tomorrow and for the rest of the month when all we'll hear about is how sore he is.'

Annabel and Jed chuckled.

'How do you decide the teams?' Annabel asked.

'It's supposed to be names drawn from a hat, but it's kind of funny how us Naylors always end up on the same team. And Jed's always played on our side too.'

Annabel frowned. 'Is that fair?'

'Absolutely,' both men chorused.

'Do you think the other team have any idea Annabel is playing?' Ben asked Jed.

Jed grinned. 'Nope. And I want to keep it that way. She's our secret weapon.'

***

For Ben, the opening bounce always brought a sense of relief as the adrenaline he'd held tightly in check was allowed free. Despite the uneven surface in the middle of the oval, the centre bounce was straight and high. Naturally, Jed tapped it away. Even though the opposition had put their tallest player in the centre—a sixteen-year-old basketballer called Tom—Jed was still a head taller than the teenager.

The first few minutes were frenetic as everyone scrambled for the ball. A few times Ben caught sight of Annabel's red braid running down her back. He held his breath once when she was tackled but she sprang to her feet and kept running and he decided to stop worrying. They couldn't catch her.

A whistle blew to signal the end of the first quarter. Their side was up by seven goals to nothing. He grabbed a bottle of water a runner handed him—the kid must have been about five or six—and poured cool water over his head before swallowing some. He considered himself fit, but Annabel was running laps around him and everyone else. There were moments during the first quarter that he was so mesmerised he couldn't do anything but stand and watch her. She was a gun.

Her long, lithe legs ate up the ground. Wherever he looked she was there, darting and dashing around the oval like she owned it. When she marked, she was like a bird, leaping into the air. At one point, he watched her and Jed handball and kick the ball to one another as if they were performing a complicated drill they'd clearly practiced before. Oblivious to everyone else, they took the ball down the ground from the centre until Annabel was thirty metres out and kicked it straight through the middle of the goals. As the crowd cheered and horns tooted, Ben glanced around and realised his teammates and the opposition had stopped playing to watch too.

Things got a little hairy at the start of the second quarter. The opposing team, clearly unimpressed that Ben's team had managed to stack their side with two former AFL players—and were winning—came out hard and fighting.

One of the Kennedy kids—who looked like he hadn't started shaving yet—went at Annabel, with a look in his eye that suggested he was about to go after *her*, not the ball. Ben's gut clenched and his heart pounded. He was on the other side of the ground and too far away from her to intercept the play.

He needn't have worried. Out of nowhere James came and shoved the Kennedy kid aside. Annabel scooped up the ball, slung a look over her shoulder, grinned wickedly, and kicked the ball to Rob who passed it to another teammate who kicked a goal. Annabel's whoop of delight made him smile.

At half time, Jed jogged over to him, taking out his mouthguard when he got closer. 'Keep an eye on the opposition. I reckon they're targeting Bel. Trust me, she can fight dirty if she has to, but this is supposed to be a friendly game.'

'Yeah, I was wondering if that's what they were doing or if it was my imagination.'

'She has what it takes to play tough, but I don't want to see her get hurt.'

'Me neither.'

As they headed towards their teammates in the huddle, Ben glanced around. He'd never seen so many spectators. Word must have gotten around that Jed and Annabel were playing, and this was a game to watch.

Annabel was breathing heavily, but the smile on her flushed face said she was loving every minute of it.

The other players stood around, catching their breath, and sucking on oranges as they heaped well deserved praise on her.

'That goal you kicked was amazing,' James said.

'How far out do you reckon she was?' Rob asked. 'Thirty, forty metres?'

'At least,' one of the girls replied. The Glengarrick Saints had a women's team who had been undefeated the previous year and a handful of girls were playing today.

'No wonder you got drafted,' one of the men said. 'I reckon you're better than half the blokes who play.'

'She's better than you Tommo,' someone called out and everyone laughed. Tommo wasn't the picture of fitness. If he had been, he would have been better suited to rugby or gridiron than AFL.

Annabel broke away from her admirers and nudged Ben with her hip. 'How're you doing?'

'I'm fine. But what about you? They seem to be focusing on you.'

'Pfft,' she said as she deftly re-plaited her hair which had come loose during the game. 'Doesn't bother me. Anyway, they'll have to catch me first.'

'I don't want you to get hurt.'

She touched his arm. 'I'm fine. It's all fun.'

The rest of the game was uneventful. The opposition realised they weren't going to win, and the game took on a more friendly tone. Younger kids were subbed on and given a chance to play opposite Jed and Annabel, both of whom took their game back a notch and allowed others to keep up with them.

At one point, Annabel stopped playing and put her arm around the shoulder of a young girl and posed for a photo. Beaming, the girl skipped off the field back to her parents, ten feet taller, having no doubt decided she was going to play football when she was old enough.

With minutes left in the final quarter, Ben flew high to mark the ball, landing awkwardly and twisting his knee. Wincing, he came down hard, landing with a thud. Annabel frowned, but kept her eye on the ball, shouldering someone out of the way to collect it and keep it in play. After kicking it to Rob, she ran over to him.

'Are you okay?' she asked, squatting beside him. She put a hand on his thigh and his skin burned at her touch.

'I'm fine. Just twisted it. Nothing serious.'

'Shall I get the doctor?' She glanced to the sidelines where he knew Nick was sitting.

He shook his head. He'd met the guy once or twice and something about his manner rubbed Ben the wrong way. 'I just need to get off and ice it.'

'Here, I'll give you a hand.'

She helped him stand, putting her hand under his armpit and hauling him up. He tried to stand but couldn't. He hoped he hadn't done something serious. Once he was closer to the boundary, he hopped over to a seat and sat.

'Go,' he urged Annabel. 'I'll be fine. There's only a few minutes to go. When it's over you can drive me home.'

She looked conflicted, glancing from him to the game.

'I'm okay. Honestly. You're having fun. Get out there and win.'

She giggled. 'We won from the opening bounce.'

It was true. The other side had only kicked three goals the entire game and it looked like it would be the biggest losing margin in the history of the carnival. No doubt next year someone would come up with a better way of choosing players to make up the teams and ensure they were more evenly matched.

She leaned in and kissed him, not caring how sweaty either of them was, before running off.

Ben smiled as he watched her.

'She's a bloody fireball, isn't she?' a voice behind him said.

Ben turned and saw Nick behind him. His stomach knotted. He didn't like the way Nick looked at Annabel. 'Yeah, she plays well.'

'Want me to look at that knee?'

'I'm sure it's just jarred.'

Nick shrugged. 'You'll want to ice it then.'

So much for a bedside manner. 'I'll do that when I get home.'

The final siren sounded, and Ben glanced up. Annabel was lined up in front of the goal, slowly turning the ball in her hands, eyes fixed on the gap between the posts. She must have been awarded a free kick or taken a mark before the siren sounded. She puffed out her cheeks, looking like her kick would be the one that decided the game even though the scores were so lopsided it was laughable.

She kicked the ball, and it went straight through the middle. The crowd roared, horns blared and Ben, forgetting about his knee, stood to his feet, put his fingers in his mouth and whistled.

'Good luck keeping her in Glengarrick,' Nick said. 'If she plays like that I wouldn't be surprised if another team doesn't come knocking on her door again. Do you know why she quit?'

'She didn't quit. She retired,' Ben said before grinding his teeth together. Annabel's decision to retire from the game and her reasons behind it were none of Nick's business.

Nick clamped a hand on Ben's shoulder. 'Good luck with the knee. Lucky for you, looks like you'll have your own little nurse to take care of you.'

Ben fumed. He wasn't sure Annabel would appreciate knowing her boss had just referred to her as "a little nurse". He was about to reply when Annabel bounced over, beaming. She glanced at Nick and smiled, but her attention was solely on Ben. His heart swelled.

'How's the knee? Did Nick look at it?'

'Nah. It'll be fine. I'll take some anti-inflammatory tablets when I get home and if it's still bothering me tomorrow, I'll get the chiro to check it out.'

'Good decision. I can always give it a massage if that helps.'

Nick scowled but Annabel didn't seem to notice.

'Let's get you home.'

'I'm fine. You have to stay and celebrate.' He pointed over her shoulder. 'There's a line-up of kids wanting your autograph and a selfie I reckon.'

Annabel grinned. 'I love it.' She dashed off, pulling her hair from the tight braid as she approached the group of admiring girls.

Ben turned to say something to Nick, but he was gone.

Chapter 19

Ben was unusually quiet when Annabel helped him out of her car when they arrived back at *Wandana*. She'd been almost tempted to drive him into Stockton to the hospital to get an X-ray, but she'd watched him test out his knee and he seemed to be able to bend it without too much pain. Whether he could stand on it was another question.

She pulled up in front of the cottage and hesitated. 'I presumed you would want to come to my place. But if you'd rather I take you to the stables, I can.'

'Your place is perfect.'

'As long as you don't expect me to be your personal nurse.'

He made a grunting sound. She glanced at him, surprised to see the muscles in his jaw working.

'What did I say?'

'You didn't say anything. Your boss made a remark about me and "my little nurse" earlier and it ticked me off.'

Annabel shrugged. She was used to those sorts of comments, although it surprised her that something like that had come from Nick. Since she'd been working with him, he'd done nothing but sing her praises. Ben must have misunderstood him.

She turned off the car and went around to help Ben out. He was able to put a little bit of weight on his sore leg and together they hobbled to the front door. She let him in ahead of her and followed him to the bathroom.

'I'll take a shower first then I might just put it up on the couch if that's okay?'

'Fine. I'll grab some ice.'

'There's an ice pack in the freezer at my place.'

'Too easy. I'll duck over and grab it.'

When Annabel returned, Ben was on the couch, both feet up. His hair was still damp, and he smelled of her shampoo and body wash. She tossed him the ice pack then headed for the shower herself.

Ten minutes later she was clean and warm. She returned to the living room and Ben shifted on the couch to make room for her. She lifted his legs gently, so his feet rested on her thighs and slowly started massaging his feet.

He lay his head back against the couch and sighed heavily. 'If you keep doing that I'm never leaving.'

She kneaded the back of his calves and this time it elicited a moan. She chuckled. 'I'm glad no-one can hear us, or they'll think we're up to something.'

He grinned at her. 'Keep doing that and we *will* be up to something and I won't care who hears us.'

She playfully slapped his uninjured leg.

'Do you miss playing?' he asked.

She hesitated before replying. 'Yes and no. Until today I didn't realise how much I missed being competitive, but I don't miss the stress.'

'You're an incredible role model for the girls. Maybe you should see if you could help coach the women's team. Or help out at the school. Jed told me you used to coach too.'

'I was actually thinking about that today. To be honest, I'd be more excited about working with the younger girls and helping out with Auskick or something.'

'I'm sure they'd welcome you.'

'How's the knee?'

He lifted the ice pack and they inspected it. 'Red. Cold.'

'Swollen.' She frowned. 'Are you sure you don't want it X-rayed.'

'Positive. Honestly, I don't think I've done anything serious. It's just twisted.'

She ran her hand up and down his thigh, pressing lightly around his knee. The rough hairs on his legs abraded her palm. He flexed his thigh muscles and she laughed. 'Now you're just showing off.'

After more slow strokes, he caught her hand. 'You might want to stop that.'

She held his gaze as she withdrew her hand and went back to stroking his leg, gently massing his muscles. His head fell back, and he closed his eyes. She was so close to him she could see a couple of hairs just above his lip that he'd missed when he'd shaved that morning. Her heart accelerated as her stomach tightened. They'd spent a lot of time on this couch kissing, but they hadn't gone any further. It was only a matter of time and perhaps tonight was the night. She had no doubts she wanted to spend the rest of her life with him, so it made sense to take their relationship to the next level even though it was still early days in their relationship.

She lifted her hand and unhurriedly brushed her thumb across his lips. His head snapped up and his eyes widened.

Leaning in, she closed her mouth over his, kissing him hard. He kissed her back and pleasure slid through her body. The ice pack slipped to the floor as he shifted position and drew her into his lap.

'Is your knee—?'

She didn't get to finish her sentence as his lips met hers again. He tasted delicious. She put her hands either side of his face and increased the pressure of her mouth against his. As they deepened the kiss, a tingling sensation flooded her body as waves of heat washed over her and butterflies took flight in her stomach.

As they kissed, Ben's hands roved over her body, quickly fanning the fire inside her. She was about to beg him to stop because the sensations were overwhelming and she didn't want their first time to be on the couch, when his hand paused.

She met his gaze.

'Let's not rush this, Bel,' he said, words simple, tone soothing.

She rested her head against his, breathing heavily.

'Is this what you want?' he asked.

She nodded.

'Your place or mine?'

She giggled. 'Given my bed is closer…' She let the sentence hang.

He picked her up and she wrapped her legs around his waist, forgetting about his knee for a second. She froze and frowned down at him. 'Are you sure you can walk and carry me?'

'Honey, when you're in my arms and your legs are wrapped around me like this, I could walk on two broken legs and it wouldn't bother me.'

She laughed and he moved towards her room. She held tight, kissing his jaw, his neck, his ear. Breathless at what was to come, she found it hard to think. When he stopped in the doorway, they stared at each other for a long moment, as if making sure they were both committed to doing this.

Their lips met again and this time there was nothing tentative about it. Nothing gentle. The kiss was passionate and steamy, and Annabel let herself melt into his arms.

Chapter 20

Late one Friday afternoon at the end of Annabel's fifth week working in the clinic, Dorothy Taylor walked in, accompanied by her grandson, Jason. Melissa had gone home early, and Annabel was alone behind the front desk. Nick was in his office finishing off his notes after his last patient.

Jason's shoulders drooped, and he hobbled behind his grandmother like an octogenarian after a hip replacement. It was an unseasonably warm autumn day, but he was dressed top to toe in layers of black. Without acknowledging her, he collapsed into a chair and slid down into it.

'I told him that if he doesn't take his medicine, the voices will start, and people will think he's gone crazy again.' Dorothy made a circular motion with one finger to her temple. 'He's loopy in the head you know.'

'No. He has a mental illness, Mrs. Taylor,' Annabel said, glad the clinic was empty of other patients. Knowing he was coming in to see Nick, Annabel had checked Jason's file, so she knew a little of his medical history and background.

Dorothy dismissed Annabel's response with a wave of her hand. 'Like I said. It's all in his head.' She angled her head towards her Jason. 'But when he started running a fever, and I didn't know what caused it, I thought I should bring him in.'

Jason's cheeks were flamed, his heavily eye-lined eyes glassy. Had he taken something?

'Nick won't be long, okay, Jason?' Annabel said.

Jason grunted.

'Silly boy. Some days I wonder if he knows how to speak.'

Annabel cringed. She flashed Jason a quick look. If he'd heard his grandmother's remark, it didn't register.

Still standing at the reception counter, Dorothy chattered on steadily, covering topics from the issues of blue-green algae in the local river, to a new movie she wanted to watch, to her latest horoscope and her opinion on who would win the latest election in America.

Jason remained mute.

'Jason? Come on through.'

Annabel looked up. She hadn't heard Nick's door open. She wanted to catch him before he saw Jason.

As Jason eased himself out of the chair and lumbered towards Nick's office, Annabel tried to get Nick's attention. Dorothy tried to follow Jason, but Nick waved her back. 'I'll see Jason on his own today.' He glanced at Annabel and gave her a tiny nod.

'But…but…he…' Dorothy stammered.

Nick cut her off gently. 'He's an adult, Dorothy. Why don't you pop down the street and have a coffee? When Jason's finished here, he can find you.'

Surprisingly, she obeyed.

'She's an interesting character,' Annabel said when she was gone.

'That's one word to describe her. I don't know many of the town's odd-bods yet, but I'm told she's one of them.' Nick laughed. 'Apparently the other one to watch out for is some guy called Saunders.' He headed back to his office and closed the door.

Fifteen minutes later, the door opened, and Jason appeared, looking much brighter, with Nick one step behind him. He put a hand on Jason's shoulder and passed him a folded piece of paper. 'There's a list of numbers here. When you're ready, give them a call. And you can come back in and see me any time.'

Jason unfolded the paper and looked down at it as though trying to decipher Nick's scribble. 'Thanks, Dr. Young,' he mumbled, carefully tucking the paper in the pocket of his black overcoat.

'Everything okay?' Annabel asked after he'd left.

'Not really. Apart from the fact he's probably got a virus, he asked me about gender reassignment.'

'Oh.'

Nick exhaled heavily. 'Poor kid. With a grandmother like that, he's in for a tough ride. Both his parents have died so she's all he's got.'

'He is in for a tough time,' she agreed.

Jason was the kind of kid Jed loved to work with out at the farm during school holidays and she made a mental note to suggest something to Nick.

The phone rang, and she picked it up. 'Glengarrick Medical Centre, this is Annabel.'

'Annabel, it's Heather.'

'Hi.'

'Something's not right with Jock.'

Annabel frowned. 'What's up?'

'Well, I think he's having a heart attack, but he says what do I know? He says he's not. It's just his indigestion playing up.'

'What are his symptoms?'

Nick was going through the mail and he stopped what he was doing and gave her a questioning look.

'When he woke this morning, he was moving funny,' Heather said. 'He slept badly. Tossed and turned all night. I told him to take a couple of Panadol. Thought it was his restless legs playing up.'

'Where is his pain?' Annabel asked.

Nick put a hand on her back and glanced over her shoulder as she scribbled Jock's symptoms on a piece of paper.

'In his back and shoulder. But on the right side not the left.'

'Where is he now?' Annabel asked.

'He's at home now but the silly bugger's been out working all morning. Thing is, I'm worried. He just told me he coughed up blood earlier. And now he said he feels lightheaded.'

'I think you should bring him in to get checked out.' She glanced at Nick and he nodded. 'Nick doesn't have any more patients this afternoon. The appointment book is empty.'

'He won't budge,' Heather said. 'I rang the *Nurse on Call* hotline and they said to call an ambulance.'

Annabel already knew Jock well enough to know he wouldn't appreciate being told what to do and he wouldn't want the fuss and bother of an ambulance.

'I'm worried Annabel. He's very pale.'

'Should I send Nick?'

'No. No. You know Jock. He won't want to bother the doctor.'

'What if I pop out and check on him? Maybe I can convince him he needs to be seen.'

'Could you? I think he'd be okay with you coming out.'

'I guess so.' Annabel glanced up at Nick. 'I'll have to check with Nick and make sure he's okay for me to finish a bit early.'

'If you could, I'd feel so much better.'

Within five minutes Annabel was in the car headed out to *Wandana* with a promise from Nick that if she was concerned about Jock, she'd call him, and he'd come straight out.

***

When Annabel arrived at *Wandana*, Heather was waiting for her at the front door. She'd almost worn grooves into the gravel with her pacing.

'Is he worse?' Annabel asked after jumping from the car and sprinting over.

'He coughed up blood again.'

'Where is he?'

'Inside. In the back room.'

'Have you called Ben?'

'He's working with James at the far end of the property where there's no mobile coverage. I can't get onto either of them. That's why I called you.'

Heather led the way and Annabel followed her through the house to the sunroom extension in the back. Annabel stepped over the threshold and froze. Jock sat in a chair looking grey and unwell. Heather was right. He had the appearance of a man having a heart attack.

He looked up when Annabel came in. 'Hello, love. Have you come to find out what Heather's so worried about?'

'I'm worried too, Jock. You look awful. What's going on?'

'Bit under the weather, love.'

'Start at the beginning. Heather said you woke up this morning with back pain. Is it still there?'

He considered it. 'It's not really a pain. More like a tightness in my chest.' He thumped a closed fist to his chest.

'Is it there now?' she asked.

'Only when I breathe.'

'Is it worse when you breathe in?'

He tried and failed, coughing, and wincing in pain. Annabel ran through all the scenarios in her head. He could be having a heart attack, but what troubled her more was the way it was harder for him to take in a deep breath. And the blood. Heather showed her what he'd coughed up in his hankie. It wasn't much, but any blood wasn't good.

She palpated Jock's pulse. Racing. He was pale and sweating profusely. Whether he liked it or not, he needed to get to hospital, preferably in an ambulance.

'I'm going to give Nick a quick call,' Annabel said, pulling her phone from her pocket.

Stepping outside, she called 000 first. Depending where the ambulance was and whether they were out on another job, it could be awhile before it made it out to the farm. The alternative was driving Jock into Stockton to the hospital herself, but if something happened on the way, she'd never forgive herself. Something in her gut told her Jock was seriously unwell.

After hanging up, she called Nick and filled him in. He agreed she'd made the right decision to call the ambulance and promised to meet her at the hospital.

Ten minutes later two paramedics arrived. After she introduced herself as a nurse and explained she used to work in the emergency department, they listened while she told them Jock's symptoms. It only took them seconds to agree with Annabel.

One of the paramedics unzipped her bag, rifled through it, and pulled out a blood pressure cuff, a stethoscope and an oxygen saturation monitor. While she wrapped the cuff around Jock's upper arm and slipped the monitor on his finger, the other paramedic went through the same series of questions with Jock that Annabel had.

The finger probe beeped erratically. Heart rate one-forty. Annabel had already felt Jock's pulse—it was irregular. Oxygen saturation levels were only seventy-eight percent. Jock needed oxygen.

Despite his protestations, when the paramedic slipped the oxygen mask over his face, Jock nodded his thanks.

Less than half an hour after Annabel had made the call to 000, Jock was loaded onto a stretcher and into the waiting ambulance. She and Heather followed the ambulance in their cars to the hospital.

In the emergency department at the hospital in Stockton it didn't take long for the staff at the hospital to diagnose what was wrong with Jock. Within moments of arriving, he was taken to X-ray which revealed nothing, then onto CT for a scan of his chest. Annabel stayed with him while Heather made phone calls to James and Ben. Natalie and Rob were away on a holiday and she left a message.

After the CT scan, with his usual sense of humour intact, Jock thanked the medical imaging staff for providing such an interactive ride at the show and told them he hoped to never see them again. The report came back quicker than Annabel expected. Jock had multiple pulmonary embolisms—blood clots—in both lungs.

'How the bloody hell does that happen?' he asked.

'Lower your voice, Jock,' Heather hushed.

'I'm not entirely sure,' Annabel said.

'So how will they fix it and how long 'til I get out of this place?'

'They'll probably need you to stay in for a couple of days while they find out why. You'll get some blood thinners and you'll be fine,' a chirpy female voice announced as she flung back the curtain.

Heather smiled. 'Hello, Vanessa, dear, lovely to see you. I didn't know you were working here now. Vanessa went to school with Ben,' Heather explained to Annabel.

Vanessa smiled. 'That's right. I was two years behind him.'

'Am I allowed to eat?' Jock asked Vanessa.

'Yes, you are,' she replied. 'Unfortunately, all I can offer is sandwiches and a cuppa.'

'Better than nothing which is all I've had since lunchtime.'

'Which was only three hours ago,' Heather reminded him. She rolled her eyes and patted Vanessa's arm. 'Seriously, Jock's like a child when he's sick.'

Not long after Jock finished his second cup of tea, Ben arrived, still in his work gear, looking flustered and apologising that they'd been out of reach. Once Heather explained Jock was fine, he visibly relaxed. He kissed Annabel's cheek before hugging his mum then shaking his dad's hand.

'You trying to fall off the perch?' Ben asked.

'Not yet,' Jock replied.

'Good. Because James and I are gonna need a hand fixing fences in that back corner. And there's all those trees to clear.'

As they were discussing farm work, Vanessa came back into the room. 'G'day, Nails, how're you doin'? Haven't seen you in years.'

They chatted briefly, catching up on what they'd been doing since they last saw each other while Vanessa took Jock's vital signs and recorded them in her charts.

'How's Zara? Do you still see much of her?' Vanessa asked.

Annabel went still. She'd forgotten to ask Ben about Zara.

'No. I haven't seen her in ages,' Ben said.

His answer was vague, but Annabel heard something catch in his voice and his face clouded over.

'Such a shame,' Heather said with a soft sigh. 'You were the best of friends. I don't know what happened between you two and why you won't talk about it but—'

Ben interrupted. 'We went our separate ways, Mum. No big deal. It happens.'

'What's she doing these days, do you know?' Vanessa pushed.

'She's a lawyer.'

An orderly arrived to take Jock to the ward and the subject of Zara was dropped, but Annabel made a mental note to ask around and find out more about the mysterious Zara Pritchard. She'd start by asking Vanessa.

Chapter 21

Just after seven o'clock Annabel left Ben and Heather with Jock and headed back to the emergency department intent on finding Vanessa and asking her about Zara. She found her at the desk on her phone.

She glanced up guiltily when she saw Annabel standing there and slipped her phone into the pocket of her scrub top.

'Sorry. It's quiet for a Friday night. Thought I'd just catch up on Facebook.'

Annabel glanced around the empty department before turning back to Vanessa. 'Are you asking for trouble?' she whispered, with a smile. If she wanted information about Zara, she needed to get Vanessa on side.

Vanessa gave her a puzzled look.

'How long have you been an ED nurse?' Annabel asked. 'Surely you know to never say that word out loud. Every time anyone says things are quiet, it's guaranteed to go haywire.'

Vanessa smiled back. 'I'm not an ED nurse. I'm usually on the surgical wards but I'm filling in here because they're short staffed. You just reminded me they warned me never to say it's quiet.'

'In my experience saying the word "quiet" can bring instant disaster to an otherwise pleasant shift.'

'Are you a nurse too?' Vanessa asked.

Annabel nodded. She was about to explain that she was currently working at the GP clinic in Glengarrick when a car roared up to the front entrance, tires screeching, horn blasting.

'And there we have it,' Annabel said as she and Vanessa bolted towards the main doors.

Annabel didn't even stop to consider that she didn't work there. Her brain went straight into work-mode.

The doors whooshed open and three teenage girls entered, sobbing uncontrollably. As Annabel faced them, adrenaline sped through her, firing up her heart rate. It was at that moment she realised how much she missed working in ED.

'She's not talking,' one of the girls said.

'I think she's really sick,' one of the others added.

'Who?' Annabel asked.

The girl pointed towards the door. 'Hannah. She's out there. In the car. A friend drove us here.'

Annabel peered into the car and sighed. It was a sight she'd seen many times in her career. The question was, had the girl drunk too much alcohol or had she taken drugs?

A boy who didn't look old enough to be allowed behind the wheel of a car carried the girl into the waiting room and deposited her in a chair. Her long blonde hair hung in a stringy mat, covering her entire face. She wore teenage girl standard-issue high-waisted skinny leg jeans and a cropped T-shirt, the exact replica to those of her three distraught friends.

As Annabel held open the doors and ushered them into a treatment bay, she tried not to gag as the sour stench of regurgitated alcohol and food hit her. Like most nurses, she handled blood and broken bones better than vomit.

Vanessa looked shaken and unsure what to do.

'See if you can grab details from the girls about what happened. I'll assess Hannah,' Annabel said.

'Are you sure you don't mind? That'd be great. The others are on their tea break, but they'll be back soon.'

Annabel turned to the driver of the car. She saw a mix of desperation and fear in his eyes.

'Follow me,' she commanded. Between them they half-carried, half-dragged the girl to the cubicle.

'I dunno know what happened,' he mumbled. 'We were at a party. She was fine then suddenly she went all floppy like this.'

Annabel brushed the girl's hair aside and her heart skipped its next beat. Hannah was Ben's niece. Her face was smeared with dirt and vomit.

Filled with an increasing sense of urgency, Annabel turned back to the boy. 'What's your name?'

'Noah.'

'Help me get her onto this trolley.'

He unceremoniously dumped Hannah onto the bed where she lay on her back, eyes closed, arms outstretched.

Annabel glanced over at the hysterical girls and chose the one who seemed more together than the others. 'What's your name?' she asked.

'Maddy.'

'You stay with me. The rest of you can go back to the waiting room.'

'Is she going to be all right?' Maddy asked. 'She won't die, will she?'

'Not on my shift,' Annabel muttered.

She turned her attention back to Hannah. It was difficult to reconcile the girl in front of her with the sweet seventeen-year-old she'd met at dinner the first night she'd arrived in town. Annabel hadn't seen Hannah since as she'd been away at boarding school in Melbourne. What was she doing in Stockton?

She glanced around to see where Vanessa or her colleagues were, but the department was empty. Not knowing what else to do, she started her emergency assessment.

Airway was fine. Breathing was fine. Hannah was conscious, but not speaking. She was pale too and her blood pressure was probably in her boots.

'What happened?' she asked Maddy as she gently lifted one of Hannah's eyelids then the other.

Pupils were equal and reacting normally. She wrapped a blood pressure cuff around Hannah's skinny upper arm. Her skin was icy cold. Possibly hypothermic. It had been a cold day and the evening had gotten colder and Hannah only wore a singlet top and jeans.

'I don't know what happened,' Maddy said, shivering.

Annabel glanced around and saw a blanket warmer. She pointed. 'Go and grab some hot blankets and take some for you and your friends and bring a couple back for Hannah please.'

While Maddy darted off, Annabel found the IV trolley. She was surprised at how much her hands trembled as she wrapped the tourniquet around Hannah's arm and felt for a vein. The extra tension of working in a foreign environment on someone she knew must be hitting her.

Maddy reappeared with an armload of blankets just as Annabel slid the cannula into place and flushed it with normal saline. She fixed the dressing to Hannah's arm before discarding the sharp and tidying up the IV trolley. She labelled blood tubes and checked Hannah's blood sugar levels which were higher than she would have expected. When she was done, she connected Hannah to the monitors and took an ECG before taking two blankets from Maddy and wrapping them around Hannah.

Annabel turned her attention back to Maddy and folded her arms across her chest. 'You must know something.'

'We were at a party, then, well, I don't know.' Maddy's voice trailed off.

Guilt emanated from her in waves but shaming her wouldn't get the answers Annabel needed.

'You can trust me, Maddy,' she said.

Maddy bit her bottom lip. 'We had a fair bit to drink,' she admitted.

'How much?'

'I don't remember.'

'What about drugs?' Annabel asked carefully.

Maddy ducked her head, refusing to meet Annabel's gaze.

'Please don't lie to me, Maddy. It won't help Hannah. I'm not going to report you to the police, if that's what you're worried about, but I need to know what happened, so that I can do the right thing for Hannah.'

Maddy glanced up.

'Do you understand?'

Maddy nodded, wide eyed. 'Are you going to tell my mum?'

'Not right now. It's not important. But I need to know what Hannah had to drink.'

'She only had coolers, I swear.'

'No drugs?'

'Not that I know of.'

'But there *were* drugs at the party?' Annabel pushed.

'Yeah, but Han's not that stupid.'

Vanessa appeared, looking flushed and flustered. 'Sorry. Active chest pain arrived at the same time. Are you okay? Need anything?'

'I'm fine.'

'Good.' Vanessa rushed off, back towards Resus.

Annabel found paperwork and started a chart, scribbling a note. At her previous hospital, standing orders for alcohol overdose were to start an IV to rehydrate but she didn't work here and had no idea of the hospital's policies and protocols. Technically, she shouldn't even be here, but she wasn't going to stand by and wait for someone else to come and see Hannah.

She went back into the cubicle and did another set of observations. Hannah's oxygen levels were lower than normal, and her heart rate was too high. Annabel put her hand to Hannah's skin. Still cold. She needed to be reviewed by a doctor, but judging from the noise coming from Resus, everyone was caught up in the middle of the code.

Hannah lay on the narrow trolley between them, with an unknown alcoholic cocktail slivering through her veins, and no-one knew anything. Annabel resisted the urge to grab Hannah's friends and shake the information out of them, but she knew it would be pointless.

When Annabel heard Nick's voice, she exhaled in relief. Ducking out of the cubicle she waved him over.

He frowned as he walked towards her. 'What's going on? Why are *you* here?' He put a hand on her shoulder. 'I had a call from one of the doctors. She said the whole place is out of control and asked me to come down to help. Thankfully I was already at the hospital seeing Jock.'

Annabel gave him a quick rundown of what she already knew about Hannah—which was very little—except the girl reeked of alcohol and that she suspected drugs were probably involved.

'Do you know if anyone has contacted her parents?' Nick asked.

'I don't know. But they may not have had time to get hold of them. It's a madhouse in here.' She stuck her head out the cubicle again. 'Is the department always this short-staffed?'

'I have no idea. Like you, I don't work here. Anyway, you keep an eye on Hannah. If it's only alcohol in her system, she'll just need some fluids and she can sleep it off at home.'

'And if it's more?' Annabel hoped Hannah hadn't taken drugs, but she might not have done it willingly.

Hannah still lay limp, with arms like loose spaghetti. She occasionally whimpered, but otherwise wasn't responding to Annabel's repeated requests that she open her eyes and wake up.

'We'll deal with that later. I'm going to find whoever is in charge and see where I can help. Give me a shout if you need me.'

'Thanks, Nick.'

He gave her a quick hug, then headed over to Resus. While Annabel enlisted Maddy's help to remove Hannah's dirty clothes and put a fresh gown on her, she thought about Nick's hug. A few times since the football game he'd been overly familiar with her, finding moments to touch her arm or shoulder, but she'd put it down to them being a good team and him feeling relaxed working with her. Hopefully he wasn't getting some wrong idea. If so, she'd have to make it even clearer to him that she and Ben were an item and he needed to back off. The last thing she needed was for Ben to think something was going on, especially after what had happened between Chantelle and the paramedic she had the affair with.

Ten minutes later Noah and the other girls reappeared in the cubicle. 'Is it okay if we go home now?' Noah asked.

Annabel was about to answer when Nick reappeared and caught him by the shoulder, spinning him around. 'How old are you?'

'Eighteen,' Noah mumbled without looking up.

'Don't lie.'

'Seventeen.'

'And you drove here?' Nick asked.

'On the back roads. Been driving since I was a kid.'

'Well you can hand over your keys right now because you're not driving anywhere tonight.'

Noah growled as he fished his keys from the pocket of his jeans. 'How are we supposed to get home?'

'I don't know. Get a taxi.'

'Yeah, right because there's plenty of taxis in the middle of this hell-hole town.'

'Not my problem.'

As Noah and the girls shuffled off, Nick and Annabel stepped away from Hannah's side.

'How old is she?' Nick asked.

'Seventeen.'

He shook his head. 'What possesses these kids to be so incredibly dumb?'

'She's not a bad kid,' Annabel said, coming to Hannah's defence. 'Someone probably spiked her drink. Do you think she'll need to be kept in overnight?'

'Let's see how she responds to another litre of fluid. I'll check on her again in an hour. You're doing a great job, Bel.' Nick wrote another order for IV fluids before heading off to see another patient. This time she wasn't imagining the way he'd looked at her. A loud warning niggled in the back of her mind.

'Annabel?'

She turned to see Heather standing there, face ashen. Fear clawed at her belly. 'Is something wrong with Jock?' she asked.

Heather shook her head. 'No. Nothing's wrong with Jock, but Natalie called. She said Hannah's here.'

'She is.' Annabel led the way back to Hannah's cubicle. 'We think she's had a bit too much to drink, but she'll be fine.'

Heather wrung her hands. 'Natalie and Robe are aware for the week and we're supposed to be watching her.'

'You can't blame yourself, Heather.'

'If I'd known Hannah had planned to go to that party, I would have stopped her, but I was so focused on Jock being unwell.'

'You didn't put the alcohol in her mouth,' Annabel said, keeping her voice low.

Heather sighed as she wiped the sheen of tears from her cheeks. 'No. But Natalie and Rob taught her better than this.'

Annabel touched Hannah's hair. 'I obviously don't know anything about raising children, but I do know that kids will try things out no matter what their parents teach them. They come to an age when what their peers say is more important than what their parents say. I've seen it happen lots of times.' She paused, searching for something that might bring comfort to Heather. 'We all make silly decisions sometimes.'

Heather looked up at her. 'Annabel?' She stopped, bit her lip, shook her head. 'Annabel, I might be out of line here, but please be careful around Nick Young. I've heard he can be...' Her voice tapered off. 'Just be careful okay. I saw how he looked at you before.'

Annabel inhaled and exhaled sharply. 'There's nothing between me and Nick. We're colleagues. That's it. I promise.'

But the warning sounded louder. She thought back to all the times they'd talked between patients. It was rarely work-related. Nick was fascinated that she'd played semi-professional football and always brought the conversation back to that. Or he asked about her and Ben and their relationship, which, now she thought about it, was odd.

'*I* know that, but I wonder if Nick does,' Heather said.

'He knows Ben and I are a couple.'

'Hmph. Let's just say it hasn't stopped him before. Rumour has it that he's broken up more than one relationship. That's why he moved to Glengarrick.'

'I'll keep my eyes open and I can promise you I won't let myself be drawn in by him. Yes, he's charismatic, but I'm not interested in him. Nothing has happened between us and it won't. Ever. I love Ben too much. If Nick does anything inappropriate, I'll resign on the spot.'

Heather's shoulder sagged in relief. 'Thank you, Annabel. It would kill Ben to lose you after what happened with him and Chantelle. Until he met you, I didn't think he'd ever find someone to love again. You're so good for him.'

Annabel hugged Heather. 'He's good for me, too.'

'I'll stay here with Hannah, sweetheart. You've had a long day.'

'What about Jock?'

'He's busy keeping the nurses in line.' Heather gave a rueful smile. 'Or driving them bonkers. I didn't miss them rolling their eyes as I left.'

'Where's Ben?' Annabel asked.

'I'm not sure. He took a phone call and left. He may have headed home.'

'I'll ring him and see where he is,' Annabel said, 'and see if he wants me to bring home something for dinner.'

The last thing she felt like doing was cooking tonight and she imagined he felt the same way after a long day working on the farm then coming into Stockton to see his dad.

She turned to leave then stopped. 'Can I ask you a question, Heather?'

'Of course, sweetheart.'

'What's the deal between Ben and Zara Pritchard?'

Heather frowned. 'Nothing. Why? Has Ben said something?'

'That's just the thing. He never mentions her except in passing, but I get the feeling there's more to their relationship than just friends. Were they ever a couple?'

'Gosh, no. Nothing other than friends. Unless I'm mistaken, there's never been anything romantic between them. Zara was like another sister to Ben.'

Annabel frowned. Heather's words should have given her a sense of relief, but they didn't. If they were such close childhood friends, it made no sense why Ben didn't talk about Zara and why he seemed to act weird whenever her name was mentioned. 'Georgie told me she's pregnant.'

'I had no idea until Vanessa mentioned it earlier today,' Heather said. 'I didn't even know Zara had a partner. To be honest...' she leaned in and lowered her voice, '...I'd heard she was bisexual. I don't know what happened, but about a year ago Zara seemed to slide off the face of the earth.' Another frown appeared. 'Now I think about it, I remember being surprised she didn't come back for Daisy's baptism. She and Georgina used to be incredibly close too.'

'Georgie told me she was overseas at the time,' Annabel said.

'Oh, right, I didn't know that either.' Heather put a hand on Annabel's arm. 'Honestly, sweetheart. If you're worried, ask Ben. He'll tell you. He has nothing to hide. Especially when it comes to Zara.'

For some reason Heather's words did nothing to alleviate Annabel's concerns and she left the hospital intent on asking Ben what the deal was with him and Zara.

Chapter 22

Ben was driving home from the hospital when his phone rang. He glanced at it in the holder on the dash. No caller ID. Hoping it wasn't the hospital saying Dad had taken a turn for the worse, he swiped his finger across the screen.

'Ben Naylor.'

A slight pause. Presuming it was a telemarketer, he almost hung up.

'Nails.'

He recognised her voice straight away. Zara.

'Hi.'

'I… er ….um…I…' she stammered. 'I know it's been awhile since we've spoken. . .'

Months.

Ben pulled over to the side of the road and took the phone off speaker so he could hear her more clearly.

'I got your text message. That's great news about you and Annabel. I look forward to meeting her.'

'Yeah. It's great. She's great. How are *you* doing?'

The silence stretched so long Ben had to check his phone to make sure the call hadn't disconnected. Sometimes they lost service on this stretch of road.

'Zara?'

He heard a shuffling noise.

'I have cancer, Ben.'

At first, he wasn't sure he'd heard her correctly. Who had cancer?

'Nails? Did you hear me? I have cancer,' she repeated softly.

The air rushed from his lungs and it took him a second to catch his breath. 'God, Zara, no.' Cancer happened to old people, not his friends. Not Zara. 'How bad is it?'

'It's treatable, but they want to bring the baby on early so they can do surgery and I can start chemo.'

He swore softly and let the implication of Zara's words wash over him.

They'd discussed just about everything when he'd agreed to be a sperm donor. But obviously they'd never discussed *this*. Suddenly the car felt like it was closing in on him and he realised how selfish he was being. This wasn't about him; it was about Zara.

He got out and inhaled deeply. In a nearby paddock a horse glanced up then put its head down and kept eating. His mind whirled. How was he going to tell Annabel?

'It's in the breast…growing quickly…difficult to diagnose…but fortunately they don't think it's advanced…maybe a mastectomy…definitely chemo and radiation after the baby is born…genetic testing…hopefully it hasn't metastasised to other organs in my body…if it's in my lungs or bones I'm screwed… but the doctors think I'll be fine. It shouldn't be terminal…'

Terminal? He forced himself to tune back in and focus. Of course, it couldn't be terminal! Terminal meant Zara would die, which meant…

'What about the baby?' he interrupted. 'Will it be alright?' He softened his tone, realising how blunt he must sound. 'I mean how far along are you?'

'I'm just over halfway. They'll try to get me to thirty weeks and induce me.'

He swore again.

'They think I've found it early enough.'

He had no idea what to say.

Zara didn't say anything else either, and the silence kept going, as if she was waiting for him to speak. But he had no words. Nothing. He couldn't even organise his thoughts into a straight line.

'I'll be fine, Nails, you know me.'

Why was she comforting him? He should be saying something to her.

'I am so sorry, Zars.'

'I'm not *dying*.'

She laughed, but he knew her well enough to tell it was strained.

'I'll be fine, honestly. It's just a little hurdle.'

Some hurdle. But then again, if anyone was stubborn enough to stare cancer in the face and beat it, Zara would.

'What's the treatment and when do you start?' he asked. 'As soon as the baby arrives?'

'I'm not sure yet. I only found out about it this morning.'

'This morning?' He ran his hands through his hair. 'Have you told your parents?'

'Not yet. I wanted you to know first. I'm on my way to Glengarrick now. I didn't want to tell them over the phone.'

'Why do you sound so calm?' he asked.

'Trust me, I'm not calm. The emotions have rolled in a thousand different directions since I found out.'

'Are you in any pain?'

'None.'

'And the baby is okay?'

'For now, yes.'

There was another long beat of silence. He sucked in a deep breath and exhaled slowly.

'Nails, I have a favour to ask.'

'Anything. What can I do? What do you need? Just tell me.' This was his best friend. Zara. He'd do anything for her.

'If something bad happens to me, I need you to raise your son.'

Ice slivered down his spine. A son?

'Bloody hell, Zara. Nothing is going to happen to you. I won't let it.'

And not just because he didn't want to lose Zara. He didn't want to lose Annabel and if she knew he'd fathered a child—a son—without telling her, their relationship was probably doomed. There was no knowing what she might do. And he wouldn't blame her if she walked out. This was something he should have told her right at the start. Right up there when he had the conversation about his PTSD. He ran his hands through his hair. This couldn't get any worse.

'Call me tomorrow after you've spoken to your parents, Zars. I want to see you, okay?'

'As long as you promise you'll give me a hug. I could really use one.'

'Deal.'

After Ben hung up, he let out a shout of frustration so loud a flock of galahs lifted out of the gum trees in surprise. He couldn't go home yet. Not until he figured out how he was going to break the news to Annabel.

He slammed a fist on the bonnet as memories of his childhood with Zara assailed him from all sides. His stomach felt like it had fallen into a dark bottomless crevice and for a second, he thought he was going to throw up. He sucked in a deep breath and swallowed down the panic. It couldn't be possible. There had to be a mistake. Maybe he should call her back and encourage her to get a second opinion.

Zara couldn't have cancer because if anything happened to her, he couldn't raise her child. Could he?

***

The lights in both the cottage and in his little flat above the stables were on, but Annabel's car was parked closer to his place, so he presumed that's where she was. He pulled up and parked alongside her car. After taking the call from Zara he had no idea how long he'd sat on the side of the road, heart racing, head whirling, but clearly it had been awhile if Annabel was already home from the hospital. He should have sent her a message at least so she knew not to worry.

He let himself in. The flat smelled incredible. A mix of Annabel's favourite candle scent and something cooking on the stove.

She looked up with a smile when he entered the kitchen. 'How's your dad?'

With Zara's shock phone call, he'd almost forgotten about his father. 'Um, he's fine. Good. Driving the nurses crazy already.' He kissed her lightly on the lips. 'Hey, thanks for looking after Hannah. Mum called and told me what happened. Big day for everyone.'

'Did you get my message? I was going to pick up take away for dinner but when I didn't hear from you, I just grabbed some ingredients to make soup.' She indicated the pot on the stove. 'Hope that's okay.'

'Yeah, sorry, I should have called.'

'Your mum blames herself for Hannah,' Annabel said.

'Yeah. She would. Natalie and Rob are on their way back home, so they'll sort Hannah out. She's normally a good kid.'

'I reckon her drink was spiked at that party. These things happen.'

'They won't happen again.' He went to the fridge, took out the orange juice and poured himself a glass. Anything to buy time. 'Listen, can we sit for a minute?' he asked, keeping his tone as casual as he could. 'There's something I want to tell you.'

Annabel's head snapped up and she stopped stirring the soup. 'What?'

His heart hammered against his chest. He hated that he was going to hurt her.

She turned off the stove and came to him. Her usual smile was gone, her eyes full of a mix of fear and concern.

He took her hands in his and rubbed the back of them with his thumbs. 'You know how much I love you, right?'

'Yes. And I love you too.'

Her voice quavered and his heart almost broke in half. He tried to swallow. 'I'm so sorry, Annabel. I've made a huge mistake.'

Her face paled and she snatched her hands away. Jumping to her feet, she gaped at him. 'What?'

He stood and reached for her, pulling her stiff body into his arms. 'Not about us,' he said hurriedly. His nerves hummed in his ears. 'I mean it, Bel. I love you so much. I never thought I'd find someone who understands me like you do. I didn't think I had a right to find love again and because I have, I treasure it every day. I treasure *you* every day. But I have to tell you something and I don't know what your reaction is going to be. All I can hope is you know how much I love you.'

Tears formed in her eyes before she hastily brushed them away with the back of her hand. 'You're worrying me, Ben. Whatever it is, just tell me. I'll deal with it.'

He inhaled and exhaled slowly. 'When I turned thirty, I did something really stupid.' He ran his hands up and down his thighs. 'I was a…a…sperm donor,' he mumbled.

Annabel gasped. 'For Zara?'

He dropped his gaze and nodded twice.

'Is Zara having your baby?' she asked.

He looked up and met her eyes, which were filled with tears. He shook his head. 'No. Zara's having *a* baby. Not mine.'

Her eyes flashed. 'Didn't you do biology at school, Ben?' she asked coldly. 'Your sperm. Her egg. Voila. That's how babies are made.' Red spots burned on both cheeks. 'Did you sleep with her?'

'No! She used IVF.' As if that made it better.

Annabel crossed her arms over her chest and glared at him, waiting for him to explain.

'I...ah...I told Zara I never wanted to be involved with the baby.' As the words came out, remorse and regret and embarrassment flooded through him. What kind of a person was he that he'd agreed to do this? 'I know it was a stupid decision, but we were young and thirty was this milestone birthday and both of us were single and Zara always gets what she's wanted.'

Every word from his lips was an excuse.

'What's changed? Have you reconsidered and decided you want to be a father now? Do you want to be with Zara, not me? Is that it?'

'No. God, no. That's not it. That couldn't be further from the truth. I want to be with you, Annabel. You have to believe me.'

She waited.

'The thing is...Zara has cancer...breast cancer.'

'She what?' It was barely a whisper. 'Is it...?' She left the question hanging. 'How long have you known?'

'About an hour.'

'You only found out *today*?'

He nodded. 'I knew she was pregnant when the clinic called me months ago, and I sent her a text to congratulate her, but she never replied. I haven't spoken to her until today. She called me out of the blue and told me about…about…the cancer. And about her…my…the baby. She's having a boy.' He ran his hands through his hair again. It was so hard to look Annabel, the woman he loved, in the eye. Why had he gone along with Zara's crazy plan? 'If something happens to Zara, she wants me—us—to look after him.'

'Are you kidding me?' Annabel took two steps back. 'No. No. There's no way.'

'It might not even come to that. Zara said the cancer is curable. But just in case—'

'No, Ben.' She put up a hand. 'You know I'm adopted. I can't. I can't and won't raise another woman's baby.'

'This isn't another woman's child, Annabel. He's mine too.'

At that, Annabel burst into tears and without a word, turned on her heel and walked out, slamming his front door behind her.

He didn't follow her.

After cleaning up the kitchen and putting the soup into a plastic container he turned off all the lights and sat in the dark wondering how he'd gotten into such a mess. Georgie called and let him know Annabel was safe. After telling her his side of the story, he turned out all the lights and finally fell asleep with wet cheeks and a freshly hurting heart.

He stirred once during the night thinking he heard Annabel, but when he woke as the sun was just coming up, there was no sign of her, not even a text from her telling him where she had gone.

And he felt worse than ever for not chasing after her.

Chapter 23

The second Ben dropped his bombshell about Zara and the baby, Annabel knew she had to leave. She couldn't stand there and listen to Ben explain or justify what he'd done. She needed space to clear her head and time to think about what she was going to do. She wasn't naïve enough to think that running away would solve the problem, but until she'd got her head around what he'd told her, she couldn't stay in the same house as Ben.

She didn't run far.

When Jed opened the door to her hesitant knock, Annabel fell inside.

Amidst a tsunami of tears, she poured out the whole story to Jed and Georgie. They listened quietly, taking it all in, not choosing sides. But by the time she'd finished talking about it, she was no closer to knowing what to do.

Georgie gave her arm a gentle squeeze. 'You look shattered. You're wearing that shiny-eyed look that tells me you're only one step away from crying again. Do you want to stay the night here?'

It was late, and Annabel could barely keep her eyes open. Georgie was tired too. She'd already stifled a few yawns.

'Thanks. That'd be great.'

Georgie showed her to the spare bedroom, found a pair of pyjamas for her and told her to get some sleep.

The next morning, Annabel staggered into the kitchen. Naturally, she'd slept badly.

'How're you feeling?' Jed asked, handing her a coffee.

Georgie was at the table, feeding Daisy in her highchair. 'Have you decided what you're going to do yet?' she asked.

Annabel shook her head. The night before, she thought she'd made up her mind. She would leave Ben. He could start a life with Zara and their son if that's what he wanted. But now she wasn't so sure.

'I don't know what to do.'

'Have you spoken to him yet?' Georgie asked.

'No.'

'You need to call him, Bel,' Jed said. 'You can't solve anything by avoiding him.'

She sighed. 'I know.'

There was at least a dozen missed calls from Ben and more than twice that many text messages. She'd read every single one, tears streaming down her face as Ben had poured out the depth of his love for her. Every message ended with the same words: *'I'm sorry. I love you. Come home. Please.'*

Jed handed Annabel a coffee and she wrapped her hands around the mug. 'I know it's stupid, but even though I know he loves me, I can't stop picturing Ben with Zara.'

Georgie looked up and frowned. 'Ben wasn't *with* Zara. I know this sounds crass, but he just filled a cup with his sperm. That was an act of service, not love. Ben loves *you*, Annabel, not Zara.'

Jed nodded in agreement. 'I've never seen him like this. He adores you.'

'Then why did he lie? Why didn't he tell me about this up front? Doesn't he realise that what he's done has changed our entire lives. We were planning a future together. Children of our own. And now this?'

'Firstly, he didn't lie. He just never told you about it. But as soon as he found out, he told you. If you ask me, that took guts.' Georgie sighed softly. 'After you went to bed last night, we called Ben and asked to hear his side of the story. He explained everything. As I suspected, Zara talked him into doing it. You have to know Zara to understand she's a steamroller when she wants something.' She rolled her eyes. 'If you ever want a lawyer on your side, she's a damn good one. I know her, and I know Ben. He's a softie and he wouldn't have been able to say no to her. He never could.'

'But why didn't he tell me earlier?' Annabel repeated. She wasn't sure she would have understood why he'd done it, but at least she would have known from the start. Then she could have decided if she wanted to pursue a relationship with him.

Georgie shrugged. 'Only Ben can answer that.'

Annabel squeezed the bridge of her nose. She had a whopping headache.

'Ben loves you, Bel,' Jed said. 'And I know you love him. I've never seen you so happy either.'

Annabel sighed. 'I know.' And Jed was right. She *did* love him. They'd even talked about getting married one day.

'I'm not saying anything about this whole situation is right, but none of this is the baby's fault. He didn't ask to be conceived by a sperm donor. He didn't ask to be raised by a single mum. He didn't ask for his mum to get cancer. From where I sit, this little baby is the one most at stake here. He's the innocent victim in all of this,' Georgie said.

Annabel stared at Georgie, finally seeing it from Ben's—and Zara's—perspectives. She knew what it felt like to be a child that didn't ask for bad things to happen. Her own father's name was listed on her birth certificate as unknown and her mother was only fifteen when she'd had Annabel and given her up for adoption. As crappy as her upbringing was, at least she knew who her parents were. If Ben chose not to be part of this baby's life, the child would go through life like Annabel had, always wondering who her biological father was. She couldn't willingly do that to him.

She looked from Georgie to Jed. 'Are you saying you think I should say yes to taking Zara's baby?'

Jed shook his head. 'Right now, from what I understand, all Zara wants from Ben—and you—is for you to look after the baby *if* she gets too sick and can't look after him herself.'

'But what if she dies?' Annabel asked.

Jed chuckled. 'I'm not playing down the seriousness of her cancer, but you haven't met Zara Pritchard yet. She's too stubborn to die.'

Georgie nodded. 'Honestly, I think Ben just wants to do the right thing by the baby. And by Zara. But he won't do it if that means he will lose you.' Georgie touched Annabel's arm. 'He's already lost so much.'

'Surely there's someone in Zara's family who can look after the baby.'

'Her parents would step in of course, or one of her sisters, but Ben is biologically the baby's father. Legally and morally he'll want to do the right thing.'

'He's a good man, Annabel. He will want to do the right thing by everyone and that includes you,' Jed said.

Annabel stared at the floor. 'I know.'

Thick silence fell. The idea of a future without Ben filled her with nothing but panic. Even though his news had rocked her to her core, she still loved him.

His face slipped into her mind, the way an old-fashioned slide would slip into place on the projector. She let the image stay before her then closed her eyes and blinked it away. Without doubt leaving Ben would be the biggest mistake of her life. But she needed some space to think through the ramifications of what he'd told her. Even if Zara didn't die, there was every likelihood Ben would want to have something to do with the baby. His son. How was she supposed to accept that?

'Are you happy for me to stay here for a couple of days?' Annabel asked after a while. 'Just until the dust has settled.' The cottage was too close to the stable block and she didn't want to risk bumping into Ben as they were coming and going until she knew what she wanted to say to him.

'As long as you let Ben know you're here.'

Annabel nodded. 'I'll send him a message now.'

Chapter 24

Startled from sleep in the middle of the night by a ringing phone, Ben glanced around, momentarily confused by his surroundings. It took him a second to get his bearings. Instead of in bed with Annabel, he was on the couch in his flat. Again. Wincing, he swung his feet to the floor. The couch was too short for his long frame and his back was stiff. He'd chosen the couch because he couldn't bring himself to sleep in their bed without Annabel to curl up beside.

The phone stopped ringing and his heart started fluttering in his chest. Maybe it was Annabel calling him.

He hadn't slept properly since she'd walked out even though he knew she was okay—she'd sent him a message to say she was staying with Jed and Georgie—but knowing she was still in Glengarrick and didn't want to see him was just about killing him. He'd lost count of how many times he'd kicked himself for not telling her about Zara at the beginning of their relationship. He wasn't sure how he'd cope if he destroyed another relationship.

The phone started ringing again and he finally found it, lodged between the couch cushions. No caller ID, so it wasn't Annabel. Maybe it was Zara and there was something wrong. Heart racing even faster, he swiped his thumb across the screen and brought it to his ear.

'Ben Naylor.'

'Ben. This is Sergeant Scott Davis from Stockton. We have a problem.'

Instantly alert, Ben scrubbed his eyes and checked the clock. 1:47a.m. He'd never met Scott, but he knew him by reputation, and he was a good cop. He wouldn't call unless it was serious.

'What's going on?'

'Special Ops are going to need you,' Scott said.

Ben's heart rate doubled. 'I'm on leave.'

'Doesn't matter. Call them. It's urgent.' Scott hung up.

Without stopping to think about the time, Ben called his former boss, Bob.

Bob answered on the first ring. 'Nails. You were my next call.'

'Scott Davis just phoned. What's up?'

'We have a situation I need you to check out for us.'

'You know I'm still on leave.'

'Yeah. But this is going down in your backyard. I need you there. It's going to take me a couple of hours to assemble the rest of the team and get them up to you.' Bob gave him the address of a property halfway between Glengarrick and Stockton.

'That's about fifteen minutes from here.'

'I know.'

'What's going on?'

'Call me when you're in the car and on the way and I'll give you the details.'

It took Ben less than ten minutes to shower and pull on his uniform. Adrenaline coursed through him as he grabbed a banana and bottle of water, scooped up his keys and exited the house. As he jogged to his car, he hadn't realised how much he'd missed the rush of heading out to the unknown. Time off had been nice, and spending it helping his dad and James was good, but it wasn't rewarding like this. Being a cop was who he was.

But was he ready to throw himself back into the unknown? What if he couldn't handle it?

After getting in the car, he paused and concentrated on his breathing the way he'd been taught by his psychologist, focusing, and centring his mind. He could handle it. He was ready.

After entering the address into the GPS, he called Bob again as he headed down the driveway towards the road. 'I'm in my car now. According to the map it'll take me twelve minutes to get there. What's going on?'

'A report has come in that a guy wearing a bra loaded with explosives has been threatening to blow himself up. Name of Bruce Saunders.'

Ben had never heard of him.

'When was the report made?'

'Two weeks ago.'

Had he heard Bob correctly? At the gate, he eased his foot off the accelerator. 'Did you say two *weeks*?'

'Yeah, a friend of this Bruce guy made a call to Stockton police two weeks ago. According to the friend, Saunders has been wandering around local towns in the region for the last six months claiming he has explosives strapped to him. The information was passed onto the detectives at the Arson and Explosives Squad in Melbourne.'

'And what? They sat on it?'

'Looks that way,' Bob said.

'What the heck? Surely that information demanded an immediate response. Someone made a complaint two weeks ago and no-one's acted on it?'

Ben heard the edge in his voice. It was hard not to be annoyed. He'd been called out in the middle of the night for something that had been going on for weeks, possibly months by the sound of it. What made it urgent now? And why was he getting involved when he was on leave?

'You're right. It's an oversight.'

Ben raised his eyebrows but kept quiet. He continued driving, keeping his speed well below the limit. There was no rush now.

When Bob didn't say anything else, he asked, 'So, is this guy for real?'

'Yes.'

'I've heard nothing about it. Glengarrick's not that big. I would have heard if a guy was walking around town making claims like that. What did the arson squad detectives say when you called them?'

'They're treating it extremely seriously, and they've prioritised an operation to arrest the guy.'

'I'm confused. Why am I driving out to the middle of nowhere at two o'clock in the morning when they already have the wheels in motion?'

'The friend who called it in was assaulted earlier today, right after Saunders threatened to kidnap a kid from the local primary school in Stockton.'

Ben swore. If the man's behaviour was escalating, that wasn't good. But the idea of walking onto this bloke's property to check things out was even less a good idea. Perhaps he should think about back up.

'How concerned are we?' Ben asked, before realising he'd said "we".

'Very concerned. That's why SOG have been called in. Saunders is a paranoid schizophrenic but doesn't like taking medication. According to his mate he's also one of those conspiracy theorist blokes. We checked his social media. He has a YouTube account full of rubbish. Thinks the new 5G tower is the government monitoring him. People say he became a recluse after his wife died and it's only been the last few months he's been seen around town.'

'Allegedly wearing a bra filled with explosives. Great.'

'There's more,' Bob said.

Ben figured as much, or he wouldn't have been called out in the middle of the night. As a negotiator, his role was specific.

'We had a call from Wayne Pritchard down at the pub earlier tonight. Apparently Saunders had been heavily drinking all day and was getting too vocal. Pritchard kicked him out and he didn't go easily.'

Ben exhaled. 'And there we have it. The quadrella. A grieving, intoxicated, conspiracy theorist with an untreated mental health condition. I'm starting to wish I hadn't answered my phone.'

'You should also know,' Bob continued, 'Saunders has threatened local officers in the past.'

Ben's mouth went dry, and his stomach balled into knots. He didn't need to check his hands to know they would be trembling.

'I might not be currently working, but why haven't I heard about this guy until now?' The members of the Glengarrick police unit were great blokes and Ben knew them all socially. A heads up would have been nice. 'What's the deal? Am I just going to check things out, or is this a hostage situation?'

'Nothing like that. Just go and meet the guy. Keep things nice and cordial. Find out if it's all a bunch of bull, or whether he does have explosives strapped to his body. And see if you can find out if he's about to blow himself and the entire town up.'

At an intersection, Ben slowed, checked there was no one coming, and turned left. 'Let me get this straight. This guy is well known to authorities, he's a paranoid schizophrenic possibly off his meds, he's probably drunk or hungover, and who knows whether he's taken illicit drugs. He assaulted a mate earlier today, threatened to kidnap a kid and he's been seen walking around town with a bra-load of explosives strapped to his body for the last six *months*.' Ben tried to laugh. 'You sure this isn't some early April Fool's joke?'

'No joke.'

'Explain again why he hasn't been picked up sooner.'

'Scotty Davis visited him a few months back and asked if he was wearing a bomb. He gave him some evasive answers and Davis concluded he was bluffing.'

'What do *you* think?' Ben asked.

'No idea. That's why I'm sending you in. His mate reckons he's irrational but wouldn't hurt anyone which is why he was surprised with what happened today. Sounds like up until now he's enjoyed the attention and the reaction he gets. He's that kind of guy. Wait until you get to his property. Apparently, he has a rocket-shaped mailbox and uses alfoil wrapped dinner plates as special satellite dishes to keep the feds from listening in on his conversations.'

'And add grief to the mix.'

'Yeah.'

'Poor bloke. But a recluse normally wouldn't strap a bomb to himself and wander around town making jokes about blowing it up.'

'I think that's why after what happened today with his mate, they're taking the threats seriously.'

'Why wasn't he arrested straight away?' Ben asked.

'His mate wouldn't lodge a formal complaint.'

'Why not? What about the others? If everyone's so concerned about him.'

'No one wants to get involved, especially not his neighbours. Like I said, when you see his place, you'll understand why everyone keeps their distance.'

Ben came to another intersection. He checked the map on the screen. He was minutes out.

'So, all we have is a history of small-town gossip and no-one's put their money where their mouth is. No-one's been prepared to forcibly bring this guy in and get him admitted to hospital, so he can get the help he needs?' It was a statement as much as a question.

'Yeah. That's about it. Apparently, he's afraid the "men in white coats" would take him to a psychiatric ward. I suggest if you chat to him you don't mention anything about hospitals.'

Ben slowed as he approached the gate to the property owned by Saunders. His headlights lit up the rocket and his eyes widened.

'Holy cow. You should see this place. It's like a fortress.' Barbed wire curled around a high fence and Ben spotted security cameras. 'Unless he lets me through the front gate, I won't be doing any negotiations with this bloke. Place is locked up like a drum.'

'Yep so I heard. That's why I called you. When it comes to negotiations, you're the best.'

Ben chuckled. 'Thanks, mate. I appreciate it.'

'You're welcome back any time.'

'Yeah, I know. Ask me again after I get through tonight.'

If he got through tonight.

***

Still, chilly nights always amplified noises, but at least at wasn't raining, Ben thought as he stared at the gate and cattlegrid in front of him. Saunders had padlocked the simple wire farm gate. If that wasn't enough of a deterrent, the "Danger, Keep Out", "Private, No Trespassing" and "No Entry" signs were a visible warning that no-one uninvited was welcome on this property.

Headlights flickered in Ben's rear view mirror. On an isolated road at this time of night, it was most likely another cop. Ben drove his car off the road, switched off his lights and waited.

The unmarked car pulled alongside him and the window rolled down.

'G'day,' a fresh-faced, wide-eyed constable greeted him. 'Are you Senior Sergeant Ben Naylor?'

'I am.' It had been months since he'd thought of himself as a cop.

'I'm Josh Ryan. From Stockton.'

They shook hands through the open car windows.

'How long you been on the force, Josh?'

The young man grinned. 'About six months.'

'You a local?'

Josh nodded. 'Lived in Stockton all my life.'

'You know this guy?'

Another nod.

'Why don't you fill me in?'

Josh manoeuvred his police vehicle behind Ben's, got out and the two men leaned against Ben's car, staring towards the darkened farmhouse.

'He's totally paranoid,' Josh said. 'I've heard he has CCTV cameras everywhere. I'll bet he can see us here now.'

'I''ll bet he's asleep.'

'Nah, rumour is he doesn't sleep, thinks he needs to stay awake through the night to watch over the place. He sleeps during the day.'

'Do you know what happened to his wife?'

'First wife still lives around here. Second wife died in twenty-twelve. He went downhill after that.'

A rustle in the trees caught their attention and they both fell silent. When a mouse darted across the road, Josh let out a relieved laugh. For all his bravado, Ben betted the kid was almost wetting his pants.

'He reckons the Pakistanis are trying to take over his property,' Josh continued.

'What?'

'We had a heap of door-to-door salesmen a few years back. They weren't scammers, but they were all from overseas. Saunders used a shotgun to get them off his property.'

Ben raised an eyebrow.

'He's nuts. He reckons the CIA fly drones over his house all the time. We've tried to tell him it's farmers checking their crops and sheep, but he doesn't believe us.'

'You've met him personally?'

'Heaps of times. He comes into town a fair bit although not as much lately.'

'Do you think this IED is real or fake?'

Josh screwed up his face. 'IED?'

'Improvised Explosive Device. Is it real?'

'Oh. Yeah. Nah. I've seen it. Looks fake to me.'

Ben resisted the urge to roll his eyes. He tipped Josh had never seen a real bomb, let alone a fake one.

'Can you describe it to me?' he asked.

'It has three triggers. One on his chest and one on each shoulder. He explained the purpose of the shoulder switches. They're so he can detonate the device by tilting his head if his hands are ever tied or handcuffed.'

'You're kidding me.' Ben shook his head in astonishment. 'Does he know you're a cop?'

'Oh yeah. He said he didn't want to hurt the police because we're just doing our job.'

'Do you know if he wears the device all the time?'

'Never takes it off. At least I haven't seen him without it over the last six months.'

'How closely have you been watching him?'

'Pretty close. We know he drove to Stockton yesterday to visit his mother; she's in a nursing home. Then he went to see his brother.'

'Do his family know what's going on?'

'Yeah. His brother told us Bruce showed up at the hospital with the bomb strapped to him and said everything was going to go down soon.'

'What does that mean?'

'Dunno.' Josh grinned. 'Guess that's what you and I are here to find out.'

Hardly, Ben thought, but kept his mouth shut.

Josh also told Ben the house was allegedly boobytrapped and Bruce claimed there was a tank buried in a pit with enough explosives to blow the top off the nearby mountain as well as explosives buried all over the property. Ben wasn't stepping foot over the fence without proper backup and right now, Josh wasn't it.

'Let's walk a bit,' Ben suggested, pushing himself off the side of the car.

They walked about a hundred metres and came to another gate which was also locked. On the other side was a long, pine tree-lined driveway. From this vantage point, they could see the farmhouse. Next to the gate was a three-metre high rocket-shaped mailbox.

It was over two hours before the CIRT team arrived from Melbourne. Ben greeted his colleagues and donned his vest and protective equipment and, leaving a disappointed Josh at the front gate, walked onto the property, his heart in his dry mouth.

Within seconds a light came on at the farmhouse and Bruce appeared at this front door. He disappeared briefly before returning, carrying a can of soft drink and a torch. He paced his front porch in an erratic manner.

'Stop right there,' Ben shouted.

Bruce complied.

It took Ben a long time to convince Bruce to remove his shirt and show them the bra and ignition switches. Despite repeatedly being asked, he refused to remove the device, lie down on the ground, and give himself up.

'The only way it's comin' off is when it blows up,' Bruce told them.

'Guess we'll have to keep him talking,' Ben said to one of the other negotiators.

For the next six hours they worked their way through a range of subjects including Bruce's late wife, his cars, his daughter, his mother, his work, his motorbikes. He shared his distrust of the government, not just the Australian government, but all governments, talked about his fears of being monitored by agencies which didn't exist as far as Ben was aware. He denied having a mental illness but said he'd spent time in a mental health facility once. No-one seemed to have any knowledge of that, so they avoided that particular discussion point.

Saunders was surprisingly chatty and more lucid than Ben had expected, and he like felt he and the other negotiators built up a good rapport, even sharing the odd joke. At times Ben recalled the last time he'd talked someone off the ledge, but he was able to put those thoughts aside and deal with the situation at hand. To fill in time, he even told Bruce all about Zara and the baby and Annabel. Bruce's only comment about that was he thought Ben was an idiot if he let Annabel go. Ben already knew that.

'It's ending tonight,' Bruce said at one point, 'although I'm worried it's going to hurt.'

'It doesn't have to hurt, mate,' Ben said, 'if you surrender and take off the device. We're here to help you, not hurt you.' He must have said that a dozen times already.

'Are there bombs anywhere else?' one of Ben's colleagues asked.

'Could be,' Saunders replied evasively.

At times during their negotiations, he got restless and told them to step back, 'because I don't want to kill you.' He'd count down backwards from ten, but his hands never went near the trigger. At one point he started crying, then he burst out laughing. It was the strangest negotiation Ben had ever experienced.

***

After seven hours of stand-off, just as dawn was breaking on Monday morning, Saunders asked what time it was. Those were his last words.

Two hours later, around nine-twenty, without him appearing to do anything to initiate it, a massive explosion ripped through the house behind him, shaking the earth. The sky was momentarily lit as a huge fireball shot into the air and seconds later, without a word, Bruce raised both arms to his shoulders and triggered the device. There was a second smaller explosion, a blinding flash and he was gone.

Amid the scene of devastation one thing remained standing— the home-made rocket letterbox. The explosion flattened everything else and debris including chunks of metal, masonry, iron, and timber were thrown hundreds of meters away. How the letterbox still stood was astonishing.

Two senior constables from the special operations team were hurt in the explosion. One was airlifted to the Alfred in a serious but stable condition. The other was taken to the Stockton Hospital.

Police blocked off a six-kilometre radius from the property following the explosion as they worked to make sure no other bombs were present.

Ben had never seen anything like it in his entire career. His first thought, after making sure everyone on his team were safe, was to let Annabel know he was okay. Without doubt, she would have heard the explosion, figured he wasn't home and put two and two together. She'd be worried sick.

When she didn't answer, and his call went to voicemail three times, worry slipped in. Then he remembered she hadn't spoken to him since he'd told her about Zara and the worry turned to something more. Regret. Saunders was right. He was an idiot.

Chapter 25

Early Monday morning, Annabel sent Melissa a message, calling in sick for work at the clinic. She felt like she was running on autopilot. She had slept poorly for the past three nights, and she knew if she went to work, she wouldn't be able to concentrate. Jed and Georgie were being lovely letting her stay with them, but Jed had given her an ultimatum the night before. She had to talk to Ben. Today.

She decided to grab a takeaway coffee from the *Silver Spoon* and go for a drive to clear her head before heading home and finding him.

Annabel spotted Nick as soon as she walked into the café and her heart sank. He had his head down, reading a book. Given she'd told Melissa she was sick, her boss was the last person she wanted to see. She was about to order her coffee from Renee and wait outside when Nick looked up, smiled, and beckoned her over. She sighed. She couldn't pretend she hadn't seen him now.

'You don't look that unwell,' he said, closing the book and standing to greet her.

'Mental health day,' she replied, hating that she had to justify why she needed a day off. She'd worked full-time since starting in the role and it had been much more challenging than she'd expected. If he asked for a medical certificate, she'd be furious.

'You take as long off as you need.' His hand skimmed over her arm in a gesture of support and stayed there longer than necessary.

Her skin tingled and she took a step back, putting a bit more distance between them. She really wanted to get her coffee and go.

'Do you live here when you're not at work?' she asked, keeping her tone light. It felt like every time she came into the café he was here—sometimes even between patients he ducked in to get a coffee. Maybe it had something to do with Renee, who was happy to tell everyone she was single, and looking.

'I don't like being at home. My house is too empty.'

Annabel felt a momentary flash of pity and pushed it away. After Heather mentioned Nick's reputation, Annabel asked Georgie what she knew about him. Georgie did some digging and discovered he'd left his wife and two small children after having an affair with the practice nurse at his former clinic in Melbourne. No wonder Heather had warned her to be careful.

'You got time for a coffee?' he asked. 'I don't have a patient until nine-thirty.'

The voice in her head shouted "no" but she didn't want to be rude. At the end of the day, he was the one who employed her. She checked her watch. 'Sure. I guess. I have a few minutes. I was going to get a takeaway and go for a drive, but I can stay for a little while.'

'My shout.' He shot out of his chair and headed over to the counter.

It was a miserable, overcast day, matching Annabel's mood. Rain had threatened all morning. The fire in the wood burner stove had been lit and it was glowing brightly, but it hadn't had enough time to warm up the café yet. Annabel wrapped herself in one of the polar fleece blankets Georgie kept in wicker baskets at the front door for her customers.

'How's Jock?' Nick asked when he returned, bringing two coffees with him—neither of them in take away cups. He sat opposite her.

'He's good. He came home from hospital yesterday morning.'

Heather had called her, clearly not knowing anything about her argument with Ben, or that she wasn't at the cottage, and told her Jock had come home from hospital and was happily recuperating, loving all the attention. Annabel imagined he was being doted on by Heather and his granddaughters.

'And Hannah?'

'They discharged her on Friday night.'

'With a shocking headache, no doubt.'

'I'd say so.' She hadn't followed up with Natalie to find out how Hannah was. 'Thanks for your help at the hospital. Are they usually so understaffed?'

'I honestly don't know. But I heard you made an impression.' He tilted his head to one side. 'I might need to watch out, or they'll poach you.'

Her face heated. 'I'm sure that's not going to happen. Sorry to leave you in the lurch at the clinic today. I just need a day off.'

'I'll be fine. I'll manage.' He winked. 'Just.'

For the next few minutes they chatted about patients. Annabel mentally applauded herself for sounding professional and detached and told herself there was nothing personal about this conversation, simply two colleagues catching up on the news about their patients.

Deep in her gut though she sensed Nick saw her as something more than that. Until Heather had said something, she'd brushed aside her feelings, but there was no denying he was sending out signals. His flattery of her and her nursing skills had been nice to begin with, but now they made her skin crawl. If he continued to make her feel uncomfortable at work, she was going to say something.

'Amelia Waterman brought her baby in again on Friday afternoon after you left,' Nick said.

'Again?'

'I don't think she's coping.'

Amelia was a sixteen-year-old single mother Annabel had seen every third day since she'd started working at the clinic. Her baby, Eli, was two months old. "Not coping" was an understatement. Annabel wouldn't be surprised if Amelia decided to place her son up for adoption which might be the best for both mother and child.

'How's Eli doing?' she asked.

'Not well. He's lost more weight, but Amelia won't let me refer him to a paediatrician.'

'Did she let you immunise him this time?' So far Amelia had resisted Annabel's suggestion that her baby really needed to be immunised.

He shook his head.

'Can't we do something? Get a social worker involved?' Each time Amelia bought Eli in, Annabel's heart broke. She pictured what it might have been like if her own mother had kept her. Even though she didn't have a close relationship with her adoptive parents, in their own way they loved her, and she'd been well cared for.

'There's nothing we can do. At least she's bringing him in regularly and we can keep a close eye on him.'

'I suppose.'

She finished her coffee. 'I should get going.' As she stood, a loud boom sounded, rattling the windows. She frowned. 'What was that?'

The chef poked his head out of the kitchen. 'Did you hear that? Was that thunder?'

'Wouldn't have thought so at this time of year,' Renee replied. 'But I have no idea what it was.'

'Sounded like a gunshot,' Nick said.

Annabel shook her head. 'No. I've heard gunshots on the farm. That was more like an explosion.'

Renee shook her head. 'Weird. But there are no sirens. Can't be anything too serious.'

'I hope not,' Annabel replied. She turned to leave, but Nick caught her arm at the wrist.

They were the only two in the café, but he leaned in and lowered his voice anyway. 'There's something I want to say before you go.'

Her stomach knotted.

'I saw Ben yesterday. He looked like crap. I asked him if he was okay and he said you two had had an argument. I guess that explains the mental health day. Hope you can patch things up.'

Annabel stayed silent. There was something disingenuous about Nick's words. She knew Ben well enough to know Nick would have had to pry any information about an argument out of him. Nick was making it sound like they'd sat and had a man-to-man chat. What had most likely happened was they'd bumped into each other at the petrol station or newsagent or some place as equally innocuous.

'I'm here anytime you need to talk, Annabel. Not as a doctor. As your friend. I know what it's like when a relationship isn't working.'

His eye contact lasted too long, and the moment stretched out between them, filled with nothing except the faint sounds of music coming from the café sound system and cutlery and crockery being stacked. In the distance outside, a siren wailed, breaking the awkward moment.

Annabel gathered her scattered thoughts. 'Thanks for your concern about Ben and I, but we're fine. One little argument isn't enough to rock our relationship. We're all good.'

Nick's eyes moved across her face as though he was trying to read between the lines. 'Yes, but are *you* okay?' he asked, staring at her. There was no mistaking his meaning. His concern wasn't for Ben or their relationship, it was for her.

Annabel stared back, folding her arms across her chest. 'I'm fine..'

'I'm sorry if that came out wrong, but I'm worried about you. I'm concerned because I heard Ben suffers from PTSD.' His gaze narrowed. 'That must be hard.'

'Ben's mental health is none of your business,' she snapped.

Nick held up a hand in surrender. 'Fair enough, but remember I'm here for you if you need me,' he repeated.

'Thank you. I appreciate it. You've been a good friend.' She put her emphasis on the word "friend" and hoped he picked up on it. She needed him to get the message loud and clear.

'If you ever want things to be more than friends…' He let the sentence hang and the space between them felt like it was closing in.

Walk out, a voice yelled inside her head. *Walk away now.*

She took two steps back. 'No, Nick. We can never be more than friends. We are colleagues. That's all.'

'Can't be? Or you don't want to be? We can be discreet.'

Her mouth fell open. What the hell? Was he suggesting they have an affair? A shiver ran down her spine followed by waves of shame and guilt and fear. How had she gotten herself in this mess? She should have listened to her gut instinct about Nick from the moment she met him. She still remembered how she'd felt that first day she bumped into him at the real estate office. How had she been so blind to not see him for who he was?

She wanted to be sick. Was this how affairs happened? Was it that easy? Did it just take one glance? A shared laugh? A distant partner? She shivered. This was probably how it started with Chantelle. Or with Scott and Nicole again.

She shook her head. Until Friday she and Ben weren't distant. Sure, they'd had an argument, but the only reason she'd put distance between them was so she could sort out her head and work out what to do about Zara and the baby.

She needed to see him, and they needed to work things out together. Ben hadn't caused the distance between them. She had. It wasn't his fault. The blame lay squarely on her own shoulders. She'd pushed him away as if punishing him for a decision he'd made before they'd even met.

Nick's voice cut into her swirling thoughts. 'Don't overthink it, Annabel. Say yes. I know you sense it. There's something between us.'

'There's nothing between us,' she said, hoping no-one could hear the conversation. She glanced around. Thankfully the café was empty after everyone had gone outside to find the source of the noise.

Nick put a hand on her arm. 'Don't push me away.' He tried to catch her in a sideways hug. 'I know there's a connection between us. I can wait until you know it too.'

Calling on her football playing days, she shoved him away with a sharp elbow deep into his ribs.

He grunted as he released her, wincing as he massaged the spot that would have a bruise later. She glared at him coldly. 'I won't be at work for the rest of the week. Or the week after that. You can find yourself another nurse.' Turning, she stormed out of the café.

On the footpath, Annabel stopped in surprise. Rain had set in, but there wasn't an umbrella in sight. Instead, dozens of people huddled in groups of twos and threes and fours, all talking, faces animated, their backs turned against the rain like horses standing in a paddock. There were cars everywhere. Annabel counted six police vehicles.

What the heck is going on?

The drone of a helicopter caught her attention and she looked up and saw a police chopper hovering overhead readying itself to land on the school oval. A large white van emblazoned with the Channel Seven logo drove slowly down the main street and pulled up near the mechanic, illegally parking and taking up four parking bays. Two men jumped out and started unloading camera equipment. They were clearly on a mission. But for what? What the heck had happened that there was a news crew in Glengarrick?

'Did you hear what happened?' a woman asked as she rushed past.

'No.'

'Huge explosion on a property out near Stockton. I heard there was a hostage situation.'

Fear caused bile to rise in the back of Annabel's throat. If there was a hostage situation, they usually called Ben. Surely not this time. He was on leave. She grabbed her phone and noticed three missed calls from him. She rang him back, pressing the phone to her ear, trying to block out the animated voices and sounds around her.

He answered on the first ring. 'I've been trying to call you.'

'I'm sorry, my phone was on silent in the bottom of my bag. I just saw your missed calls. Is everything okay? I heard there's been an explosion.' The words tumbled out. 'Are you okay?'

'I'm okay,' he hurriedly assured her. 'But I wanted you to know in case you hear about it from someone else. Two cops were injured.'

'I saw the police helicopter.'

'Yeah, they've airlifted one of the guys to the Alfred in Melbourne. The other one, a young local guy has been taken into Stockton for observation.'

'Oh my God. What happened?

As Ben filled her in, Annabel listened in total disbelief. Out of the corner of her eye she saw Nick exit the café. He stopped to talk to someone before getting in his car and driving off.

'I have to stick around here for a bit longer, but I'll be home later today. Is that alright?'

'That's okay. Not a problem. Do what you need to do. I'll be at home waiting for you.'

There was a beat of silence. 'I love you, Annabel. And I'm so, so sorry.'

She swallowed. 'I love you, too, Ben. And I'm sorry too.'

'We'll talk tonight, okay?'

Tears pricked her eyes. She nodded. 'Okay,' she somehow managed to say.

Yes, they needed to talk, but right now she was just grateful Ben was safe. If she lost him, she wouldn't cope.

Chapter 26

The town buzzed with people and activity all morning. At one point, the line of people waiting to order food from the café snaked around the corner and Annabel, despite having no experience working in hospitality, called Georgie and offered to help. Georgie gratefully accepted and moments later arrived with Jed to help Renee.

Annabel recognised a lot of people, but there were dozens she didn't know and she presumed they were either locals who had come in from their farms to hear the news or they were from out of town, hoping to glean some gossip.

At two o'clock, after the rush had settled and Georgie told her to go home, she spotted Ben walking down the street with some other police officers, but he didn't look up and see her. She figured he'd need to debrief, and knowing that could take hours, she might as well head home. It was going to be hard to be patient. She wanted him home so she could hold him in her arms and tell him how much she loved him. There was nothing—not Nick, not Zara and a baby—that could come between them. What they had was good. It was strong. It was worth fighting for.

***

It was after four o'clock when Ben knocked on the door of the cottage. When she opened it, his half smile was tired and wary.

'Okay if I come in?'

She nodded as she opened the door wider and stepped back to let him pass. 'Of course.'

He looked shattered. Three days' worth of stubble covered his face and dark shadows ringed his eyes. It was unusual to see him unshaven.

Like her, Ben bore the hue of someone who had barely slept, but unlike her, his expression hinted at the devastation he'd witnessed both before and after the explosion. She desperately wanted to reach for him and let him know she was there for him, but she held back. There were still too many other unspoken things between them. Namely Zara and her baby.

Ben pulled off his dripping jacket and hung it on the hook at the door before taking off his boots.

'Still a bit wet out there?' she asked.

He shook his head and water sprayed everywhere. 'Raining cats and dogs. I think it's poured all day. I've never felt so drenched in my life.'

She walked ahead of him into the lounge room and he followed. She'd lit the fire and he went straight to it, facing it and rubbing his hands together.

'Do you want to take a shower first?' she asked. 'Get into some dry clothes?'

He turned to face her. 'Do you mind? I can go back to my place and shower there.'

'Don't be silly. Most of your things are here anyway.'

He went to her and hugged her tight. 'Thank you.'

It felt so right to be in his arms again, but she gently shoved him away, pretending she didn't want to get wet, when really she wasn't ready to be so close to him yet. 'You're soaking.'

He kissed the top of her head. 'I'm hungry too.'

'You're always hungry.' She gave him another little push. 'Get in the shower and I'll make you something to eat.'

'Give me half an hour.'

'If you take any longer, I'll come and check to make sure you haven't gone down the plug hole.'

'Is that a threat or a promise?'

***

Ben took much longer than half an hour. When he snuck up on her in the kitchen and wrapped his arms around her, she stiffened. Releasing her, he took her hand and drew her into the loungeroom. She sat while he threw another log on the fire and stoked it until the flames roared.

'Do you want to talk about what happened this morning?' she asked.

He shook his head. 'To be honest, no. I've had enough talking.'

Her heart stalled for a second as hurt washed over her. If he wasn't willing to talk to her about the stress of his job, she wouldn't be able to help him deal with it. Not that she was an expert on PTSD or anxiety, but surely if he wouldn't open up to her, there was no point continuing their relationship.

She started to stand. 'I'll get you something to eat then.'

Ben caught her wrist and gently tugged her back down. 'I'm sorry, that came out wrong. I'm happy to talk—I want to talk— about us and about Zara. I *don't* want to talk about the explosion. At least not yet. I've just spent the last few hours debriefing it with my bosses and I just want to forget about it for a while.'

She nodded. 'Fair enough.'

He sat beside her on the couch and angled his body to face hers, searching her eyes. 'I'm okay, Annabel, honestly. And I'm not avoiding talking about it, I just need to clear my head and talk about something else for a while.'

'Were you scared?'

He nodded. 'At times, yeah, but the team were great. Thing is, it made me realise how much I love my job.'

She stared at him. 'You want to go back to it?' He couldn't live in Glengarrick and do his former job.

'Not to special operations, no. But I want to go back to work as a cop. It's what I know. What I love. It's who I am. I love being here on the farm but at the end of the day, all I'm doing is helping Dad or James. It's in my blood but it's not in my heart.'

'What will you do?'

'There's a job in Stockton and I—'

'You're going to take it?' she interrupted.

'Not until you and I have talked about it. I want to know where things are with us first.'

She exhaled slowly. 'I quit my job today.'

He stared at her. 'Why? Because of me? Because of Zara?'

She shook her head. 'No. Nick Young wanted more than a doctor-nurse-colleague relationship.'

Ben's eyes darkened. 'I knew there was a reason I didn't trust that guy.' A frown formed. 'What are you going to do? Are you going to move back to Geelong?'

'Not at all. I love it here in Glengarrick.'

'But if you don't have a job, what will you do?'

'There's bound to be positions at the hospital in Stockton. In ED. I'm sure I could get something there.'

'Really?'

She nodded. 'I want to stay here.' She looked into his eyes and saw the love in them. 'I want to stay with you. My future is not in Geelong, it's in Glengarrick.'

Ben exhaled softly and smiled. 'I hope you know how much I love you, Annabel Norton. And how sorry I am. I never imagined one decision a year ago would hurt anyone the way it has. It was so stupid of me.'

She nodded and licked her lips. 'I get that.'

'I wish I knew where to start to make things better between us.'

'You could start by telling me about Zara.'

He let go of one of her hands and rubbed his palm over his jaw. In the quiet it made a loud scratching sound.

'I can't even begin to describe how shocked I am by Zara's news. And I'm upset.' He closed his eyes, as if words or explanation failed him.

She got it. Words failed her too. She stared at him, waiting for him to continue.

'I haven't slept much the last few days,' he confessed, taking both of her hands again.

'Me either. I shouldn't have walked out on you.'

He squeezed her hands. 'It's okay. I understand why you did. You needed some space.'

She smiled as she returned the squeeze. One of the things she loved most about Ben was his ability to understand her. No one else had ever done that.

'I'm so sorry if I hurt you, too, Ben. That wasn't my intention.'

'We're both hurting. That's why we need to talk about this. I don't want to do anything unless we do this together.'

'Have you seen her yet?' she asked, trying to ignore the tug in her gut that felt strangely like jealousy.

Even though both Jed and Georgie kept telling her Ben and Zara were more like siblings than friends, it still felt weird. Maybe once she saw them together, she'd feel more at peace. Then again, it might make things worse. What if she saw them together and it looked like they were a perfect couple who just didn't know they were supposed to be together? It's all she'd been able to think about. What if Ben was supposed to be with Zara, not with her? Her thoughts were so conflicted she wasn't even sure she wanted to voice them.

'No, I haven't seen her. Not yet. We've spoken on the phone a couple of times. She's in town though. She wanted to come and see her parents this weekend and I told her we'd catch up if you—' he hesitated '—if you're happy for me to see her.'

'What did you tell her?'

'The truth. That you're finding it hard to get your head around all this. Just like I am. I said I can't see her unless you and I have had a chance to talk about it and you're happy for me to see her. For what it's worth, Zara feels terrible. This is not what either of us planned when she asked me to be her sperm donor.' His Adam's apple bounced as he swallowed. 'She also said she wants to meet you before the baby's born.'

A flicker of unease went through her. 'Why?'

'Knowing Zara, she'll want to apologise. To ask you to forgive her. Us. To try to get you to see she's not a bad person.'

'I'm sure she's not.' From what Annabel had heard about Zara, she wasn't a bad person. She sounded like a normal person who'd made a bad decision when she's asked her friend for his sperm.

'I can't bear to lose you, Annabel,' Ben said softly. He pulled her into his arms again.

Annabel stiffened. 'Why do I sense a "but"?'

'I don't want to lose you,' he repeated, 'but I want to go and see Zara tomorrow. And when the baby is born, I want to meet him too. I want to be part of his life, even if Zara fully recovers. I need you to be okay with that. I know it sounds crazy, but from the moment Zara called me and told me she's having a boy, I haven't been able to stop thinking about him.'

She met his steady gaze. Her heart pounded in his ears. Could she live with that? Could she deal with knowing the man she loved had fathered a child with someone else? It was all so confusing and confronting. What would they tell him when he grew up?

'I guess you want to know if he'll look like you,' she said. It was as much a question as a statement.

He nodded. 'Yeah. I do.'

She swallowed. 'I'm happy for you to meet him, but I don't know whether I can,' she said carefully. 'At least not straight away. It's going to take some getting used to.'

'And I'm not rushing you. I'm simply asking your permission to let me go and see Zara and to see him when he's born.'

'You don't need my permission, Ben.'

'No, I don't, but I'd like your blessing.' He steepled his fingers and implored her with his eyes. 'I know this must be breaking your heart and I'm so, so sorry. I totally understand how hard this is for you.'

Annabel massaged her temples where a headache had formed. It might be hard for her, but it was nothing compared to what Zara was facing. At least Annabel didn't have cancer. She couldn't stop thinking about Zara having to deal with a cancer diagnosis while she was pregnant. The worry of that hanging over her must be awful. If Annabel were in her shoes, she'd be terrified she might die and leave her son an orphan.

'I'll meet her,' she said hurriedly, before she changed her mind. 'And I'll meet the baby too when he's born. I can't promise you anything more than that.'

Ben reached over and took her hands. 'Thank you, Annabel. Thank you.'

'You must be exhausted,' she said after a long beat.

He nodded as she sank back into the couch and yawned. 'Exhausted and sore from sitting in the same position for too long.'

'I could give you a massage after dinner,' she offered softly.

'I'd love that.'

He sat back up and turned to face her. Running a finger down the side of her face, he smiled before putting his arms around her and pulling her into his lap. She turned her head to the side and leaned into his embrace, enjoying the moment of closeness despite knowing there was still so much ahead of them that they needed to work through.

At least they were talking. And they loved each other. That was the best place to start.

Chapter 27

The next day, Annabel headed into town to see Zara. Georgie had told her she was staying at her parent's pub. On the drive in, she had to pull over three times to steady her breathing. Despite knowing she was doing the right thing going to meet Zara, she felt sick. She should have called first.

Annabel hadn't told Ben what she was doing either. Even though they'd had a long talk and cleared the air, she hadn't been ready to ask him to stay with her again, so he'd gone back to his little flat above the stables. She missed him.

The night before they'd spent hours talking about what they'd do if Zara got sick, what would happen if she died, and what would happen if she made a full recovery. Annabel still couldn't believe how lucky she was to have met such an amazing man who didn't want to push her beyond what she could deal with.

Getting got out of the car, she gulped in the chilly air. Winter was a month away but up in the alpine region the cold seemed to seep in earlier than it did in Geelong. She gazed around her at the endless landscape of dark green paddocks and bare trees under a leaden grey sky. The weather matched her mood.

She stood in front of the car for a moment and listened. Emptiness pushed on her ears, pressing deep into her head. She still found it unnerving at times at how quiet the country was. No cars. No horns. No people. No music. No neighbours. No dogs barking. Today there weren't even any sheep bleating in the background. Nothing except for the faint whisper of the wind through the gum trees.

Heart pounding and pushing against her chest, Annabel drew in a slow breath and let it out again. She could do this.

But catching her reflection in the car window she realised how forced her smile looked. There was no way Zara would believe she was thrilled to meet her, or happy about the situation they'd found themselves in. Because the truth was, she wasn't.

But it was hard not to feel compassion for Zara, and there were moments when Annabel thought her heart would break for Zara. In her career she'd cared for patients with cancer and it had always been tough—and they were people she didn't know personally. This time it was different. Because it involved someone she loved. Ben.

She sighed. None of them deserved to be in this place. Not Ben, not Annabel. And definitely not Zara or her unborn son.

As she continued to breathe slowly, the tension in her chest slackened and an unexpected feeling of peace settled on her shoulders as if someone was pressing down on her carefully. She looked up, and for a second the clouds parted, and a beam of sunlight cut through the grey.

She could do this. She had to do this. For Ben. For herself. For Zara. For the baby.

As quickly as it appeared, the sun went behind a cloud and it started to drizzle. Annabel got back in the car and five minutes later turned into the main street and drove towards the pub.

Zara must have been watching out the window. By the time Annabel had pulled herself together one last time, Zara was waiting for her out the front of the pub wearing a hesitant smile,

Annabel had seen photos of Zara, but nothing prepared her for how pretty she was up close. Zara was nothing like Annabel had pictured. She'd built an image in her mind of a tall, voluptuous woman with fashionable clothes and long, gorgeous blonde hair. The woman in front of her was nothing like that. In her oversized coat she looked fragile, as if one gust of wind would blow her over.

Zara's gaze swept over Annabel. Her eyes were piercing blue, but rather than being icy as Annabel had imagined they would be, they were warm and friendly, as was her smile.

Life pivots on tiny moments, Annabel thought. She had a split second to decide how to deal with this hugely significant situation.

She could turn away now or she could stay. There was no choice. She'd fought tougher battles on the football ground and faced bigger and stronger opponents.

She forced a smile. 'Hi, Zara.'

'Hi. Do you want to go for a walk?' she asked. 'I know it's cold and wet, but there's not much privacy in the pub.'

Annabel nodded. 'That's fine with me.'

They headed towards the river.

'Thanks for coming to see me.'

'I should have called first.'

Zara shrugged. 'It's all good. I've kind of been expecting you.'

Annabel glanced sideways at her. She hadn't told anyone she was planning to meet Zara, so she wasn't sure how Zara knew.

'Does Ben know you're here?' Zara asked.

Annabel shook her head.

'Will you tell him?'

'Of course.'

Zara exhaled softly. 'He's such a good man. He told me how much he loves you.'

It was Annabel's turn to sigh. 'And I love him, too.'

'I guess you must feel as if he's deceived you in some way.'

Annabel hesitated. How honest should she be with Zara?

There was no choice. Whether she liked it or not, if she chose Ben, that meant Zara and her son would always be part of their lives.

She took a deep breath, knowing every word she was about to say would expose how vulnerable she felt.

'It did feel like that at first. I was incredibly hurt when Ben told me what he'd done. I felt betrayed.'

Zara nodded. 'Yeah, I can understand that now. And I'm sorry Annabel. Neither of us thought this through at the time.'

For a long while the only sound was of their feet on the concrete footpath. Annabel tightened her coat around her and wished she'd worn gloves.

'Do you know if Ben's told his parents?' Zara asked.

'Yeah. Yesterday.'

Zara winced. 'How did they take it?'

'Shocked. Sad. But happy too. Ben said they'll do whatever you'd like them to do.'

'They'll want to get to know him.' Zara put her hand on her abdomen. 'I know what Jock and Heather are like.'

'Yeah, they will,' Annabel said. 'At the end of the day, your son is their biological grandson.'

Zara nodded slowly. 'Yeah, he is.' She stopped walking and faced Annabel. 'I didn't really think things like that through when I asked Ben to be a sperm donor. I can't believe how incredibly selfish I was.'

'What do you mean?'

Zara sighed heavily. 'All I wanted was a child to call my own. Both my sisters had babies and I guess you could say once I got the idea of having one myself, it got stuck in my head and I couldn't think of doing anything else. Ben might have told you I was in a relationship with a woman at the time. That's why I needed a sperm donor.'

'Yeah, he told me.'

'At the time I couldn't see myself falling in love and doing it the traditional way.' She rubbed her belly again. 'Now I wish I'd waited and got to share this with someone special.'

'Ben?'

Zara shook her head. 'Ben and I will never be anything other than friends. You will never have to worry about that. But yeah, if I met someone as amazing as Ben, I wouldn't walk away.'

'How did you think you'd be able to keep it a secret? Surely you must have known Jock and Heather would eventually work it out. Especially if the baby turns out looking anything like Ben.'

'To be honest, I didn't think about it. I was fixated on having a baby that I didn't give the Naylors a thought.'

'Or Ben,' Annabel said.

'Or Ben,' Zara agreed. 'It was naïve of both of us, I guess. But,' she said with a smile, 'I get the sense it's all going to work out now.' She started walking again. 'Thanks for coming to see me today. That tells me so much about you already. It tells me you're prepared to give it a go if you have to.'

Being open with Zara was easier than Annabel had expected, so she decided to keep going.

'Honestly? I hope it never comes to it,' Annabel said, staring at the ground as she walked. 'I'm adopted. I know what it feels like to not be wanted. You have no idea what it's like to grow up feeling rejected—first your biological parents, then by your adoptive parents.'

Zara glanced at her.

'I'm so sorry, Annabel. All I can say is I hope it doesn't come to a time when I need you to raise my son.'

There was a long stretch of silence.

'How is it possible to be happy and sad at the same time?' Zara asked.

Annabel licked her lips. She'd wondered the same thing many times in the last few days. 'I don't know.' She glanced at Zara. 'How are you feeling? The cancer, I mean. I'm sorry, I didn't ask.'

'I'm okay.'

'Really?'

'At the moment, yes. I don't feel unwell at all. Some days I actually forget I have this tumour growing inside me.'

'You're incredibly strong.'

Zara let out a half-laugh. 'No. I'm not. I'm pretending. For my parent's sake. For the baby's sake. Deep down I'm terrified I won't live to see him grow up.'

Annabel gulped. 'I'm sure you will.'

'Yeah, well, as long as you don't tell me I'm brave too, because I'm not. Earlier today I lost it. I was standing at the post office waiting for the woman in front of me to finish her conversation. I glanced at the magazines and staring back at me was a picture of a celebrity declaring: "I will beat this cancer!" I wanted to rip the cover from the magazine and shred it to pieces. What makes her think she gets to decide whether she'll beat cancer? *Cancer* decides who wins.'

'I can't imagine what it must be like,' Annabel said carefully.

'You know how everyone thinks you can cure cancer by running marathons? Or by getting footy players to wear pink?'

Annabel nodded.

'Well it doesn't work. You can't cure cancer by posting coded messages on Facebook. Or running marathons. I know. Because I've done all that over the years. I've supported those footy players and donated my hard-earned dollars and I've been guilty of posting strange things on Facebook like the colour of my underwear and what type of fruit I am.'

'Me too,' Annabel said.

'The thing is, I don't get to choose to beat cancer.'

'How does that make you feel?'

'Angry. I'm angry that these bloody cancer cells are having a round-my-body all-expenses-paid trip of a lifetime. Right now I wish this baby was here so that I can have the surgery and start chemo and get on with it.'

'Will you have a mastectomy?'

'Double. Just to be safe. If that's what the doctors think I need.'

Guilt crept into the pit of Annabel's stomach. She was the one who had been so selfish. All she'd thought about was how this situation was affecting her and Ben. She hadn't stopped to think about things from Zara's perspective.

'Are you afraid?' she asked.

'Of dying? Yes, of course I am.'

'No. I mean, aren't you afraid I won't love your baby?'

Zara shook her head. 'Of course not. It never entered my mind. I knew Ben would love him at once because I know Ben. That's why I chose him instead of an anonymous donor. I know him better than I know myself. He was always my best friend. He was safe. I knew my child would have good blood in him.' She gave a little laugh. 'Better than the woman I read about who used a sperm donor then discovered later, after she was pregnant, that the guy was in jail for murder.'

Annabel shuddered and pulled a face. 'Yeah, that would be awful.'

While they were working, the drizzle had turned into rain and both of them were soaked. It probably wasn't wise for Zara to be out walking in the rain.

'We should head back,' Annabel said. 'If anything happens, I'll do my best to love your son, Zara, but I'll be honest, it might be hard. I don't know. I know Ben will love him unconditionally but…'

Zara held up her hand. 'All I'm asking is that you make a decision in your head to love my son if anything happens to me. That's it. I believe love is a choice. The emotions will follow, I'm positive. I don't expect any of it will be easy…'

'No, it won't be easy,' Annabel agreed. 'Because knowing Ben belonged to you first before he was mine is tough. Really tough.'

Zara touched her gently on the arm. 'I hear what you're saying, but you need to know Ben was never mine. We were only ever friends. That's all. You have to understand that. His whole heart belongs to you, Annabel. I have never seen him this way. Ever. Trust me. He adores you.'

Tears pricked behind Annabel's eyes.

'It's all going to work out,' Zara said, full of confidence.

'How can you say that?'

'Because I've met you.'

'But what if your baby doesn't love me?'

Zara smiled. 'Trust me, he will.'

Chapter 28

That night, lying on his back, Ben took in the sight of the star-filled sky swirling above them. Beside him, Annabel breathed softly. Closing his eyes, he listened to the familiar sounds of the farm and to nature's orchestra warming up for the night. In the distance he heard the cows moving around in the paddock as they grazed. A horse whinnied and another one replied. He glanced over at Annabel. She looked so peaceful for the first time in a week.

He'd been surprised when she'd called him earlier that day and told him she was on her way home from town. She'd just seen Zara and wanted to see him. The timing was awful. He'd been called to a meeting in Melbourne for further debriefing sessions. While he was there, he caught up with his old boss and arranged to interview for the role in Stockton.

After Annabel's call, it had taken all his self-control not to speed the whole way home. He desperately wished he'd been a fly on the wall during her conversation with Zara. He'd missed a few calls from Zara, but he'd chosen not to answer them. He owed it to Annabel to hear from her first how their chat had gone.

Even though there was a hint of frost in the night air, when he'd suggested they light a fire in the outdoor firepit, Annabel hadn't hesitated. He'd brought two swags and piles of blankets and they were lying under the stars, side by side. In the firepit, the flames roared and every so often a log would pop, sending sparks shooting into the night sky.

'You're not too cold?' he asked for the third time.

She turned to face him. 'Not at all. Now stop worrying.'

'Okay. I'll try.'

'I'm glad I saw Zara today.'

He waited.

'She's lovely.'

'Does she look unwell?'

'I don't think so. She's tiny. It's hard to tell she's pregnant actually.'

'How did it go?'

'It was good. Really good. We talked through a lot of things and I told her we'd do whatever she needs us to do. She only has to ask.'

Wrapped in his swag, Ben rolled over onto his stomach and stared down at her. He stroked her hair. 'Thank you. You have no idea what this means to me.'

'I think it's going to work out.'

'Yeah, it is.'

'I also bit the bullet and called my parents and told them.'

His eyebrows shot up. 'What did they say?'

'Actually, they surprised me.'

'In what way?'

Tears filled her eyes. 'Dad told me his best decision ever was choosing to adopt me.'

'Really?'

She nodded. 'Mum wasn't as forthcoming, but she told me once I'd met the baby, it would be impossible not to fall in love with him.'

'I did not see that coming.'

'Me either. Would you believe they even asked if they could be part of the baby's life? As grandparents.'

'What did you tell them?'

'I didn't know what to say. I don't think it's my decision really. It's up to you and Zara.'

'It's up to all of us. We're in this together and we have to make it work. That means promising each other to be honest if we're finding something hard to cope with.'

She nodded. 'Zara's going to call you. She really wants to see you.'

'I figured that. She rang a few times today, but I didn't take her calls because I wanted to talk to you first.'

'Thank you. I appreciate that.'

He rolled onto his back and stared at the sky again. 'I never dreamed meeting you would make me this happy.'

Annabel rolled over this time and stared down at him. 'Ditto.'

At the huskiness in her voice and the desire in her eyes, Ben's stomach hitched. Shivers of anticipation rolled across his body.

'You know what? All of a sudden I'm not hungry anymore,' she said.

'Really?' He'd planned to cook dinner in the coals once the fire had died down and she'd said earlier she was starving.

'I didn't come here for the food tonight, Ben. I came here for you.'

He went silent, staring at her. Firelight danced in the reflection of her eyes. When she leaned down and tenderly kissed his lips Ben's heart exploded with love. He reached up and tangled his fingers in her hair, tugging at the tie, until it released her hair so that it cascaded around her shoulders and fell onto his chest. Heat flooded him as she lowered her head again and caught his mouth in hers. He kissed her deeply in return. Her lips were warm, tasting slightly of salt from the potato chips they'd nibbled on earlier.

She responded by gently exploring his mouth as if for the first time, and within seconds their kiss blossomed into something much more. If he didn't stop now, he'd be powerless to stop what came next.

He closed his eyes and felt Annabel's breath on his neck. It sent shivers shooting down his spine. His senses were hyper-aware and as her mouth closed over his again, Ben moaned with happiness.

The intensity of Annabel's desire in her eyes shocked him, but he wasn't about to stop to work out what was going on in her head. She clearly wanted him, and he wanted her. Needed her.

She stopped kissing him and pulled back, searching his eyes as she cupped his cheek with her hand. The touch was soft, as if she was curious as to whether he still felt the same as he had when they'd made love the first time.

He slowly traced her cheekbone, then her nose, then the outline of her lips with his finger. 'You're so beautiful, my Bel.'

She closed her eyes and as her lips parted, he traced his finger down her neck, along the scoop of her clavicle to the hollow of her throat. He knew exactly where to touch her to bring pleasure. As did she. Her kisses were driving him wild, and desire was rushing around his body, turning his blood into molten lava.

Was she ready for this? He certainly was, but he didn't want to rush her.

When she closed the gap between them further, there was no doubt what she wanted. His body responded as he pulled her tight to him and he wished the material of the swags wasn't between them.

Their eyes locked, and without needing to say a word, they got out of the swags and stood in front of the fire, swaying slightly in each other's arms before their lips met in another tender kiss.

She moaned softly. Her breath was warm against his mouth and every fibre of his being desired more of her touch.

'Ben?' she whispered.

'Mmm,' he mumbled against her mouth.

'Can we make love?'

Silently, Ben took her hand and led her back to the cottage.

Afterwards, he lay with his head on her chest and listened to the steady and reassuring rhythmic beating of her heart. As she held him tight, skin to skin, Ben felt like he was nestled in the safest place in the world—a place he never wanted to leave. Annabel's arms.

No matter what happened, everything was going to be alright.

After a while, she stirred and shifted position and they lay side by side facing each other.

A smile formed on her lips. 'I'm never letting you go,' she said softly.

He snuggled closer and they wrapped their arms around each other again. 'Good, because I'm all yours. Forever.'

Epilogue

August, that year

Ben and Annabel were at the kitchen table in the cottage at *Wandana* having a cup of tea when Annabel suddenly leaned over, took his face between her hands, and kissed him hard on the lips.

'What did I do to deserve that?' he asked.

'It's our anniversary.'

He frowned. 'Anniversary?'

'Six months since you asked me to dance at Daisy's baptism.'

He chuckled. 'That seems like a lifetime ago.'

So much had happened in such a short space of time, yet the next six months were going to be even more hectic once Zara had the baby.

'I'm glad fate bought us together,' she said.

'Me too.'

He still wasn't sure what he'd done to deserve such an

amazing woman in his life. All his fears about getting serious had quickly evaporated and he still found it hard to believe he was planning a third wedding next year. Sure, they were going to have their share of challenges ahead of them, but they'd be fine.

'You know how much I love you, right?' he asked.

'I do,' she said, kissing him again. 'And I love *you*. More than words.' She sat back and looked at him, her face suddenly serious. 'Do you think we should have sex more often?'

He burst out laughing. 'You read my mind.' He pushed his chair back so quickly it almost toppled. 'Ready whenever you are. I reckon we've got enough time before we have to leave.' They were due at the football ground at one o'clock to watch the Glengarrick Saints hopefully win another Grand Final.

Annabel giggled and grabbed him by the arm, pulling him back down. 'Not now, you nut.'

'Okay, after I finish my cuppa then?' He took a gulp and coughed as the hot tea scalded his tongue and the back of his throat.

'Serves you right. No, I'm being serious Ben. I've been thinking. Maybe the reason I haven't fallen pregnant yet is we're not having sex often enough.'

He sighed softly. Since finding out about Zara's baby, Annabel had decided she wanted to start a family of her own and he'd been more than willing to oblige. They'd talked at length and decided that even if something happened to Zara and they ended up with her son as well as a baby of their own, they'd make it work. Unfortunately, after three months of trying, Annabel still wasn't pregnant. With Zara due any day, he was concerned once she had the baby Annabel might struggle.

'Annabel, darling, we have plenty of sex,' he assured her as he tenderly stroked her jaw.

'Really?'

He rubbed away at the frown forming between her eyes. 'Trust me, if we weren't, I'd let you know.' He kissed her on the lips. 'Right now, I'd like to take you straight back to bed and make love to you, but then we'll be late for the game and I don't want to have to explain the reason we weren't there for the opening bounce to my family.'

'But do you think twice a week is normal?' she persisted.

'I don't know. What's normal?'

There was a beat of silence before she continued. 'I was talking to Georgie the other day. She and Jed had sex at least four times a week when they were trying to fall pregnant after they lost Robbie, and now they've got Daisy and another baby on the way.'

He screwed up his face. 'You talked to Georgie about their sex life? Isn't that weird?'

'I wanted to know if we're normal,' she said. 'Maybe our bodies have adjusted to a routine and we need to change things up.'

'If you're saying we need to spice things up a bit in bed I'm all for that.'

'Can you be serious please?'

'I am being serious. Bel, let me assure you our sex life is perfect.' He kissed her again.

'Sometimes I think the entire world is pregnant and I'm the only one who isn't,' she moaned. 'You know how when you decide to buy a particular brand of car you see them everywhere? That's how I feel about women and babies. Everywhere I look another woman is pushing a pram.'

'It only seems that way.'

She sighed wearily. 'I know you're right. It's just not easy.'

He kissed her gently and once more felt a wave of love for her. He'd been besotted the moment he first saw her and now, six months later, his love and affection for her had deepened into something rich and beautiful. He couldn't wait to marry her and spend the rest of his life making her happy. Hopefully that would include a child of their own.

He stood and picked up their empty cups of tea. 'Come on, we'd better go, or we'll be late.'

Annabel grabbed her puffer jacket and Cats beanie and scarf, and he picked up the esky and they headed to the car. As he was putting the esky in the boot, his phone rang. He glanced at it and his heart rate accelerated. Zara.

He swiped his finger across the screen as he got in the car behind the wheel.

'Zara,' he mouthed to Annabel. 'Hey, Zazu, what's going on? Are you on your way to the footy ground?'

'Nope. I'm on my way to the hospital. Contractions started this morning. Looks like I'm having a baby.'

Also by Nicki Edwards

"Escape to the Country" Series (Medical Romance)

Book #1: Intensive Care

Book #2: Emergency Response

Novella: Operation White Christmas

Book #3: Life Support

Book #4: Critical Condition

Novella: Operation Mistletoe Magic

The Peppercorn Project

One More Song

Holding onto Hope

Second Chance Christmas

"Off the Field" Series (Small town Romance)

Book #1: The Final Siren

Book #2: Settle the Score

Book #3: The Last Quarter (coming 2021)

About the Author

Nicki is a city girl with a country heart. Growing up on acreage outside Geelong in Victoria, Australia, Nicki spent her formative years riding horses, hand rearing lambs and pretending the neighbour's farm was her own. After spending three years in a regional town in New South Wales in her twenties, Nicki's love of country towns and rural life was further developed.

Nicki's dream is to one day escape to the country and live on land surrounded by horses, dogs, cows and sheep. Unfortunately, until (or if) that happens, Nicki will continue to live vicariously through the lives of the characters in the books she loves to read and write.

A voracious reader, Nicki always wanted to be an author. After returning to university as a mature aged student to study nursing, Nicki juggled full time study, part time work and raising four small children to achieve her dream of becoming a nurse. But her other dream—the dream to write—never left, and in January 2015 Nicki had her first book published.

Nicki now divides her time between writing, working as a nurse in General Practice or riding her horse Monty.

Nicki and her husband Tim have four young adult children, two spoiled border collies (#mollyandindie) and an ancient Burmese cat called Roxy.

To stay up to date with her latest releases, please visit Nicki's website: http://www.nickiedwardsauthor.com/ or find her on Facebook or Instagram where she spends far too much time!